There she is!

She's stepping off the jet—a bit unsteadily. She's in her mid-twenties, all in satin, and splendid, but she walks as if on eggshells—unwilling to let the spectators know she is slightly stoned. She crosses to the limousine—and drops her bag. A hidden bottle of aquavit drops with a crash and shatters on the tarmac. Rose picks up her bag and walks on—to the concert.

There she is!

IN CONCERT LIVE! She finishes the blues, and in the light and the love sent by her audience, she looks like a new person—animated, receptive . . . consuming every last ounce of energy in her being. *How can anybody give that much?*

She's not *anybody* . . .
she's
THE ROSE

The Rose

A novel by

Leonore Fleischer

Based on the
Original Screenplay by
Bill Kerby and Bo Goldman

Story by
Bill Kerby

WARNER BOOKS

A Warner Communications Company

Dedicated to

the men in my past who have brought me down
and the men in my future who'll take me back up
—L.G.F.

I

At Mach 0.82, the silver Learjet nibbled at the sky, a child's dream of Christmas. Thirty thousand feet above the ground, it sparkled like a toy, a silver airplane model hanging by a thread of cloud. On its glittering fuselage was a painted red rose, long-stemmed and bleeding diamond dew. If you could see it, you'd recognize it right away. Millions did. It was the symbol of The Rose.

Locked inside the sealed environment of the private craft, Rose pressed her forehead moodily against the icy glass of the little window. She looked out, but she was seeing nothing. Her small face, which was usually bright with her energy, was now pinched, her eyes expressionless. The corners of her wide red mouth turned down in a frightened scowl. Under the clouds beneath the plane's bright belly was southern Pennsylvania; in half an hour they'd be touching down at LaGuardia Airport in New York. The apprehensive line between her arched golden brows deepened. Her hand trembled, and she reached for the half-empty bottle on the little table at her side. Without bothering to grab her glass, she took a long pull straight from the bottle. The warmth of the Aquavit eased her a little, but she kept the bottle clutched nervously in her hands, as she stared out at the cloud formations, her stomach forming a knot around the drink.

Behind her, the guys in her backup band were mellowing out with long tokes of hash, passing the pipe around like Indians on a blanket. Rock music rose from a portable cassette deck and the guys' laughter rose with it; the potent smoke making them high and happy.

"Knock it off, for Chrissakes!" Rose turned on them suddenly, savagely swiveling around in her leather chair to glare at them. "If you feebs wanna get high, take a bus!"

Dennis, the road manager for the group, gave a whinny of laughter. "Cool it, Big Star," he yelled back. "Somethin's buggin' your ass, don't lay your trip on *us*. Wiggle on back here and have a poke of this good stuff, mama. Come get your head together." He waved the hash pipe amiably in Rose's direction.

Rose swiveled back without a word. Dennis was right; she shouldn't take her bummer out on the band. They were cool, and they minded their own business. She raised the bottle to her lips. Most of the time, she minded hers, too. Live and let live.

Most of the time, there were a few things that Rose enjoyed more than traveling in her own private plane. She really got off on the star trip; in the seventeen months she'd been on top, it hadn't had time to grow stale. She loved her own swivel chair, up in front, and her own little table. She got goosebumps every time she looked at the big red rose painted on the fuselage, where everybody could see it and know it meant her, The Rose. She adored the carpeted walls, the private bar, the mirrored johns, one of them reserved for her own exclusive use. Sometimes she wished the whole world could see her sitting on her own private potty in the Rose Room. The boss's seat.

All over America, there were small runways where the private jets landed, and the ground crews in their coveralls came running up to service the plane. Rose really dug to watch them; she enjoyed going into the cockpit and hearing the tower call her own craft down over the radio. She even got a kick out of the flight plans and navigational charts. All to move *her* ass, all to fly The Rose.

Rose usually enjoyed having the guys on board —the backup band and the roadie, Dennis, and their changing assortment of ladies and groupies. She didn't mind the guitars and the amps that crowded the aisle; the big stuff—the synthesizer, large sound system, lights and all the other electronic paraphernalia of a traveling bigtime band—went by bus and truck. Rose also used to travel by bus and truck, but not anymore, and never again. Now she went first class, and, usually, she loved every minute of it.

But not today. None of it made her happy today— not her swivel chair, or the painted rose, or her own john, or the melting cloud formations under the wings as they dipped down toward New York City. In the back of the plane, Rose could see that the band was really stoned now, laughing and grooving. She caught sight of a pair of girl's feet high in the air, and she knew that somebody was getting it on. Many times it had been she, but not today. Not today.

Hell, she brooded, it wasn't even her plane; it was leased from the corporation she owned by the corporation Rudge owned in a deal so complicated it turned out to be a tax shelter. The whole fuckin' plane—pilot, navigator, flight plans, leather chair, expensive toilet paper, fancy soap, plastic glasses in the bar—all no more than a deduction at the end of the fiscal year. Nothing was the way you expected it to be, nothing.

Only two things were certain: one, that Rose was tired, deep down to the bone, and two, Rudge was pissed off at her. Not as pissed off as he was gonna get when Rose talked to him, but plenty all the same. She stared gloomily out the window at the ground below, coming up fast under the wing. Tiny toy houses held turquoises in their yards—bright squares, ovals, and circles that glistened with gemlike beauty in the summer sunlight.

Yet Rose knew that the houses were cracker boxes, and the turquoises were nothing more than plastic backyard swimming pools, stinking of chlorine, probably leaking, too. Nothing was the way you ever thought it was going to be.

Down there on the airfield, Rudge Campbell would be waiting for her, madder than hell and waiting for explanations. Rose could picture him, sitting in the back seat of the limousine at the edge of the runway. He'd be listening for the engine, his battered cowboy hat tilted forward over his ice-green eyes. Rudge's eyes were colder than a cobra's. The car's engine would be idling so that Rudge could enjoy the full benefit of air conditioning on a hot day. His lizard-skin Tony Lama boots would be propped on the leather jump seats, and his arms would be folded calmly as he waited for Rose's plane to touch down. But his cybernetic mind would be ticking, ticking, ticking under the cowboy hat because—in repose or not—Rudge Campbell never rested. By the time the little Learjet had taxied to a stop, Rudge would have worked out the details of at least three more deals in his head.

He wouldn't yell at her—not at first. That wasn't his style. He'd give her a quick, cold grin and his eyes would be hooded. He'd save his wrath until he got her alone. Rose put the bottle to her lips and slugged down a long one. She shivered. If he was mad now, what was he going to be like after she'd talked to him? She'd have to look into those eyes of fathomless green, lakes hidden in a mountain forest and fed by winter snows. And she was going to have to tell him. But first, he'd be demanding an explanation about the album. Shit.

It wasn't her fault, damn it! If anybody was to blame, it was Rudge, not her! If he wasn't such a fucking slave driver, if he didn't keep her working so hard for so many hours, she wouldn't be on the thin edge of exhaustion all the time, and she wouldn't be fucking up. It wasn't the booze that held things up; it was those grueling hours without any sleep. The booze only helped to get Rose through the night and into the studio the next day; late maybe, but there.

Cutting an album that the company expected to ship platinum was not the same as making a voice recording in a Chillicothe dime store. It took everything that Rose had, every electric surge of energy from her huge voice and tiny body. And nobody was giving her a minute to lay back and cool out. So the sessions had run overtime and the bills had mounted up, and Rudge had blown his stack. Good session men and good technicians didn't come cheap, and Rudge demanded only the best. The best facilities cost the earth, ten thousand a day—that was for studio time and equipment alone—so Rudge wanted them in and out of the studio in less than a week, with a dynamite album. But it hadn't happened that way. They'd left Nashville with the album less than half completed; Rose hadn't laid down but two good tracks. If they hadn't had a scheduled sold-out concert at the Garden in New York, they'd still be in that goddamn studio, with Rose half dead on her feet.

Normally, Rudge would have been right there with them in Nashville. He usually never let Rose out of his sight or the sound of his voice. He guarded her like an eagle watches a rabbit, always ready to pounce. He would have been present at every session, sitting up there in the control booth with the headphones on, his green eyes narrowed as he ticked off every riff, every lick of every track.

But Rudge had been forced to stay behind in New York, setting up the biggest tour of The Rose's career so far. It was the tour that would sell the album, and the album would also promote the tour. Glued to the telephone, Rudge had been hondeling with the press and battling the promoters and the arena owners over every percentage point, setting up the concessions that could net them an extra million dollars in T-shirt and decal rights alone. He was also auditioning opening acts. They were trying to find exactly the right one—a band that would get the audience hot for The Rose without bringing the house down. Nobody could forget how Ike and Tina had overshadowed Mick Jagger on the Stones' last tour. The Rose wasn't looking for competition on her own stage.

So, while Rose was wailing in a studio in Nashville, Rudge had been trapped in New York, chewing on the telephone wires, keeping one ear to the rail. He was calling Nashville every hour on the hour, and what Dennis had been forced to report hadn't made Rudge Campbell happy. Delays, tracks that were laid down wrong take after take, Rose drunk, Rose sleepy and not coming in on her cues, Rose boozy and out of voice, Rose missing for a day and a half. As his digital brain had given him a readout of the mounting costs, Rudge grew more and more pissed. Rose was going to have to answer a lot of questions when the wheels touched the ground. She took another drink, emptying the bottle. Shit. There was a fresh one somewhere in her poke. She rummaged around until she found it.

She was going to have to face him, tell him what was eating at her. She was worn out. But she knew that would cut no ice with Rudge. To him "worn out" was no reason, no excuse, not even an answer. He couldn't even imagine it. Tired? Fuck *that* noise! The Rose was a Star, and Stars continued to shine, worn out or not. Life was the most exhausting gig of all, he would say. Plenty of time to rest in the grave, he'd tell her; she could hear that rotten Limey accent of his, mingling with the street parlance of New York. The Rose didn't have the time to get tired; she was The Rose.

Seventeen months. She'd been a Star for seventeen months, and every minute of every hour of every one of those fuckin' seventeen she'd been tired out of her mind. In less than a year and a half she had cut three albums— two had shipped gold and the last one platinum—and

12

she'd played one-night gigs, benefit concerts, and two
road tours that had cut across the face of the nation. Also,
out a flashbulb going off in her face. She had done a cover
story for *Rolling Stone,* which was run in three consecu-
during that time she couldn't take a drink or a piss with-
tive issues. At first, the reporter had practically climbed
into bed with her. By the time they'd reached the third
issue, the reporter *had* climbed into bed with her, and
young America had learned every fact there was to know
about The Rose, from the size of her nipples to the flavor
of her douche. For seventeen hellish, hectic months The
Rose had been living in a goldfish bowl in the middle of
Grand Central Station. Now she had to change the water
or she would float belly up and die.

If she could get Rudge to understand and agree.

The Learjet was taxiing to a stop. And there, on
the edge of the tarmac as she knew it would be, sat the
black Cadillac limousine, its one-way glass windows
rolled up. Behind that impermeable tinted barrier sat
Rudge, an Englishman dressed as a cowboy, waiting for
The Rose. Waiting and angry. Rose gave a little shudder.

She waited until the rest of the group had filed off the
plane. First Danny and Norton, the lead guitarist and the
bass guitarist, trotted down the steps, encumbered by their
Fenders. Neither of them ever let anybody handle their
axes. Next came Dennis, loaded down with the small
amplifiers, then Whitey, the second lead, strolled noncha-
lantly down the gangway, empty-handed. He always sent
his guitar with the truck, which also carried the band's
huge speakers, the floor amplifiers, the keyboards, the
lights and gels, the control boards, and miles and miles of
thick, ropy black electrical cable.

After the guys, the girls left the aircraft one by one.
Only Norton was married; Whitey had a most-of-the-time
old lady, but she waited for him in the Idaho hills, where she
raised goats and wove ponchos out of their organically
dyed shearings. The other girls were temporaries—group-

ies, mostly, and an occasional stewardess or waitress or secretary picked up by Dennis on his travels. What all the girls had in common was long legs, long hair, and short attention spans. They were thrilled to be allowed on the Star's plane, and they would cheerfully fuck anybody in the band or anybody else in the entourage. The band referred to them collectively as The Mice.

There was also a rock 'n' roll photographer, a long, lean, intense-eyed girl wearing a micromini and tall boots. Over her tiny breasts she had strapped a bandolier made of film cans. In three of the cans were rolls of film. In the five others, dope and pills of every description. She was fucking Whitey, and it looked like it was getting heavy. Maybe Whitey's old lady was going to be stuck with the goats.

When the plane was empty, Rose stood up unsteadily and started for the door. Wooops, forgot my poke, she said to herself.

Rose's "poke" was her trademark. She weighed about ninety pounds without it, and a hundred and twenty with it. It was a large sack of tough canvas; once, it had been bright green, but now it was faded and scuffed. Rose had sewn appliqués and braiding around it, not only to patch and reinforce it, but also in defiance of the bag's advancing age. In it, Rose carried just about everything she could lift—scarves tangled with the vitamin bottles, lemons were mixed with her pots of makeup, honey had spilled on the copy of Hermann Hesse's *Siddhartha,* which she had been meaning to read for three years now. All the way down at the bottom of the poke was Rose's money, but she hardly ever had to search for it, because Rudge signed for everything with credit cards.

Lifting the bottle of Aquavit, she stuffed it into the poke and made for the door of the plane. Her gait was somewhat unsteady, partly due to the amount she'd been drinking and partly to the outrageous harlot shoes she was wearing. In this day and age, 1969, when everybody was into organic and natural, Rose had dug out of some ancient thrift shop a pair of open-toed, sling-back, high heeled slippers, and she never let them off her feet. In them, she felt tall and glamorous, the Joan Crawford of rock 'n' roll.

The sunlight hit her strongly as she reached the doorway, and Rose squinted in pain. Fumbling around in her poke, she found her plastic-framed sunglasses and put them on. That was a little better. She looked out. Ooooooh, it was a long way to the ground. Six steps. Hell, she could do it.

And she did, in her own way. On the third step, her long, floating, hand-batiked scarf tangled in the railing of the ladder, pulling her off her precarious balance. Down she went, tumbling down the last three steps and twisting her foot under her on the soft surface of the landing strip. The bottle of Aquavit rolled out and smashed, oozing onto the tarmac.

The limo door opened and Rudge stepped out coolly, unfolding his jeans-clad legs in their millionaire cowpoke's three-hundred-dollar boots. He stood watching Rose coldly, waiting to see if she could get up and walk before he lifted one finger.

He saw a thin, small-boned young woman in her middle twenties, her pointed face hidden under a billowy frizz of golden hair. Tight satin jeans, appliquéd with sequins, rhinestones, and roses, clung to her slender thighs and small buttocks. Her breasts were disproportionately large, but firm and bobbing as she struggled to her feet. They were only thinly disguised by an Indian blouse of tye-dyed spangled chiffon. She stood up and made a few feeble passes at dusting herself off. On her arms was her usual complement of bracelets—at least twenty of them, jangly, sparkly things of silver, plastic, wood, gold. Whatever had captured her fancy. Rings caught the light on most of her fingers; feathers were entwined in her hair. She wasn't conventionally pretty, but she made you draw your breath. She was stunning, outrageous in her satin and velvet and finery, a medieval minstrel in the twentieth century, a sock in the eye to straight people everywhere. Millions of girls tried to copy her style, but there was only one Rose.

Well, she had all her fingers and toes, Rudge noticed. Nothing appeared damaged; nothing seemed to be missing. She'd have to tell *some* story to talk away twenty-eight thousand dollars' worth of extra studio and union-musician time. *Some* story.

Rose caught his eye and smiled tentatively. Rudge drew his lips back in an answering smile. Each of them smiled, star and manager, and each knew pretty well what the other was thinking behind that smile.

The band and The Mice began loading the instruments and the small amps into the Chevy van that was pulled up behind the Caddy. Without a word, Rudge took Rose's arm and propelled her into the back seat of the limousine. Both pretended gravely not to notice just how loaded The Rose was.

The smoke-glass windows cut the sunlight off at the pass. As the limo turned off the landing field and onto the access road that led away from the airport, Rudge reached for his crocodile briefcase and spun the combination-lock digits. Rose sighed. They were open for business.

He owned an apartment on the Avenue Foch in Paris; he had stayed in it three nights over the past four years. He was remodeling a brick house in the newly fashionable London borough of Islington, but in four years he hadn't had a chance to select the nineteenth-century fireplace mantels. He lived in a duplex high over Central Park, but the refrigerator held only a shriveled wedge of lime and a rotten piece of Camembert. He ate on the run, slept on his feet, and was umbilically attached to a tele-

16

phone. His office was his real home and hard work his only milieu. There was only one true love in Rudge Campbell's life, and you spelled that m-o-n-e-y.

Besides the money itself, and the ways of spending it, what it represented in terms of wheeling and dealing was what Rudge loved best. The power of making a deal, of outfoxing the dogs, coming up with the bloody game in your teeth. Winning put the blue in the sky and the red in The Rose. And yet for the first twenty-odd years of his life, he wasn't even Rudge Campbell.

When he'd come squalling angrily into the world on a bleak day in early January 1933, he wasn't Rudge Campbell at all.

"Thomas Patrick, d'ya hear me, woman? I want him named after me. He's the first boy in the family, in't he? Thomas Patrick!" Callahan's shout escalated into a roar.

"Reginald," countered the baby's mother, stubbornly. "Oi want 'im to 'ave a better chance at life than a common name loike Thomas will give him. Oi've always fancied the name Reginald. It's refoined-like."

"Reginald!? It's soppy! A bloody soppy name for a bloody soppy arsehole! What's wrong wiv a workingman's name, then? You want him to end up some bloody soppy clerk in some bloody soppy office, earning three bob a week instead of a man's wages?"

"It's better'n the fish market, in't it?"

"Whut's wrong wiv Billingsgate, then? It's good honest work and it puts bread and drippin' on the table, dun' it? *Reginald!*" Thomas Patrick Callahan's rough voice dripped scorn. "A name fer a bleedin' ponce or a flippin' fairy."

A Liverpool Irishman, a navvy, who had lost his dockside work when the Depression blanketed England in gray misery, Callahan had drifted south in search of work, and had ended up in London, filling barrels in the Billingsgate market, where the nation's fish and seafood were

17

shipped to the nation's tables. He'd lucked out. He also lucked out with Lily Green, and had married her. Lily had been born and raised in London, within sight and smell of Billingsgate, and she was heartily sick of it. She was a great reader of the society pages in the penny newspapers, and she yearned after any pathetic hint of the upper classes.

Now the maternity ward at Charing Cross Hospital was echoing with the Callahans' row, and the other patients began to register their complaints. With an indignant rustle of starched skirts, Matron bustled in stiffly to throw Thomas Patrick out and, in his absence, Lily Green Callahan signed the boy's birth certificate.

Reginald Thomas Patrick Callahan, she wrote laboriously, and so he was christened. Naturally, for years after, he was never called anything but "Reg." So much for social aspirations.

Reg Callahan was born with a stink in his nostrils, the stink of the river Thames at low tide, mud crawling with nameless sewage, and the reek of the fish barrels on the dock. Slimy wharves shone phosphorescent with tonnage of fish and seafood, heaped into barrels, baskets, kegs, and casks, all loaded and ready to be trucked out. Hake and plaice and winkles and cod, lobsters and prawns with waving feelers like giant insects, hundreds of dozens of oysters from Colchester and Whitstable. Reg's father wore a leather apron smeared with fish blood and toiled down at the docks, while Reg's mother sold fish from a barrow in the Islington High Street on market days. The boy was five years old before he tasted meat, and six years old before he became aware that there were aromas in the world apart from mud, sewage, seaweed, and fish.

Later in his life, when money had made all odors sweet to Rudge/Reg, he would often order Dover sole or lobster Newburg for the sheer pleasure of sending a cost-

18

ly dish back untasted. No matter how exotic, how well prepared, how expensive, nothing could persuade Rudge Campbell to put a mouthful of fish between his lips.

London in the Depression was a drab and gloomy place to raise a family, especially a family that grew by one with every year that passed. It seemed to Reg, looking back, that he was always hungry and always cold. Why was it that none of his childhood memories included a summer day? Only the chilblained winters would come back to him—wet, raw, rheumy. His overcoat was always too short or too thin to keep his legs or bottom warm; at night there were never enough blankets to go around. The only advantage in sharing a bed with his older brothers was that they could help to warm him. They always made the littlest one sleep down at their feet, like a dog, to take the chill off the bottom of the bed.

In a family the size of the Callahans, everybody had to work. Young Reg was often kept out of school to help his mother at the fishbarrow. He was only eight, but he could count up lightning fast, without using his fingers or even a pencil, and he could make correct change. He could *make* it, but he didn't always *give* it. Every now and then, when an infallible hidden voice told him that Missus wouldn't be counting her change, he managed to slip a farthing or two, maybe even a copper, past the customer and into his own pocket. He was so artful as he did it, his thatch of black curling hair making a frame for the wide green eyes in his choirboy face. The same infallible little voice told him never to "do" a customer twice; so the ladies made no complaint, and Mum never found out.

From his pocket, Reg would transfer the tiny hoard into a cardboard box he kept hidden behind a loose brick at the back of their old house. The Callahans resided in the downstairs flat of a grimy tenement in London's East End, a short walk from the docks where Dad worked. Nobody ever used the backyard for anything but the weekly laundry, and Reg soon discovered that behind the old bricks was the perfect hiding place for his treasures. He had no idea why he was saving every farthing and ha'-penny, yet something told him that money—even the tiny sums in his possession—was the key to a locked door.

When Reg was only six and a half years old, the war broke out. Hitler invaded Poland, and England declared war on Germany. A patriotic fervor swept over the docks; here was the chance to feed England while earning a few extra bob a week. After 1940, there was the nightly terror of the raids; Jerry would come over at least twice a week and he always dropped his dreaded load of destruction on London's docks, the arteries of supply to all of England. Reg soon became accustomed to the sight of the bloated barrage balloons, the sound of the screaming sirens, and the dull boomings of the anti-aircraft guns. He even got used to being awakened in the middle of the night by the shriek of the air-raid alarms and to being dragged down to the cellar for safety, or to the shelter in the Underground station a few streets away. Every week the docks were bashed by bombs, but still the dockers managed to carry on.

When Reg was ten years old, his character was shaped by a single revelation. By 1943, London had been battling the air raids for three years; they were almost nightly occurrences in the East End. But this raid was different. Jerry came over in full force, flying so low you could just about make out the black bent crosses stenciled on the fuselages of the bombers. Not trusting to the cellar, the Callahans made for the Underground. Cots were set up there at all times, so that Londoners, seeking shelter, might sleep in safety if not in peace.

All night long they could hear the heavy thudding of the explosions, the deep sonorous booms reaching their terrified ears even in the cavernous heart of the Underground shelter. There seemed to be no letup whatever, and it wasn't until eight the following morning that the Callahan family emerged with the others from under the earth, their faces wan with apprehension.

"Holy Jasus," breathed Tom Callahan, crossing himself.

"Dear Lord," whimpered Lily Callahan, her eyes wide with horror.

It was gone, all of it. Every stick and stone and brick and street of the London they knew had vanished in the night, as though smashed down by the angry fist of God. The cinema where they could occasionally afford the twopenny seats—gone. The bakery that had sold them the cheap cream buns and the jam rolls for Sunday's tea—gone. The betting shop where Tom Callahan would take a chance with a weekly sixpence on the football pools—gone. The fish and chips shop—gone. The greengrocer's—gone. The corner kiosk where the old man sold Callahan his daily *Standard*—gone. And the Roman Catholic church where they used to hear Mass every Sunday—it, too, was gone, no longer a landmark, its stone spire punctuating the weeks of their lives. Everything familiar had disappeared overnight. The Callahans stood stunned as they stared uncomprehendingly at a stony ground leveled flat by the Germans.

But what of their own house? What about their own furniture and clothing and everything else they owned in this world? Wailing loudly in fear, Lily ran blindly down the crooked, smoking, rubble-filled streets, past the fire trucks and the exhausted rescue workers in their round helmets, past ambulances and corpses, over shattered glass and twisted steel girders and fallen beams with great protruding nails. She ran crying toward home, and Thomas and the kids ran howling after her. When they turned the corner of their street, the weeping became sobs, and the sobs turned into screams.

21

They'd been bombed out. Windows had been blown out all over the street. A direct hit had carried away all of No. 21 Ashdown Street, even the lowest-floor flat. Their house was a jagged ruin, bits and pieces of destroyed furniture strewn about the streets like the broken toys of a pampered child. Pockmarked walls exposed the shameful tatters of peeling wallpaper to the chilly morning. One direct hit, and everything had disappeared in smoke and flame. Even the cat.

Reg's green eyes didn't blink; they stared in wonder at the total destruction around him. Nothing. He recognized nothing. His mother was lamenting loudly and his father was screaming furious curses, but Reg didn't hear them. He could only stare. His entire world, his every landfall, his very own terrain, had been taken from him overnight. There was nothing left to hold onto.

Unless . . . Suddenly, Reg turned and ran around the ruin of the house to where a bit of the back wall still stood. He checked the foundation of the house and, by some miracle, the loose brick was still there and still loose. Reg pulled and tugged at it and it fell to the ground.

The cardboard had all burned away, but in the ashes, Reg's little cache of coins lay gleaming as though freshly minted. The coppers had melted a little, and three or four of the ha'pennies had fused together, but the threepenny bits still held their shape. When Reg reached in and touched them, the coins burned his fingers with their metallic heat.

Blowing on his blistered fingers, the ten-year-old boy contemplated his money with narrowed eyes. He had a sudden vision of the future, and a great truth was revealed to him on the spot. Nothing in this whole world was permanent. Nothing except money. They can come in the night and take everything away, mash it flat, make it disappear. But money lives forever; it possesses a life of its own, apart from the rest of the world. If you can accumulate enough of it, there's nothing they can do to you.

You will not come to any harm. But how much of it was enough? He would spend the rest of his life finding that out. The lesson he'd learned was his revelation: Nothing is true, permanent, or of value in this life except enough money. Forever after, Reg Callahan would be guided by that revelation, and only by that revelation.

Oddly enough, on the same morning that this vision came to Reginald Thomas Patrick Callahan, on the other side of the Atlantic Ocean a baby girl was born whose life and death would be also shaped by that boy's vision.

The Rose.

She sat beside him now in the limousine, pale and apprehensive, as the car glided through the dimness of the Queens Midtown Tunnel and burst upon the crowded byways of Manhattan. It was Rudge's great gift that he knew just when to chastise her and when to treat her like royalty. He knew her so well that their instincts meshed, and words were often unnecessary between them. Right now Rudge knew it had to be Kid Gloves City for The Rose. Not only would she respond better to kindness, but also the thin, vague threat of catching it later would remain hanging over her, making her more anxious, more pliable to his wishes.

And he was going to need her pliable. They had a big New York concert ahead of them; immediately after that, they had to finish recording the album. Then there were two major tours, back to back; he had the details just about worked out. Rose had been drinking a lot, and it was going to have to stop. If she thought that she was tired and overworked now—well, she hadn't seen anything yet. The hard work was just about to begin.

Rudge smiled gently at Rose and brushed back a tendril of her curly hair. Rose smiled back nervously and shut her eyes.

II

In the wild mountain ranges of Manhattan's top office buildings, RC Associates Ltd. was Mount Everest. You needed courage, endurance, warm clothing, and a Sherpa guide to make it to the top in the cutthroat music business, but Rudge Campbell hadn't been cold in ten years. His suite of offices possessed—no, *commanded* —two of the finest views of this city of stone and steel and glass. If they ever built a more luxurious office suite than Rudge's, he'd move. Meanwhile, he was content with the entire sixty-third floor of the most prestigious address in the business. Furnished in wall-to-wall Louis XV mixed with rock-pop-psychedelic 1960s *kitsch* art, Rudge's offices were designed to impress, and impress they did.

Exciting as his own office was to look at, it was primarily a workplace, the bridge of the ship Rudge commanded. Dominating the room was a large, glass-topped desk. Actually, it was an antique dining table worth many thousands of dollars, but with Rudge's technology spread out on its gleaming surface, the table resembled an electronic control center. On one corner of the desk was a large telephone console, almost a switchboard, its panel covered with buttons that lit up constantly instead of ringing. This, and the conference-call squawk box that sat next to it, connected the rest of the world to Rudge.

Most of the time he ignored it. Somebody in the outer office would get it. That's what they were paid for. An unobtrusive black telephone near it bore a dial empty of telephone number. This was Rudge's sacred private telephone; its number was changed every third week, like the password given to a military guard. When the black phone rang, Rudge was on it like a cat on a herring. Only a handful of the most important people in Rudge's professional life had that number; it linked him directly to large sums of money.

Also squatting proudly on the desktop were not one but two Rolodex files, each one bulging with neatly typed cards, some in Rudge's own code. They were out of reach of everybody other than Rudge himself, and he never let anybody approach them. Every night, the Rolodexes were locked away in a steel safe; it was Rudge's last act before turning out the office lights; he was usually the last one to leave. The precious files—updated daily—contained the private numbers of head honchos in every phase of the rock 'n' roll business—from the telephone in the Mercedes-Benz limo of the president of Atlantic Records to the unlisted number in the boudoir of the latest bird that the hottest deejay in the country was balling.

Two of the office walls were floor-to-ceiling windows looking out on New York; through them you could see the rivers that surrounded this island city, and the many kinds of shipping that kept it a vital port. The other two walls were covered with a woven gold fabric, a satin Jacquard reproduction of a pattern of Marie Antoinette's. It had cost fifty dollars a yard at Schumacher's, but it might as well have been burlap. Because nothing of it showed. Rudge's walls were plastered with old Avalon Ballroom posters, Andy Warhol silkscreens of film stars and soup cans, an original Milton Glaser portrait of Bob Dylan, a football banner for Arsenal—Rudge's favorite team in England—and dozens of photographs and posters of The Rose. Her face was everywhere—beaming in triumph as she raised her arms high at a concert, singing, laughing, signifying, wailing, getting down. Here was a picture of The Rose grinning with Mick, Bill, and Charlie, while Keith glowered off in a corner and Brian looked stoned. A picture of The Rose and Janis Joplin admiring each other's bracelets. Janis wore a large crushed-velvet hat trimmed with ostrich plumes, and The Rose's breasts were bare. Now a blowup of The Rose back-lit and sweating in front of twenty-five thousand ecstatic fans. Her eyes were shut and her hair was plastered in wet tendrils on her forehead and cheeks; she looked like a young martyred saint. Shining above the photographs of The Rose in all her moods and personas were three magnificently framed records—two gold and one platinum—and the photostat of a check for record royalties, made out to Rudge Campbell in the amount of three quarters of a million dollars.

The opposite wall was almost Spartan, dominated by a huge schedule board, larger than anything in the room except Rudge's desk. It was The Rose's schedule—concerts, recording dates, interviews, and the tours that Rudge was finalizing now.

There were other offices in the suite. They were allocated to the "associates" in Rudge Campbell Associates Ltd. Other artists were handled by Rudge's associates; the bands were all boys and girls on the way up, since Rudge dumped anybody he thought was on the way down. But The Rose was handled personally by Rudge himself, and only by him. None of his associates had access to her at any time. Rudge's personal suite consisted of an outer office, where callers were kept in a holding pattern until Rudge announced that they could enter the palatial room with its breathtaking views, a private bathroom complete with sauna, and a smaller office that was used mostly as a storeroom for file cabinets, press kits, buttons, posters, T-shirts, and other giveaways, all of which carried the face and the long-stemmed red symbol of The Rose.

On the floor of Rudge's office was a unique Swakara rug, its size making it virtually priceless. And lying on her belly in the center of the rug, The Rose herself was going over the contact sheets of her latest set of "official" photographs, giggling now and then like a happy child when she saw a picture she liked, frowning more often at the pictures she didn't. In her sequined shawl and lacy blouse, she looked like a kid dressed up for Halloween. Rudge shot her a sharp glance as he picked up his IBM minirecorder with its magnetic belt. It was time to lay down the law to her. He'd held his tongue yesterday, allowing her to cool out. Besides, she'd been too drunk to listen. But now, as she pawed her way through the glossy contact sheets looking for her favorites, he felt that it was time.

Time. To Rudge Campbell, the only mortal enemy was time. Every minute counted in the race with life, and he could never do fewer than three things at once. Right now he was nodding his agreement or disagreement with the pictures Rose was holding up for his approval, while puncturing the tip of an Uppmann cigar smuggled in from Castro's Cuba, while dictating the day's instructions into the recorder.

"August 14, 1969, 2:45 P.M.," he began. Rudge always dated and timed his transcriptions so that nobody could fuck up his latest orders, which were subject so sudden change. "Dennis, tell George to send an extra camera crew to Florida. Set interviews with Rose's family for cutaways during the TV special. In Europe, we're booked into London, Paris, Berlin, Frankfurt. . . ."

"This one almost makes me pretty," said Rose softly, holding a contact sheet up for him to see. Her face was tired and very vulnerable.

"You are pretty," said Rudge automatically, but his

28

eyes flickered over the photograph. As usual, she was right. It was usable.

"Bet your booties," said Rose with a defiant lift of her chin. She didn't feel pretty. She had never felt pretty. She also had no real faith in the special aura of originality and style that set her apart and made her unique.

Rudge turned his attention back to the dictating machine, reeling off dates and figures as Rose, bored now with the pictures, shoved them aside and grabbed at the last bite of the Reuben sandwich wrapped in oily paper that lay on the priceless rug. She washed the last large mouthful down with a swig from her glass of Aquavit and, still hungry, looked around for something else to eat.

"No chips?" she pouted.

"The hogs ate 'em." Rudge clicked off the recorder and tucked the telephone receiver under his chin as he reached for Rolodex No. 1 and thumbed through it. Rudge kept more files than the CIA and the FBI, and many of the cards on file bore cryptic notations in Rudge's handwriting. Always, they referred to the price he had to pay or the price that would be paid to him. These cards held the measure of a man's worth, sometimes the price of his soul.

"Rudge?"

Something in The Rose's voice begged for his attention. He knew fragility when he heard it. The cracks in Rose were beginning to show. Rudge cradled the receiver and turned to her.

"Yeah?"

Sitting up on the rug, Rose pulled the gossamer tie-dyed and sequined scarf around her shoulders as though its flimsiness could warm her.

"Sinners in hell all want ice water," she said softly, meditatively.

Rudge recognized the signs. When Rose dragged out her country "wisdom," it meant that something heavy was coming. He flashed her a frigid grin. "And they'd get it, too, if *you* had the concession," he told her.

Rose threw back her head and a raucous shout of mirth issued from her. Everything about her came from the earth, except her hair, which was fire. And her voice—that huge and complex instrument, fashioned of all four elements: air, fire, earth, and tears for water. Rudge was always surprised that somewhere in that tiny body of hers so large an animal as that voice was caged.

"Hand me them peanuts," she ordered, scrambling to her feet.

"They're cashews," replied Rudge, handing over the Lalique bowl.

"Whatever. I need something new," she said abruptly.

Rudge glanced at her sharply, aware that Rose wasn't talking about peanuts or cashews. He kept his lips pressed tightly together, waiting for the girl to have her say.

Rose bit her lips, searching for the right words. You had to be so careful with Rudge. He had a way of taking your words and twisting them around until you no longer understood what you wanted, only what *he* wanted. And Rudge *had* to listen, *had* to understand, because there was only the two of them, in this together.

"It ain't fun anymore, man," she said, looking earnestly into his green eyes with her blue ones. She shook her frizzy head, and that vertical line appeared between her brows again. "It ain't fun, it's somethin' else. I'm not good, not singin' good. It's important how I sound now . . . I can't be half assed. It's gotta be good, doncha see? And that's what's drivin' me crazy. . . . I'm crazy. It's nobody's fault," she pleaded, holding out one hand, covered in sparkly rings, for him to take. "Maybe I got too much work," she ended softly.

But Rudge ignored her outstretched hand and avoided her eyes. Stone-faced, he turned away and stared out the tall window at Fun City. His voice bit down hard. The almost-southern American overlay vanished, leaving only the London accent—flat, unemotional, threatening.

"We all work *too* hard," he snarled. "Sometimes in the morning my pee is so tired I have to wake it up with a shot of vodka before it'll come out. Now, *that's* tired."

But Rose shook her head, still determined to get through to him. She knew how angry he was when he dropped his shitkicker pose. His leather vest, his hand-tailored Levi's, his ostrich-skin boots, his heavy silver concho belt, the straw cowboy hat that was the Rudge trademark—God help any *real* country boy who got in Rudge Campbell's way.

"Rudge, I need me some time before I lay down and die," she said stubbornly. "I want a year to myself after the Florida concert."

There it was. She'd come right out with it and it lay between them, ticking like a bomb.

"You come into an inheritance or something." It was not a question. Rose turned her face up to him, seeking for his eyes. "I need time to rest. I . . . I . . . can't dredge up the sincerity anymore. It's not real."

"Wrong!" shouted Rudge, his face taut with anger.

"Don't tell *me* 'wrong,' Charlie," Rose shouted back, suddenly furious.

Rudge's hand slapped down hard on the glass of the tabletop. "I'm runnin' the fuckin' Green Bay Packers here and you're givin' me sandlot in Dixie," he hissed at her, his eyes blazing.

Rose waved one small hand in frustration. Strain was pinching her face together, making it look smaller than ever. "I don't want a year off a year from now. I need it *now!*"

"Jeezus!" snapped Rudge, his face an angry white. "What *do* you want? You got twenty-nine people working for you."

"I'll be a goddamn cadaver soon!" yelled Rose. "Who needs twenty-nine pallbearers?"

31

Rudge whirled toward her, throwing his arms out wide. "Okay, you want 'out'? Let's call in the dogs and piss on the fire."

Despite herself, Rose had to laugh. "Remember when I taught you that?" she wheedled, trying to put Rudge into a better mood.

But Rudge was dead serious, and not to be side-tracked into nostalgia. "I'll tell you what I remember," he said frostily. "I remember three million dollars' worth of dates we're talkin' about canceling here. This is a fuckin' business! Just like Chevrolet and Sara Lee! This isn't 'OOOOOhhhh, I don't feel so good today,' " he mimicked her savagely. " 'Call off the tour! Screw the promoters! *Take a nap!* '" He glared at Rose; he'd been waiting for just this moment and he was determined to pursue his fullest advantage. "It's up against the wall now. So don't anybody give me any 'tired *artiste*' bullshit or I'll give them two dozen bad-ass lawyers and *this* to blow their fuckin' brains out with!"

Savagely, Rudge ripped open the top drawer of his desk and pulled out a .38 revolver, slamming it down so hard on the desktop that the glass shattered.

Rose stood frozen, recognizing murder in Rudge's eyes. Sometimes he terrified her, and this was one of those times. Silence crackled between them; each of them had made a statement; now they both knew where they stood.

"And if anybody thinks I'm jivin'," added Rudge quietly, "take a good look up here in my eyes."

Rose took a look, a good look. He wasn't jivin'. She heaved a long, silent sigh. Two tours, back to back. She was facing two tours. One of them was the big European gig that had taken Rudge months to pull together. It would carry her across most of Europe; she'd never been there. Still, she doubted she'd have a chance to see anything but the inside of the Customs sheds and the concert halls.

But first, the big swing home. Kicking off here, in

New York City, with the concert tonight at Madison Square Garden, The Rose was to head for the Southland, playing concerts in Memphis, New Orleans, and Savannah, and ending up with a gig in Lawrence, Florida. Home. Lawrence, Florida, local girl makes good and gets a hero's welcome. Oh, yeah. God, she was so damn tired she'd like to lay down an' cry. Her full red lips began to tremble.

Rudge, seeing Rose's face, changed his tactics. Besides, he'd won, hadn't he? He could afford to be generous. He stroked her bare arm with one finger. "Rose," he whispered, "you're one of the very best singer-ladies in the history of the world. Pure and simple. Don't fuck it up, Sweetcheeks," he pleaded softly, his eyes intent on her face. He paused, watching her carefully. She appeared to be coming out of it. "You want to eat some Chinese?"

Rose grinned. "All nine hundred million of them," she cracked. Rudge howled more loudly than the joke deserved, then he pressed his forehead against hers, looking deeply into her dark-rimmed blue eyes. He held up his thumb and, slowly, almost reluctantly, Rose pressed the ball of her thumb against his, in their own private ritual of long standing.

"Rack jobbers rule," they said in unison. It was the magic formula that made a joke out of glum necessity.

The intercom on Rudge's desk buzzed suddenly, and the brittle voice of Rudge's secretary came in on the box. "They're here," Mr. Campbell. "It's three o'clock."

Three o'clock. Shit, they'd forgotten. The press conference. Rudge looked quizzically at Rose, and she nodded back.

"Send them in," he instructed, pulling off his denim jacket. and throwing it hastily over the gun and the broken glass of the desktop. The office door opened and the rock 'n' roll press swarmed in.

In the long and sometimes grubby history of journalism, nothing quite like the rock 'n' roll press had ever been seen before. Stringy-haired, spaced out, stoned, they were nevertheless a surprisingly powerful lot. They had dedicated their lives, these minimally talented and often barely literate young men and women, to the proposition that the most important thing in the world was rock 'n' roll music, with sex and drugs running neck and neck in second place. And they managed to convince their readers of the same proposition. Therefore, *Creem, Crawdaddy, Cheetah, Rolling Stone,* and other fanzines were flourishing, and these scarecrow kids were making money. They were quick to idolize, and faster still to criticize a former idol. They could hype an album into a hit, hype a singer into a star, yet they themselves were woefully vulnerable to hype.

So the rock 'n' roll press was hyped twenty-five hours a day eight days a week. Gifts were showered on them, in the form of free food, free grass, free music, free parties, free T-shirts, buttons, tote bags. They were invited everywhere, cozened and honeyed and kept stoned. Some of them had even become celebrities, and had groupies of their own.

Wherever there was a superstar of rock, there the rock 'n' roll press gathered in greatest numbers, animals at the water hole at sundown. The Rose was a Super-superstar, queen of the rock 'n' roll singers—outrageous, sexually exciting, razzle-dazzle—in short, good copy. This was the beginning of the biggest tour of her career . . . first the hometown swing, and next, Europe. Yet, there had been rumblings—noises coming up from Nashville that the album was in trouble, that Rose was drinking too hard and playing too hard. Trouble in Paradise, their favorite story lead. Besides, they were personally curious. There was a fragility about The Rose that came across to even the crassest of them. They recognized that so much of her toughness was simply a coverup, a veneer, and they wanted to be around when the veneer started to crack, so they could file their stories.

34

Reporters scrambled for the closest position to Rose, but the photographers elbowed them out of the way, snapping pictures of Rose, of Rose and Rudge, of Rose again, Rose posed obligingly on Rudge's desk, even hoisting up her long velvet skirt to flash a little thigh for the cameras, camping and smirking.

"I don't want any out-of-town reporters talking to her," yelled Rudge over the pandemonium. "They give her germs."

"Hiya, Rose!" called the music critic from *Creem,* and Rudge pounced on him in an instant.

"And you! Next time you put a slam on the band, you'll be filing from a gopher hole. In Peoria!"

The questions started up suddenly, a barrage of them from all quarters of the room. Still smiling, Rose picked out the ones she wanted to answer, ignoring the ones she didn't.

"What have you been up to, Rose?"

"Oh, same as everybody else. Hangin' out, havin' a good time, stayin' stoned. Gittin' laid!" she leered cheerfully.

"Ask her what the advance is for The Greatest Show on Earth," said Rudge drily.

"Is the hometown concert sold out?" yelled another reporter.

Rose opened her mouth to reply, but Rudge cut in hastily. "I think there are still four or five seats left in the parking lot going for a bill apiece. After that, we're clean."

"Rudge here wants to put a roof over the place so's we can hang them from the chandeliers," joked Rose, but Rudge interrupted her again.

"We're taping it as the big finish for our television special. All the networks are fighting for it. I've already sold it to fifteen countries foreign. I see a gross of at least seven million and change." His voice was gloating, complacent.

"And *I* do the singin'," Rose pointed out wryly.

"How do you feel about going home to Florida to do a concert?" called a voice from the back of the room.

Rose's smile faded as she put on what she always called her "baby Jesus look." "They're my people down there. I understand them, they understand me," she said simply. What a crock of shit! she thought, her memories touching for a scorching moment on her childhood at home, then veering away again.

"You look tired, Rose," a young woman reporter commented.

"If you had to work for a living, Sweetcheeks, your ass would be draggin' too," snapped Rose. Then she took a deep breath. "After I play my hometown, I'm thinkin' about takin' a year off."

A year off! A murmur swept through the crowd of reporters, and they began to scribble furiously in their notepads. Rudge's head snapped up and his green eyes darkened in anger.

"Sure, she's takin' a year off," he said sarcastically. "The Virgin Mary's comin' off the bench to fill in for us."

Relaxed, the reporter laughed; they were on familiar territory now, but Rose held up one hand. "I'm not kidding," she said quietly. "I really think the hometown concert is gonna be *it* for a year or so."

"She *is* kidding," gritted Rudge. Then he changed the subject ferociously. "You all got your tickets for tonight's concert? You know where they're going to boogie after? Got your press badges? It's gonna be a closed party —caviar, champagne, the best of everything and more than you'll be able to stand. They tell me Twiggy is gonna be there, and you guys don't want to miss Twiggy, right?" Glaring at Rose while he jollied the reporters, he managed to bring the press conference to an end. It was obvious to Rose that she was gonna catch it when he got her alone, so she jumped off the desk and mingled

36

with the reporters, letting the photographers have a field day with candid shots.

When the last reporter left the room, Rudge whirled about angrily, ready to do mayhem on Rose. But she had vanished; she had slithered out with the group of them and down in the elevator. Even now, she was looking around wildly for her limo.

"Where's the car!?" she demanded of Dennis, who was waiting for her downstairs. "I'm a *star*, man! After a performance, a star should just disappear!"

"It's my fault," shrugged Dennis. "I thought the performance would last for more than thirty seconds."

Rose turned on him, livid with rage. "I want a car waiting for me, man!" she screamed hoarsely at him. "I don't care if I even went to Kansas fucking City, you have a car waiting for me! Understand?"

But before Dennis could say a word in his defense, Rose was off the curb and yelling, "TAXI!!" at the top of her lungs.

The street resounded with the slam of the taxicab door, and Rose was off in a cloud of exhaust fumes and summer heat. Dennis didn't get a chance to say good-bye or even ask her where she was going.

"The Roberts Hotel on East Eleventh," said Rose, sitting gingerly on the torn vinyl upholstery of the passenger seat. It smelled funny in here; the driver had been smoking cheap cigars. And the damn cab had no springs left. She was used to springs, to the deep, dark, smooth, and comfortable ride of a Cadillac limousine.

All the way downtown, her thoughts kept bouncing around in her head like those little loaded "jumping beans" she'd had as a child. Rudge, and the angry look on his face when she'd fucked him over in front of reporters. Well, he deserved it, man! Pulling that fucking gun and raving on and on, piss on the fire. It wasn't as though she wanted *out*—just some time to get her act together. A chance to rest; her body, her mind, her voice—everything was wearing down. Like tonight. Tonight she was scheduled to sing her ass off to all of Madison Square Garden. Every seat sold out weeks ago. All the deejays playing her old songs on the radio today, and talking about her new album already, waiting for it, making their listeners salivate in advance. That was a laugh. They didn't have but two or three usable cuts. Life was nothing but a race over a series of hurdles. Jump over one, and another one came up just a few feet farther on. Even the thought of it—the concert tonight, the album, the tour, the hometown concert—made Rose tired. Hurdles. Nothin' but hurdles.

And the fuckin' freak press with their creepy questions. You look tired, Rose. How does it feel to be goin' home, Rose. Fuck them. They all thought they were stars. Fuckin' everybody in the music business thought he was a star. Put a pencil or a camera into a freak's hands, and suddenly he's a goddamn star. What did they know?

As the taxicab rattled past Fourteenth Street, Rose found herself getting anxious. She wasn't eager for this meeting, and she would have avoided it if she could. But no way. Lonnie had once meant too much to her for her to stiff him now. His voice on the phone had brought back a flood of memories of San Francisco. When there had been no real hassles, and everything had been cool and mellow. Had it been only a couple of years ago? Maybe three? It seemed a lifetime away. Damn it, it *was* a lifetime. There was no going back to those days, even if she wanted to. Which she didn't, easy though they'd been. Too much had happened to her since then.

When the cab pulled up to the faded old hotel with its tattered excuse for an awning, Rose had to struggle with herself not to tell the driver to turn around and take her back uptown. Shrugging, she pulled herself out of the cab and threw the driver a five-dollar bill for a two-dollar fare. She had seen him checking her out in the rear-view mirror. He thought she was a hippie freako and wouldn't pay. Little did he know.

She fluffed up her feathers and patted down the velvet on her jeans and sashayed into the lobby, listening for the tiny gasps of recognition, watching for the stares.

And she wasn't disappointed. The Roberts, an ancient hotel, once elegant, was now used almost exclusively by rock 'n' rollers on the way up and on the way down. The stars who knew how to mind their manners stayed at the St. Regis or the Navarro on Central Park South, or even the Gramercy Park Hotel. The stars who couldn't mind their manners were stuck on the outer fringes of Manhattan in the big plastic motor inns, where they couldn't do too much costly damage. The Plaza Hotel would not even register a rock star; they'd had one experience with the Beatles and that was enough for them.

But the sidemen and the session men and the musicians who had never cut an album stayed at the Roberts, where the rooms were cheap and where nobody hit on them. The seedy lobby was always bustling with the hangers-on of the music business, male and female groupies and plaster-casters hoping to fuck their way up the long and endless ladder that led to Mick or Paul.

There was also a fairly public drug scene going on right there in the open. Small-time dealers completed lobby transactions for smoke, uppers and downers, confident that the narcs wouldn't bother with them unless they were peddling the hard stuff. The fuzz hated dealing with those hippie weirdo freaks, so longhairs were always cooping or nodding out in the Roberts lobby; anything went, short of a sleeping bag on the floor.

It looks like the third day of a music festival in Schenectady, thought Rose, as she stepped inside. She was recognized on sight, and a tremor shook the lobby of the Roberts Hotel with a ground reading of 8.6. Enjoying the sensation she was creating, the whispers of

"Rose, it's The Rose, man! Far fuckin' out!," she wiggled up to the front desk. A couple of wide-eyed groupies approached her, but she shook her yellow head and they backed off. It was cool; Rose wasn't wanting any. Maybe another time.

"Lonnie Peters, honey," she told the open-mouthed room clerk. No star of The Rose's magnitude had set a foot in this roach-infested lobby in the two years he'd been on the desk.

"Room 317, Rose." He almost stammered.

"Right on," grinned Rose, and headed for the elevator.

But her smile disappeared as the elevator doors closed behind her. Lonnie. Lonnie Peters. Could she face him? Was she strong enough? Once she had loved him so much, and he'd been there for her, strong and loving and gentle, just as she had needed. He'd been her old man; she was his lady. They had lived and loved in a bedroll on the floor of a room in San Francisco, a room covered with posters of Che and the Airplane at the Fillmore. They had smoked their joints and made their plans for a future they would spend together, Lonnie on bass and Rose on vocals. They made plans and they made love—long, sweet, stoned-out nights of kissing and licking and loving.

Whew! Lotta memories there, Rose, she told herself. Long time ago. Yet, she remembered every minute of it; it came back in a rush. Lonnie—her big, gentle Lonnie. He was barrel-chested and hairy and strong. He didn't talk much, but his eyes said it all-deep, warm brown eyes, eyes that could be trusted. She'd had a lot of lovers since that time—lotta one-nighters and two-weekers and even an affair that had lasted four months, but there had never been as strong and dependable a man as Lonnie for The Rose.

Dependable. What a laugh, a real thigh-slapper. Rose remembered running down Fillmore Street, carrying

40

a peacock feather and a bottle of sweet wine. She'd scrambled up the ramshackle wooden stairs to their room, smiling all over at the thought of Lonnie. But the room was empty, and it took her a minute to figure it out. The bedroll. The bedroll was gone, and so was Lonnie. He'd split without a word, without a note, without a last kiss or a good-bye. None of the other guys in the band knew where her Lonnie had gone. Was it another woman or just a gig in another town? She had never found out, never heard from him again.

Until yesterday. Until the phone had rung in her hotel room, and Lonnie's voice came over the wire, pleading with her to come down and see him. "For old times, Rose. You remember old times, don't you, Rose?"

She remembered old times. Unconsciously, she rubbed at her face, feeling again the sweet soreness between her cheek and her neck. That was where he would bury his mustache, when he fucked her, slow and creamy or fast and heavy.

"Hot and sweet," he used to say. "Hot and sweet. You're the hot fudge on my sundae, mama," he used to tell her. "I could eat you to death."

Room 317. She was standing right in front of the door. The aged brown paint was peeling off the door in long, ugly strips.

"I need to see you again, mama. Come down, please, Rose." His voice on the telephone had peeled back her skin and exposed all her nerves.

Rose took a deep breath and knocked. A few seconds later it opened, and he held his hand out to her.

This wasn't Lonnie. It *couldn't* be. The man she had loved in San Francisco was a big man, with a heavily muscled chest and strong, powerful thighs. His hair was glossy, the curls tight and crisp, the eyes gleaming with energy.

The man in the doorway couldn't weigh more than a hundred and twenty pounds, and all of it bone. His hair was dry and bushy, like kinky, straggly wire, and it was dirty. His eyes were dull, and his hands and fingernails were so filthy that, at the sight of the hand extended to her, Rose recoiled on instinct.

"Rose. You look wonderful, mama. Thanks for comin'."

It was Lonnie's voice. Incredibly, this decrepit wreck was her Lonnie. Almost blindly she followed him inside. The room was tiny, no more than seven feet by ten but, even so, there were two other people in it. A girl lay on the messy bed, her eyes shut, her head nodding. She couldn't have been more than sixteen years old, maybe less. Her straight hair hung limply down below her waist, and her tiny breasts were bare. All she was wearing was a torn pair of dirty jeans. Across the room, squatting against the wall, was a pimply freak in a ragged T-shirt, scratching violently at his face and neck. The skin was already torn and abraded.

This is no scene for me, she thought, not for The Rose. She turned to go, but Lonnie's clawlike hand had already fastened on Rose's wrist, and he pulled her farther into the room.

"My lady. You were always my sweet mama, Rose," he crooned at her, and Rose could see past his cracked and grinning lips to his once-strong teeth, now rotting in his head. His breath was foul.

"Let me show you something, Rose. Look. Look, Rose. You're gonna really dig on this." Lonnie pulled open the top drawer of the rickety old dresser. Rose looked inside and gasped, her eyes two wide blue pools of horror.

The drawer was filled with large plastic bags, neatly sealed with several windings of tape. Each bag must have weighed a pound at least, and was filled with a white powder. Rose recognized it instantly, and backed away as though the drawer were a pit of live vipers.

42

"Are you crazy?!" she demanded. "Let me out of here."

"For you, Rose. Good junk. And all you gotta do . . ."

"Get away from me, you creep!" shrieked Rose, panic-stricken. "I'm clean! I'm through with that stuff! For good!" She tried to shake off Lonnie's hand, but his iron grip tightened. He might be wasted, but he was still strong. The girl on the bed didn't open her eyes, and the freak against the wall only scratched more nervously, tearing gashes in his face.

"Let me outta here!" Rose demanded, kicking at Lonnie's shins and knees with her high-heeled shoes. "Let me go, you demented freako!"

"Wait, Rose, listen! There's a fortune in that drawer, maybe a million bucks, maybe more. I'm in with the big guys now, moving big stuff. We cut it on a four. It's you and me, babe, just the way it used to be. Remember, Rose? Honey, you can move this stuff fast, with all your big connections to the money. Deal it for me, baby, and we'll split fifty-fifty. Maybe half a million bucks, Rose. All for you. No problem. And we'll be back together, right? My sweet hot fudge, remember, Rose? Remember how it used to be?" His voice was shrill and whining, but he clung to her wrist like a drowning man.

A wave of nausea passed over Rose, and for a minute there she thought she was going to pass out. It took all her willpower to keep her eyes open. She forced herself to take deep breaths until the darkness passed away from her eyes.

Wow! Lonnie. She couldn't believe it. This freak scene, with the cola cans and candy wrappers on the floor, and the syringe on the night table. She knew this scene. She herself had lived it once. A million painful years ago. She shook her head, in denial of her memories, in denial of the evidence in front of her eyes. Lonnie,

43

her Lonnie, so big and strong and quiet. A wasted, strung-out junkie who was probably right now under the steel eyes of the Feds. Any minute now, he could be behind bars, maybe for life. Pity choked her, but she forced it back. She had to get out of here. Now.

"Lonnie," she said very quietly and calmly, "let go of my wrist. Let it go, papa."

At once, she felt the grip of his fingers loosen, and she was free. She took a few steps backward.

"Lonnie, be cool, man. Just be cool. The Rose isn't mad at you," she said, edging back toward the door. "But this isn't my scene anymore, man. It's not my scene. I can't cut it, papa. Not anymore. I've been there." She wanted to cry out to him: Why did you split, Lonnie? Why did you leave me without a word? How did this happen to you? But she controlled herself, seeing in his dead eyes no answers, not even any questions.

"Hey, man," she stammered, opening the door. "Come and hear me sing. Tonight, at the Garden. Okay? Come and listen to the music. I'll leave your name at the door. Okay, Lonnie? I'll sing a song just for you." Her hand was on the doorknob. "Just for you, man." The door was open, and she went tumbling out. Oblivious of her high heels, she ran clattering down the stairs, afraid to wait for the elevator.

She ran across the lobby in a panic, without a thought for the freaks and groupies watching her. Pushing through the revolving door, she screamed for a taxicab, loudly, desperately. But before one could pull over to the curb, Rose was retching into the gutter, dry spasms shaking her small body like an earthquake.

"Oh, Jesus. Lord Jesus God. Oh, Lonnie," she sobbed.

III

By 1969, a vast, brand new sports arena built over Pennsylvania Station had replaced the rundown, seedy venerable structure that was Madison Square Garden. The new arena had the same aura of sweat socks and liniment but it was big enough to hold the twenty-five thousand screaming stoned-out rock and roll fans who had lined up in the rain to buy tickets weeks in advance for their favorite star, The Rose.

Tonight, traffic around the Garden was a bitching fuck-up, and mounted policemen distastefully reined their mounts through the crowds of fuzzy-haired flower children. The cops would take a heavyweight championship bout any day, but they really hated these kids, who stood outside the arena burning sticks of strawberry incense to mask the smell of marijuana, and begging passers-by for "a ticket, man, you got a spare ticket?" These were the unlucky ones; the lucky ones were already inside, smelling the Garden up with reefer, and throwing frisbees and flowers at each other. By rights these losers hanging around, buying and selling Rose T-shirts, making appointments for quick sex, turning each other on, these little fuckheads ought to be home in bed. But John Vliet Lindsay, Mayor of Fun City, had issued strict and sharp orders that these kids were not to be hit on. So the officers ground their teeth and tried to keep them in line. Peacefully. What a pain in the ass.

Around the side door, barricades had been erected to keep the kids back, and these barricades were manned by heavy security. A specially picked squad of police officers was augmented by Garden uniformed security officers, and they meant business. There were only two ways anybody could get into The Rose's concert without a ticket. First, if you were wearing one of the identification badges issued by Rudge Campbell's office. These were plastic, large, and prominent, embossed with a long-stemmed rose and the concert date, so they couldn't be used twice. The rock press got these, and the record moguls and their girlfriends, and the deejays and the rack jobbers who distributed the labels, and other movers and shakers in the music business. If you wanted a back-stage badge, you had to call Rudge Campbell Associates Ltd. two weeks before the concert date. There you spoke to a flunkey with a Rolodex. If you were legit, a badge was issued. Otherwise, you could talk yourself blue. High-school and college newspapers counted for shit; so did fan clubs. Nobody got in the back door without a backstage badge.

Unless. Standing quietly at the door was a short, square nonentity with a clipboard, an eye like a falcon, and the memory of a computer data bank. The list contained privileged names, given to this young man by Rose or Rudge or guys in the band. Special friends could get in if their name was on the list, and the young man was paid to recognize special friends when he saw them. Like Sammy the Dealer with his happy pills, everybody's friendly connection. Or some groupie whom one of the guys was balling. Or even, God help us, a mother or a father or a cousin.

Or Bill Wyman or Tina Turner or Janis Joplin. If you were a star, you got star's privileges backstage. But

46

security guards and city police didn't know Bill from Tina from Janis. The boy at the door knew every face in the music business, even the session men. The Rose practiced professional courtesy and was meticulous about allowing her fellow musicians to watch her any time she performed. An important function of the young man at the door was to keep the police from hassling the celebrities who, badgeless, flocked backstage to see The Rose.

Inside the Garden, the lights and sound system had been set up, the electrical system checked, the acoustics checked and balanced. Miles of black cable had been uncoiled and snaked everywhere across the stage, connecting the mikes to the amps, the keyboard to the control panel, the technicians to the musicians. The light show was ready. The stage was ready, and the audience was growing restless. No rock concert in the history of music ever got started on time—well, maybe one of John Denver's—and the kids were accustomed to being kept waiting. But they were still kids, with itchy behinds, and they were skittering like fleas all over the auditorium, sometimes snagging a better seat, sometimes begging a joint or a roach, more often getting collared by security and tossed back up into their own seats.

There were men moving around the stage, but they weren't musicians. They were sound engineers, technicians checking the mikes for feedback, making minute electrical adjustments. At the four corners of the stage, which had been set up in the middle of the arena, stood eight tall guys in jeans and bandana headbands. They had long hair and broad shoulders, and they wore western-style mustaches. In short, they were cool. They were also security, paid for by Rudge. This muscle was there to prevent anybody from rushing the stage and trying to get his hands on The Rose.

Whenever she sang, The Rose projected an enormous sensuality—raw sexual energy. It was common for

47

the kids—girls as well as boys—to rush forward to try to touch her, kiss her, feel her large breasts, grab at her hands or her legs. Her energy turned them on and made them burn, and they wanted her. Somewhere in his or her heart, each of those kids was convinced that he would be The Rose's perfect lover, and all he had to do was to get up onstage where The Rose could have a look at him. The tall, cool, mean machines in the Levi's were paid a great deal of money to handle these kids firmly, before even so much as a finger touched even so much as the tip of The Rose's shoe. Except for beepers and walkie-talkies, they were not armed, but they didn't have to be. Rudge's security people knew guerilla tactics and street moves that were quicker and more effective—and gentle—than any weapons. Nobody got hurt at a Rose concert; it was bad for business.

It was getting on for nine-thirty, and the concert had been scheduled for eight. By now, the rock freaks in the audience were so stoned they were suffering from terminal munchies. They'd gone broke buying paper cups of Coke and seventy-five-cent Hershey bars, and even the smart ones, who'd brought M&Ms by the sack, had already pigged out and were licking at the empty paper bags. The limousines had stopped pulling up to the side door, and the wheelers and dealers and stars were sitting comfortably in the reserved seats and preparing to be entertained.

Rudge checked his watch and nodded to Dennis. Now. It was time to send out the warmup act for their twenty-minute set. Rudge had decided on a piano-playing balladeer, definitely on the way up and also definitely not in the same class with The Rose. No competition there, just some mellow entertainment until the Star herself came out to shine.

The audience settled down to listen to the music, and Dennis hurried backstage to goose the band. The Rose hadn't appeared yet, but the limo driver had phoned from the car to say they'd be on their way. That meant ten minutes; fifteen at the outside, plenty of time. There was a freight entrance all the way around the other side of the Garden. It had a wide, strong concrete ramp over which the trucks and vans carrying the sound and light equipment had traveled. Security was tight there, too, and it was through this wide entrance that The Rose's Cadillac would drive, delivering the Star safe and sound backstage where she wouldn't be mobbed by her fans.

The band had been given the hockey players' locker room as their dressing room and hangout. Tables had been set up with deli and smoked fish, beer, wine, soda, and organic apple juice. The room was filled with the band's hangers-on, all wearing backstage passes. Most of these were girls—pretty, vapid, pale, and pencil-thin. They'd ironed their hair so that it hung down to their little round tushes in one straight fall, and most of them wore Indian cholas, those thin backless blouses that exposed birdlike shoulder blades and let their tiny erect nipples show through in the front. These girls lived for one thing only: to ball rockers. They slept in the afternoons, wings folded around them, and woke only with the night—to get high and get down. It wasn't music that turned them on, it was musicians. The sight of those stringy guys in the band tapping their high-heeled boots in rhythm while they banged on their huge Fender axes made these little girls cream. If they'd been alive during World War II, they'd have gone up on the roof with sailors.

"Twenty minutes," yelled Dennis, sticking his head in the door. "Hey, what the fuck are all these people doing in here?" He came into the room and stood there scowling, his hands on his hips.

"Well, Dennis," grinned Norton, who had been practicing some runs on the bass, "one is my sister, and Eulalie here is my stepmother. Mom, meet Dennis the Menace."

49

"You two, *out!*" snapped Dennis at the nervous groupies. "And that goes for all of you. Anybody not on-stage with the band, get out of this dressing room now!"

"Hey, man!" protested Danny, who was tuning his twelve-string.

"Outside!" yelled Dennis, and the girls began to drift out reluctantly, one or two making feeble pleas or protests, to which Dennis listened stone-faced and un-moving.

"Come on, man! They're not doing anything," Whitey said.

"Yet," Danny put in wickedly. He'd been looking forward to a little head before showtime.

"Everybody out! I don't care whose old lady or chickee you are; I don't care what you're showing or blowing or snowing. Just get the fuck out of here and leave these so-called musicians alone." There were days when Dennis hated his job, and this looked like one of them. He always had to play the heavy; it was his function to get the group, intact and with their heads relatively to-gether and their instruments approximately in tune, out on that stage.

"Magic time, everybody," yelled Rose, barging in full-steam to the dressing room. She grabbed the last of the baby groupies who was finally leaving and kissed her full on the mouth.

"This one is dynamite," she whooped. "Save some for me."

Dennis slammed the door behind the last of the girls. Rose drew a deep breath and looked hard at the band. Her eyes held a strange glitter, and she was jittery and skittery, totally hyper.

"Smells like jockstraps in here," she announced and marched up to her lead guitarist. "You got the tunes; lemme see the list." Danny handed her his instrument, which had the list of numbers, in the order in which the set would be performed, Scotch-taped to the back of the ax.

Rose scanned it quickly. "Let's cut this one," she snapped.

"You always like that one, Rose," Danny replied mildly. He was accustomed to this number from her. It happened before every concert.

"Well, how about this one?"

"Honeybunch," Norton began gently, "it's okay."

"No, it damn well isn't," retorted Rose angrily, her large breasts heaving, her fists clenched.

"Rose—" Dennis put out a placating hand.

If I want to cut a song, that's it!" screamed Rose, close to hysteria.

"Let's cut it," nodded Norton, the oldest member of the group.

Struggling to get hold of herself, Rose tried a feeble smile. "I'm sorry . . . Jesus dogshit," she shrugged an apology, "I shoulda gone to college." She rummaged around in her poke, coming up with an elaborate stopwatch, which she handed to Danny.

"Here."

"What's this thing for?" asked the mystified Danny.

Rose looked him square in the eye, and her voice was level, but with a strong undercurrent of uneasiness.

"I got thirty-five good minutes in me tonight," she told him. "When I go on, hit the button. Keep track of my time. In thirty-five minutes, we stop, that's 'all. *That's all.*"

Abruptly she turned and headed for the locker-room door, which Dennis held open for her. When she had gone, Dennis and the guys stared at one another for a long silent minute.

Then Danny shook his head. "Jeez, that's a new one," he said, puzzled.

The band ran out on the stage to the screams and applause of twenty-five thousand rock 'n' roll freaks. As the guys plugged their guitars into the big amps and got a last-minute sound check, the sidemen came out to lesser applause. Nicky Butler on drums, Leo "deLion" Henderson on keyboards, two saxophones, and a trombone. The sidemen were not the nucleus of Rose's original San Francisco band; they'd been added for the tour, and they were among the best in the business.

Norton laid down a rhythm riff with a strong bass line and Danny and Whitey picked it up and they were off, jamming. The crowd was yelling and cheering so loud they couldn't really hear the music. But the band and the audience knew that this jam was only a warmup. The real show would start when The Rose appeared—five-feet-one of purest dynamite with a fuse that could explode all of Madison Square Garden. The Rose was whom they'd come to hear; The Rose had all the answers.

In her dressing room, Rose sat and stared at herself in the mirror. She appeared to be in a deep trance, never taking her eyes off the face reflected in the glass. She had made up her face and put glitter on her eyelids, and star-shaped beauty patches on her cheeks and her chin. In her spangled shawl, covered with bits of tinsel sparkle, she looked like a small clown before the red nose went on. Without leaving the mirror, she reached for the bottle of Aquavit that stood on the dressing table and tilted it up, taking long, deep swallows. Then, slowly, still in her trance state, she stood up.

The bottom half of her had been sewed into the tightest velvet jeans she could find. A large rose appliqué of bright satin wound its long stem around her thighs and buttocks; the flower itself bloomed on her crotch, directly over her mound. A wide embroidered belt from Afghanistan circled her tiny waist. She wore no brassiere, and her ample titties bounced inside a flimsy tank top, covered by a chiffon blouse hand-painted in many colors, over which she had thrown her long spangled scarf. The outfit had a cheap, tawdry look, belying the fact that it had cost many hundreds of dollars and had been commissioned from the nineteen-year-old boy who dressed Mick Jagger, George Harrison, and Eric Clapton.

Now that she was standing, she killed the bottle and flung the empty into a corner. Then she bent forward at the waist, almost parallel to the floor, and bounced her body twenty times, limbering up. That wasn't easy to do in sling-back high-heel shoes, but she managed. Her face red, she stood up again and began to pant.

Her breath came fast, fast, faster. Short exhalations were followed by a long series of mighty whoooooooshes, shaking all of her little frame, rocking it like a tidal wave.

Whooosh. Whooosh. Whooosh. She'd learned this tiger breathing from a former lover who was into Tai Chi Chúan. Her chest expanded, contracted. Whoosh. Whoosh. Her face turned dark red and her eyes began to bug out. Whoosh. Whoosh.

The door opened and Dennis, the manager, came in. Whooosh. Whooosh. He stood watching her, familiar with her ritual, the stoking of the rocket fuel that would launch her performance into space. Whooosh. Whooosh.

Suddenly, abruptly, she stopped, drained, yet feeling the new energy beginning at the soles of her feet and working its way up through her body. She had expelled all her demons; new ones were being born, and the concert would be the labor room.

Her dressing-room door was open and she could hear the band out on the stage, pumping out rocking music. She wanted to be there. She *needed* to be there.

"This is your night, woman. You own it! *Let's go!!*" Dennis grabbed Rose's hand and they ran up the ramp backstage.

"Rose, please," said Dennis seriously as they sprinted for the stage, "don't say 'motherfucker' tonight. This is New York. There are important critics out there. Let's not say 'motherfucker,' okay? Okay, Rose?"

One microphone stood alone in the center of the

stage. As the spotlight suddenly hit it, a bestial roar, almost terrifying in its intensity, rose from the single throat of the vast audience. Apocalypse was here.

Grinning, strutting in her high heels and her tight jeans, Rose acknowledged the applause, the waves of love and enthusiasm by grabbing the mike with a shout.

"Hi ya, motherfuckers!!!!!!!!!!!!!!!"

At that, the audience reached Nirvana and passed into the realm of the Beyond. Their screaming broke all previous decibel records for the Garden. Thirty kids rushed the stage, only to be intercepted by the long-haired security police and catapulted right back into their seats. Rose stood with her hands on her hips, grinning at her audience, eating up their noisy worship.

Under the lights, the sleazy effect of her spangles disappeared. Except for her prominent breasts, she looked like a young archangel. Her hair was an electric halo around her shining face, and her glittery costume glinted and sparkled softly, magic lights enfolding her. Give her a sword and she could kill dragons.

Balling her small hands into fists, she raised her arms high above her head. "Drugs! Sex! Rock 'n' roll!" she yelled into the microphone, hearing responsive cheers. "Drugs! Sex! Rock 'n' roll! DRUGS!! SEX!! ROCK 'N' ROLL!!"

The audience took up the chant, shaking the Garden to its highest rafters. *Drugs! Sex! Rock 'n' Roll!* The Rose knew! God*damn,* but The Rose really knew.

Now the band was swinging into its first number with Rose, and Danny pressed the button on the stopwatch. Thirty-five minutes.

Prancing, wiggling, steaming, and sweating, The Rose was singing like a maniac, whipping the mike cord around like a live thing, rubbing up against Danny and Norton, shaking her ass, stomping her feet, grabbing her audience and whipping them around just like the cord on her microphone. Sweat plastered her golden hair to her brow and her cheeks as she pranced and jived across the stage, workin' the music for every last drop of high. It was a big hunk of music and it got the set started like an express train. Her voice, amplified by the extravagant sound system, filled every corner of the arena and echoed off the ceiling.

She was music personified, this little girl gyrating up there on that stage, singing the songs she'd made famous. She stinted on nothing, giving them her energy, her talent, her body, for them to see and hear and. How they wanted to touch her, to become a part of that eternal female mystery of the earth, a part of the sweet darkness and sharp brightness that was The Rose.

They did what they could, standing up on their seats and waving their arms high in time to the music. The aisles were filled with dancing kids, shaking and grooving, and the security cops let them dance. God help them if they didn't. The Rose needed to feel the vibrations, needed to see everybody clapping and partying to her music.

"Rose!" came calls from down front. "Here, Rose." "Here, this is for you." Hands were held out to her, clutching offerings. She danced over to the edge of the stage and reached down for the offerings. Thousands of fans had brought her gifts of roses, and the lucky ones got to press them into her hand. God, she took it! She's holding *my* rose! I want to die! The Rose gathered them in and rubbed them on her sweaty face and hair and body as she sang then threw the lovely flowers, moistened with her dew, back into the audience. There was a scramble for them, precious souvenirs.

"Rose! Look-a here!" Now bottles were being offered, in the rows nearest the stage. Rose grinned and scampered closer. My, my, what a fine selection of booze. Rudge would shit kittens. Alcoholic refreshments were forbidden onstage. She reached out happily and a bottle of Jack Daniel's was thrust into her hand. She finished another chorus and took a long swig, making a face. Jack Daniel's was for pansies. Gimme somethin' *tough,* oh, yeah. Other hands pressed forward, and she caught a glimpse of her favorite Aquavit, being·waved in the air three rows back. She nodded happily in its direction and twelve or fourteen eager hands, ten more than were needed, gained the honor of passing it down to The Rose.

She raised the bottle to her audience in a toast, and drank long and deep, then danced over to one of the big amplifiers and set it down carefully. The audience roared its approval, and she shook her fanny at them bending her knees so deeply it looked as though her jeans would surely split, and wagging her buttocks at them naughtily from side to side. More pandemonium.

The Rose was cookin' now, and it was hot in the kitchen. Whipping the long spangled scarf off her shoulders, she waved it like a flag, stroked the floor with it, shook it till it rattled. Then she tied it around her hips like a buccaneer's sash. The blouse was the next to go. It was soaked through and the big butterfly sleeves were beginning to hang limp. Rose stripped it off as the audience roared, and stood there in her tight jeans and skimpy cotton tank top, through which you could see her breasts loud and clear, the nipples erect with the excitement of the number.

The band drove to a hard rocking finish, with Rose wailing at the mike, dropping to her knees and collapsing on the floor, totally wiped out, enfolded in the cheering and applause of her satisfied audience. She lay there for a minute, gathering strength, then stood back up at the mike as the band moved on to the next number.

The treasurer's office of Madison Square Garden was a beehive crammed with ticket racks, old green steel tables, and dilapidated chairs and was guarded by wire mesh screens to separate it from the outside world. The tabletops were cluttered with papers and adding machines. Portly men in shirtsleeves and vests, smoking cheap odorous cigars, sat next to blue-haired ladies in rhinestone glasses, and all of them were busy tallying the stubs of tonight's concert.

Hovering over them, slender and feral, was Rudge Campbell. He had to be there when the receipts were counted; he and Rose had a percentage. Rudge had a theory that money should be hot; if you let it cool down, it shrinks a little, like muffins in a pan. Rudge wanted his money now, with smoke coming out of it; not later, when it would have dwindled by several thousand dollars' worth of "expenses." In his hand he held one of those new and very expensive Texas Instruments calculators; it was bulky, but it functioned perfectly, and Rudge couldn't imagine how he'd ever done without it.

Mounted just above eye level on the wall was a small black-and-white TV monitor showing the Garden arena. The sound was down way low, so as not to distract the bookkeepers from their labors. Every now and again, Rudge would check the monitor to see how Rose was doing. So far, the gig was going well—at least to judge by the friendly waving and frenzied dancing of the spaced-out, tripping rock freaks down there. He loved the fact that the audience was silent on the TV. Downstairs in the arena was a bedlam painful to the ears. Rudge much preferred the quiet clicking of adding machines to the screaming of Rose's fans. Money made such a pretty melody.

Holding a sheaf of adding-machine tapes, Rudge was checking the bookkeepers' arithmetic against his calculator's when he happened to glance up at the monitor. There was The Rose, gulping down long swallows from a bottle of Aquavit. Rudge's face darkened; he reached for the nearest phone that connected him with the stage.

"Dennis!" he snarled.

"Yeah, hi . . ." came the voice, muffled by the music pouring out of Rose and the amplifiers.

"Where the hell is she getting that booze, and why the hell aren't you taking it away from her? Is she pullin' it out of her cooze, or what? You said she was clean."

"She was, Rudge. It's no good. Must be a thousand bottles out there in the seats, all with her name on 'em. All she gotta do is reach out her hand."

"Yeah, well, don't let her reach."

"Don't let her reach?! You shittin' me, man."

"Don't make me come down there, Dennis," threatened Rudge coldly. "I got important business up here."

"Okay, I'll try, Rudge. But it ain't gonna be easy. They're on *her* side."

With a leap and a scream, Rose finished the number, electrifying twenty-five thousand people into galvanic applause. A fresh shower of roses fell onto the stage, tangible expressions of an audience's love. Rose could feel the adoration rolling toward her from out there, and she stood quietly, basking in it, smiling and nodding, feeling at home.

Her body was drenched with the sweat of her exertions, and her tiny sleeveless shirt clung so tightly to her that she might as well have been naked. The feathers in her hair had wilted, and most of the glitter had been washed off her face by the rivulets of perspiration. The Egyptian kohl she used to make up her eyes had smudged into a messy black mask, giving her the look of a demented raccoon. Yet she was beautiful, astonishingly beautiful, and her weary little body, drooping like a rose without water, held a majesty wonderful to see. There was a great intake of breath in the audience, and then it was expelled in a long, anticipatory sigh. They knew they were watching genius tonight. Nothing would be held back.

The band moved slowly into a long rocking riff,

bluesy, jazzy. Rose took the mike off the stand and held it up to her lips.

"I'm talkin' to the *ladies* in the audience," she said with a wicked grin. "Girls, this is for you. That guy you're sittin' with, tell him to take a hike. Let him walk, girls, let him walk, 'cause you're gonna talk to The Rose. This is for me and you. Alone. An' we know, don't we? Damn right, we do."

She looked out at her audience. They sat silent, spellbound by the soft crooning of her words. The girls and young women were nodding, hypnotized, and she could see that she had them, right there in her hand.

"Picture this. Picture this, girls. It's dark, and you're in bed. He's had his fill, used every drop of his big mama up. And now all you want is a kind word, some little touching, *any*thing to let you know he cares. But where is he? Gone, girls. Vanished. Not there. Disappeared. He's gone in search of another piece of meat to sink his teeth into. Has it ever happened to you? Well, has it happened? *Can I get a witness?*"

She paused, and from every part of the vast arena women's voices called to her. "Tell it, Rose." "Right on, mama." "Tell it like it is." "Rose, you know my story."

"I can't hear you, ladies," grinned Rose.

The shouts grew louder and more plaintive. "Tell it, Rose." "Sing it, Rose." "Go, girl." Down in front, a tall black girl stood up on her chair and cupped her hands around her mouth, directing her words up at the stage.

"Rose, baby, you gonna sing the women's national anthem," she yelled, breaking everybody up.

Rose nodded gravely. "You're right, sister. That's *just* what I'm gonna do."

Screams and cheers from all over the audience, and the stamping of thousands of feet.

"Real fine, real fine," Rose acknowledged. Microphone in hand, she was stalking the stage like a caged leopard, hips switching, mike cord lashing like a long, furry tail. Her energy level went higher with every word as she got deeper and deeper into her rap, until she was alight and signifyin'.

"And what happens when that lazy rat's ass comes crawling home blind drunk, and you have to wade through the cheap lies and the smell of another woman just to locate him?" she demanded hotly. Oh, she was down and dirty now, coming from rough country to the big city to find her sisters and tell them all about it, all about the lonely nights and the trashing and the *macho* bullshit and the stupid role-playing and the phony "freedom." She was *into* it now, bringing back memories of one-night stands and nameless faces, of cheap road food and come-stained sheets and tear-stained pillows.

"What do you say then, sisters? What do you say?" She stood stock still and faced them, eye to eye. "Do you open your lovin' arms and your lovin' legs and tell him, 'Come on in, daddy, and leave the plow out back'? Do you? Do you now?" She lowered the mike and searched their faces. The men looked uncomfortable, but the women were shinin' on, cheerin' and stompin' and wearin' the palms of their hands sore with clappin'. Oh, they had all rented apartments in Heartache City, hadn't they? Yeah, they recognized the landscape.

Rudge, sensing that something special was going on, left the counting room and headed down to the stage. He came silently up beside Dennis, who stood watching The Rose, transfixed. You could sniff the emotion in the air, like ozone after a lightning storm. Not one person in that whole arena was free from the spell being cast by The Rose. They were sharing in the same energy; the same heart's blood was flowing through twenty-five thousand veins.

Sweat was literally pouring off Rose now. She had probably lost three or four pounds this evening, and looked small and vulnerable under the spotlight, yet the strength of her voice was large enough to lift Madison Square Garden right off its foundation and carry it into space.

"Is that what you tell him, ladies?" yelled The Rose, the cords in her throat standing out with the strain.

At that instant, Danny clicked the stop button on the watch. Thirty-five minutes. Catching Rose's eye, he slid his hand across his throat in the "cut" signal.

Rose staggered and nearly fell. All at once, she felt totally drained of energy, weak, emptied. She'd had thirty-five good minutes and they were up. She turned back to the audience, who were watching her, hushed and frozen. She had nothing left to give them, nothing.

Oh, yes. She had one more thing to give. The deepest reserve of her strength, the inner untouched core of her very essence, her sanity, and her soul. She knew she had to give it all.

"Is that what you say to that low-life, lyin' sack of *shit?!*" she howled. "IS IT???!!!"

"NOOOOOOOOOO!!!!!!!!!" screamed the audience back at her. "NOOOOOOOOOOOOOOO!!!!!!!!"

As the wall of noise rolled over her, Rose grabbed the bottle of Aquavit off the amp and drained it to the last drop, throwing the bottle to the side of the stage. Then she grabbed the mike and began to wail the blues.

It was a song of pain, of empty beds and sleepless nights, a lament for the lovers who took up their bedrolls and left without a word, of the pain of being a woman and having the feelings of a woman. Anguish was in the song, and Rose's voice tore it out and held it up dripping for the audience to see, a lonely heart bleeding anguish. It was a song about loneliness, and loneliness isn't restricted to women. Men and boys sat in the audience, silent and rapt, unaware that tears were rolling down their faces as The Rose sang the blues.

She moaned them high and she moaned them low, and they were for everybody who had ever known love

61

and lost it or missed love completely, and that was every-body in the audience. Everybody, even the fat-cat record tycoons with their custom-tailored denim suits studded with silver. Even they were moved, some of them to tears. For who hasn't slept in an empty bed sometimes, longing for the embrace of another person on the achingly short trip to the grave?

She laid her soul bare to them, showing them her own pain, proving to them that she had every right to sing blues, that she'd paid heavy dues for the privilege. She moved them and she shook them and she wrenched them up and out of their seats for the final notes of the song. Trembling like a newborn kitten, she stood half fainting before the microphone, her head bowed, her hands barely able to keep the Mike from falling. Whitey stepped up to her and put his arms around her, and she laid her head down on his big, square shoulder, tears streaming from her eyes. She was totaled; not one more drop of juice could be drained out of her. She'd given it all, all to them.

And they knew it. With one mighty surge, the au-dience rushed forward to touch her, just to touch her and share in her personal magic. The Garden's security guards mobilized in force, and Rudge's men formed a flying wedge around her as Whitey helped her off the stage, al-most carrying her.

The screaming was incredible; Rudge had never heard an audience respond like this one. But then he'd never seen her give quite this much before.

He knew where it was coming from. She *was* close to the edge, way down deep below the surface, touching the bone. It came out of the weariness of her soul, just as she'd been claiming, but it was good, so good he couldn't let her stop. Never before had she had to dig this deep to find it. It had always been up there close to the top, where she could reach it easily. Not anymore. But it was so much better. She might be on the verge of collapse, but she had reached a new depth of meaning. She'd tapped into a vein of pure gold. Sincerity, shit! She had it *all*. She was on top, but she could go even higher. What he'd seen tonight had moved him, even shaken him, but he'd put it into perspective right away. No way was he going to let her off the hook. They had a contract, and it called for her to sing. Apparently, the more tired she was, the better she sang. Well?

The audience was stamping their feet, urgently pleading for more. "The Rose!" "The Rose!!" "THE ROSE!!!" they chanted at the tops of their lungs.

Rudge turned to Dennis. "She's a marvel," he told him. "A bloody fuckin' marvel, that's what she is. I'm gonna buy her a Mercedes-Benz, see if I don't."

Dennis, who had been blown away by Rose's shattering climax, nodded weakly, but could not speak.

"And now," said Rudge, "go and get her and bring her out here. We're gonna give them their money's worth. Tell her Rudge Campbell insists she let them have an encore."

IV

"Shit, Rudge. You could at least have let me change," complained Rose as she followed him up the metal stairway to the helipad. On the pad, the Bell Jet Ranger sat with its rotors idling. Across from the helipad, the lights of Long Island winked erratically at them, low to the ground.

Rudge shook his head. "We only got thirty minutes to get to Billy Ray before he splits."

"Relax." The dispatcher turned on the top step and grinned down at them. "We got it covered, champ."

"Yeah," snorted Rudge. "Everybody's got it covered," he muttered sourly. He seemed antsy, more impatient than usual.

The metal steps with their rubber half treads were proving too much for Rose's high heels and tired feet. She stumbled, and Rudge caught her in time to keep her from tumbling down the entire flight. "What's the matter?"

She could hardly be heard over the helicopter noise. "I'm hungry," she whimpered. "Feed me. Hold me. Make me happy."

Rudge's teeth pulled back in a ferocious grin, and he dived into his crocodile attaché case, coming up with a syringe.

"What's in it?" Rose eyed the hypodermic with suspicion.

"Vitamins," said Rudge solemnly. "C and B-12."

"Cookies and milk," cackled Rose, her voice cracking with weariness. She grabbed the syringe and without hesitation plunged it deep into her left buttock, right through the sweat-stained velvet of her jeans. "Kid stuff."

"Keep it that way," replied Rudge shortly.

Rose's face creased indignantly. "Look at my arms!" she yelled, waving them in front of his nose. "I'm clean so long the scars have healed."

"I'm not checking your arms anymore. That's all behind us."

Their heads bent down to protect them from the winds being stirred up by the rotors, they made their way to the waiting helicopter.

"Listen," protested Rose feebly. "Why couldn't we do this some other time? I look like shit now."

"You look like a star," said Rudge automatically. But she was right. She *did* look like shit. Her face was streaked, sweat stained, and dirty, the stage makeup nearly dissolved, but clinging in patches. Her hair was a damp tangle, a head of frizzy wire, and her expensive outfit was torn and dirty, where she had rolled on the floor of the stage. The chiffon blouse was so limp it was half on, half off her body.

"I ain't no star, man," moaned Rose miserably. "My hair's all stringy, my clothes are all fucked up. I gotta headache. I wanna go home." She sounded like a petulant little girl, overtired and cranky.

Rudge boosted her into the helicopter and climbed in after her. "Billy Ray's been begging me to meet you. I promised him."

"Then why don't he come to see me?" pouted Rose, but her words were carried away in the whine of the helicopter as they took off straight up, then swerved and headed for the Island.

Billy Ray's concert had been held the same night as The Rose's, tonight. He played the Nassau Coliseum, and to a vastly different audience from The Rose's. As the acknowledged king of country & western, he sang deep-voiced songs about rotten living conditions to middle-aged blue-collar workers and their wives. And they turned out by the thousands to hear him, the men wearing their best polyester doubleknit leisure suits with white plastic shoes and belts to match, the women in stiff bouffant or beehive hairdos thickly sprayed with self-styling Adorn, their plump legs exposed in miniskirts. His rotten-living-conditions songs had made Billy Ray a millionaire many times over.

Fact was, he was good. Maybe the best there was in c&w, and a brilliant and respected songwriter. He lived clean, saluted the flag, owned a couple of hundred tax shelters, and sent money home to his mother in Georgia. And he *had* worked with his hands, as a hard-rock miner, leaning on a pressure drill until the muscles in his arms had become bands of iron. He never thought in those days that his GIT-tar pickin' would bring him the adulation of millions and make him a very rich man.

Shit, thought Rose, was that a Winnebago or a train sittin' there. She'd never seen a sucker that big in her life. Actually, it was neither. Billy Ray's home away from home and means of transportation was a thirty-ton sixteen-wheeler, a huge semi, painted with a twelve-foot-long American flag, and fitted inside like a mansion. It was parked now in a field outside the Coliseum, and an army of New York State Troopers appeared to be guarding it. The Rose craned her neck at it in admiration as she followed Rudge up to the movable steps that led to the door in the semi's side.

"Get lost!" growled the biggest state trooper in New York.

When Rudge had a mind to, he could out-Limey David Frost. "Do you know who this lady is, sir?" he asked politely, waving one hand at The Rose.

The trooper took a short look. "A hippie with her tits out," he snapped.

"Come on, officer, Billy Ray is in there waiting for me," said Rose, becoming impatient.

"You and all these other people." They looked around. Dozens of bouffant ladies and polyester men were sitting in or standing by their sedans, hoping for a glimpse of the Great Man.

At that moment, the door opened, and a pudgy man sporting a blue corduroy jumpsuit, the uniform of the Billy Ray entourage stuck his head out.

"Dee!" yelled Rudge.

The man addressed as "Dee" guffawed. "Rudgie!" he yelled back. "Get your raggedy ass in here. S'okay, officer. This is The Rose."

Rose perked up at this and started to swagger by the trooper.

"Class, real class," he muttered at her sarcastically.

Rose turned and smiled at him sweetly, the smile of a benevolent angel. "Honey," she purred, "sugar-lambie, if you got some good head every one in a while, you wouldn't be such a jerk-off."

Instinctively, the trooper reached for his holster, but by the time his hand had touched the pistol butt, Rudge had yanked Rose into the trailer, and Dee had shut the door.

There were a handful of men inside, all strummin' and pickin' on their guitars, banjos, and mandolins, workin' on the finish of a musical number. All the men in the room were wearing the same blue zippered jumpsuit as Dee, sort of expensively tailored filling-station uniforms.

All except one. Seeing him, Rose knew why Billy Ray was called The Man in White. He was dressed from head to his custom-fitted boots in pure white, a dude-ranch western outfit from Nudie in Hollywood. The shirt fit closely to his neat body, and the pants were tightly creased down the middle. There was a crispness and a shine to him, almost equal to the shine from the rhinestones decorating the yoke of his shirt and the huge diamond ring on his left pinkie.

"Yeah, that's perfect!" he was saying to his backup, as he laid his big Gibson western guitar down carefully. *"That's* what I meant."

There was a murmur of assent, and Dee said eagerly, "Billy Ray, this here's Rudge, Rudge Campbell, that I've been tellin' ya about. And this here's Rose."

But Rose had been distracted from the introduction. A handsome young mandolin player, surely no older than seventeen, had caught her eye, and she sashayed on over to get better acquainted. "Well, *hello,* Jimmy Bob," she said, admiring his tall physique and apple cheeks.

"Aaaaah, uh, hi, Rose," the boy stammered, shy and sweet.

MmmmmmmmMMMMMMMM, she thought to herself. I do purely love me a tender piece of chicken, and this pretty boy looks like he's all white meat.

"Damn," she said, touching his arm lightly, "I wish this little cherry was in *my* band! Can you diddle that thing, Bobby Earl?" She pointed to the mandolin.

The young man's face lit up and he gave her a broad grin.

"I surely can, Rose. Wanna hear?"

Rose whooped with laughter and swished her hips over to where Rudge and Dee were waiting with Billy Ray.

"God," she smiled, "is that one fine young piece!"

"Billy Ray, this is Rose." The pudgy man made the introduction and Rose lit up with pleasure. She held her hand out.

"Pleased t' meet ya, Billy. I been diggin' on you for lots of years."

The man ignored her hand. "That a fact?" he said expressionlessly.

68

"She done one of your songs on the last album—" began Dee eagerly.

"I know," interrupted Billy Ray. "It's real nice to meet a dainty lady such as yourself." Not so much as the flicker of an eyelid.

"How'd we miss gettin' together f' all these years?" smiled Rose, still anxious to make a good impression on this tall, dour man.

"Careful plannin'," said Billy Ray. Then he laughed and all his good ole boys laughed along dutifully. The boss had made a joke.

Rose's instincts were warning her that something was definitely not right, but, gamely, she plowed ahead with the conversation.

"I wanna record a few more of your songs. I sang 'In Huntsville Prison' tonight and the place went apeshit!"

"You did?"

"Sure did," nodded Rose proudly. "You got any other tunes no one's heard yet?"

Billy Ray shrugged. "You have to talk to my publisher. He takes care of business. I'm just . . ." he paused for a fraction of a second, and when he finished the sentence every man in his entourage chimed in word for familiar word ". . . *a country boy tryin' to stay outta trouble,*" they chorused gleefully. Then more laughter; masculine, rough.

Now Billy Ray turned his small, bright black eyes directly onto The Rose. "I heard a lotta good things about your record of 'Huntsville,' " he drawled.

Rose brightened. "Y'did?" she beamed.

"Ole Dee here said it was about the best he ever heard. Said it cut Dolly's."

Pleasure colored Rose's cheeks crimson, and she gave a self-conscious "See?" glance around the room.

"But I'll tell ya the truth," continued Billy Ray in the same deep drawl. "It didn't show me much."

The silence in the room was suddenly total and palpable. Rose looked at Rudge, who returned her look wordlessly. Was this another of his country-boy jokes?

"Y-think I'm just kiddin' around, don't ya?" The black eyes had become glittering slits.

Panic fluttered in Rose's breast like a caged canary.

"I kinda hope so," she said softly.

Billy Ray shook his head. "World's too full of bull already, lady. I surely don't begrudge anybody their due, y'understand, but don't be singin' any more of my tunes, okay?"

Rose looked around wildly at Rudge, her eyes filling up, her woeful face begging for help. But Rudge was watching the disaster with a morbid fascination, unable or unwilling to act.

And Billy Ray wasn't finished with The Rose. "It'd be different if you knew what they was about," he said coldly. "An' *listen* . . ." the iron in his voice forced Rose to look straight at him. She trembled under his scorn.

"Us 'necks don't take kindly to dumpy females dancin' in here talkin' trash. Especially t' my son."

The caged bird escaped, and panic enveloped Rose in its beating wings. She turned and made her way blindly to the door of the trailer-truck, her eyes hot with her tears. She didn't even see the handsome young mandolin player's look of mingled embarrassment and sympathy. After a second, Rudge followed her, still without a word.

The parking area around the arena was almost deserted; the floodlights had been cut, and only a handful of arclights shed dim illumination. Rose had no idea where the helicopter was, but she stormed off grimly in the wrong direction. Mortification had made her nearly crazy, and her short legs kept pumping in their high heels. She knew only two things—that she had to put distance between herself and the huge flag-painted trailer of that motherfucking redneck sumbitch, and that a moving target is harder to hit.

"Rose! Hey, Rose!" Rudge called after her. She heard his running footsteps behind her.

Rose kept on grimly, rage and shame fueling her rapid pace. Suddenly she whirled on Rudge and demanded in a voice choking with emotion, "How could you let him *do* that?"

"What was I supposed to do?" Rudge sounded aggrieved, but Rose couldn't see his face through her angry tears.

"If *I* knew, what the hell would I need *you* for?" screamed Rose. "You just stood there—"

"Listen," shrugged Rudge. "He's an asshole. What can I tell ya?"

But Rose would not let him make light of her pain. "I know that, man, I know *that!* But it doesn't make me feel any better."

"Honey, you can't let that ole stuff get to you," wheedled Rudge, putting his hand on her arm. "Whatta you care about a redneck singer? You're the star!"

"Then why didn't you tell *him* that?" demanded Rose.

There was silence between them as Rudge tried to figure out how he had let her get him on the hook and how he could wriggle off it.

"I wanted to *die* in there, man," Rose said plaintively. Yet it was clear that her anger was now directed at Rudge, who had failed her, let her down, not been there for her when she'd needed him so desperately.

Rudge stared at her. Rose was limp and bedraggled; nobody seeing her for the first time could possibly believe that this small girl in the tattered finery and smudged makeup was a star. She looked like something any self-respecting cat would bury, not drag in.

"You're trying to sign him, aren't ya?" asked Rose, too quietly.

With her unerring instinct, she'd hit a nerve. "I don't believe this!" yelled Rudge to cover his guilty confusion.

71

"I really don't." He looked up to heaven for a witness to this injustice. "She's only kidding, God. Honey, I love you. Now come on!" He tugged at her arm, trying to move her in the direction of the helicopter, which was all the way across the other side of the parking lot.

But Rose was not to be budged so easily. She knew she'd stumbled on the truth, and her indignation knew no beginning or end. He'd used her; Rudge had lied to her, painting the flattering picture of two giants of entertainment meeting on terms of equality. He must have known; he must have known. Otherwise, the fucker would have brought a photographer to record her humiliation for posterity. Ah, shit!

" 'Dyin' t' meet me' . . . my ass!" she exploded. "You dragged me up here for some clout. Well, it goddamn well backfired on you——"

"Wrong!" yelled Rudge, furious, caught with his hand in the cookie jar. God, sometimes he hated this slovenly bitch enough to murder her. Her with her toilet mouth, ruining the perfect setup he'd taken months to build so carefully.

They were screaming at each other now, face to face and poison mad. They'd come to a halt in the middle of the lot, next to a battered old Chevy pickup. Suddenly the window rolled down and a goofy-looking head poked out, ogling Rose's heaving tits, most of which were showing.

"Hubba-hubba," drooled the retard.

"Get lost!" yelled Rose. Without missing a beat, she picked up on Rudge again. "Lowlifes! You and him . . . you're two of a kind!" she shrieked.

"Calm down, Rose," pleaded Rudge. He had to get her back to New York.

"Don't tell *me* to calm down," snapped Rose.

The Adam's apple in the Chevy grinned lewdly. "I'll calm down if you'll sit on my face," he offered.

Rose jammed her arm into her poke and came up

with a full bottle in a brown paper bag. She spun around and, with all her momentum, smashed bottle and bag hard in the driver's face. Coldcocked, he fell over, and his head hit the pickup's horn, setting it to blaring like an air-raid siren. People began to collect from all directions, but Rose didn't bother to notice.

Horror washed over Rudge's features. "Jesus!! You are a maniac!!" he hollered over the insistent blare of the horn. "You go through life like it was some jack-off dream."

"Fuck you!" shrieked Rose. "Fuck him, and fuck you, too!" She burst into tears and ran off. For a moment, Rudge started to follow her, but thought better of it. He had to stop this fuckin' horn from raising the dead, and he had better check while he was at it to see if this New Jersey cowpoke was alive or dead. She could have killed him; he wouldn't put it past her. He could see Rose running across the parking lot, but how the hell far could she get?

A long black Lincoln limousine with rental plates was sitting off to the side of the parking lot. Without hesitation, Rose ran to it, tore open the door, and threw herself into the back seat.

The chauffeur had been dozing at the wheel, on his waiting time. Now he jerked awake and saw Rose in the rear-view mirror.

"Lady, this one is taken," he told her mildly.

"I wanna get out of here," shrieked The Rose.

"So does the cowboy in the trailer," said the chauffeur, yanking a thumb in the direction of Billy Ray's behemoth. "He owns the car for the night."

Rose dug down deep, all the way to the bottom of her poke, and came up with a fistful of money. Crumpling it up, she hurled the bills at the man in the chauffeur's cap. They bounced off his face and neck and landed all over the driver's seat and the floor around it.

The driver picked up one bill and smoothed it carefully. It was one hundred dollars. He took another look in the rear-view mirror, seeing a small, dirty, frightened, and bedraggled girl on the edge of genuine hysteria.

"You just bought yourself a car and a driver, ma'am."

As Rudge came running over the blacktop, yelling for Rose, the driver jammed the car into gear and they took off. Furious and frustrated, Rudge watched Rose disappear into the distance, then he turned and stomped off in his iguana-skin boots toward the waiting helicopter.

Rose slumped down on the back seat, unable to believe she was out of there and maybe could relax now. She felt like ten pounds of shit in a five-pound sack. Christ, this had been the longest day of her life. Why couldn't anybody . . . Rudge . . . understand that? How many changes did she have to go through in one fuckin' day? A fight with Rudge, a concert that had sent her soaring into the sky and drained her totally, a humiliating excoriating public meeting with Billy Ray, another fight with Rudge . . . Jesus, enough already! Give me a break, Lord!

Hell, she couldn't really blame Rudge, she thought. No reason he shouldn't sign Billy Ray if he could get him. Wasn't that what business was all about? Sure he'd used her, but when *didn't* he use her? She knew him so well, but why the fuck couldn't he be up front with her? All he had to do was to tell her what he was up to, and give her a chance to wash up and change her clothes. Shit, she shoulda known better.

No, *she* shoulda known better than to mouth off like that, in front of Billy Ray. She knew 'necks well. Lawrence, Florida, her old hometown, was the geographical center of redneck country. She'd been around men like Billy Ray most of her life and she knew what they were made of. They wanted their women to dress up fine, in

74

hair-spray wigs and polyester pants suits, and keep their mouths shut. Especially about sex. The men wanted sex, all right, in large, wet quantities, but they didn't want to *hear* about it. Especially not from no woman. A woman kept her mouth shut and her legs crossed, except for her old man.

God, why had she acted like that, swaggering around and talking dirty? She knew in her deepest heart that she was gonna freak old Billy Ray out, him and his American flag and his troop of good ole boys. Mean sons-of-bitches, all of them. She'd been nervous, that's why. Nervous and scared half to death. The man was a national idol; he'd been on top for over twenty years. Why, she was a flash in the pan compared with him. And he wrote the songs.

Rudge was after *her* to write songs, too. That's where the money was in this business, in song writing, in publishing, in copyrights. Any time that anybody played a Billy Ray composition in any part of the world or over any radio station, six cents dropped into Billy Ray's pockets. At the end of a year, those six cents would have multiplied into maybe a million dollars. Not to mention what he earned when another artist recorded a Billy Ray song.

Rose sighed. Sometimes it seemed like just nothing would go right for her ever again. Billy Ray despised her, Rudge was mad at her, and her entire body and soul craved nothing but sleep.

She looked up to find the chauffeur peering at her in his rear-view mirror. Their eyes met.

"What are you lookin' at?" demanded Rose.

No answer.

"Do you know who I am?"

"Yes, you're The Rose." He answered her matter-of-factly.

Rose peered at him, but she couldn't see much of his face in the dimness of the car. Besides, he had a uniform cap on, covering his eyes and brow. But she had the impression that he was young, under thirty maybe. She waited for him to say more, but nothing came.

"That's all?"

"I'm sorry, ma'am?" he asked her politely. He wasn't quite certain what it was she wanted.

"That's all you're gonna say?"

The young man thought this over for a moment. "Well, I dunno . . ." he said at last. "I like your music." He still spoke with a lack of excitement.

Rose shook her head. "Don't go overboard," she told him drily. "You don't need to fall down and shit in your pants." She rummaged around a little desperately in her poke. If she'd been thinking clearly, she wouldn't have wasted a full bottle of booze on that asshole's head. Damn! Inside somewhere there oughtta be . . . yeah, here it was. Triumphant, she pulled out a half pint of vodka. It wasn't full, but it sure beat nothing at all. She took a long taste from the bottle, upending it and nearly emptying it. When she brought the bottle down, she saw the chauffeur chuckling as he watched her openly.

"My name's Houston," he told her amiably. "Houston Dyer."

"You from Texas?" What an asshole question.

"Yeah. Waxahachie."

"Wax-a-*what*-ie?" She'd never heard of it.

"Don't try to pronounce it. We're the only ones who can say it. Where to?"

"The Big City."

"New York?"

Rose smiled at him graciously. "Very, very good," she nodded. "You're smokin' tonight."

The young man smiled back, not offended. "Where to in the Big City?"

"I don't know." Rose thought a few seconds. "I'm hungry. Feed me." She leaned over and handed the nearly empty bottle into the front seat. Houston Dyer took

76

it and tilted it back for a swallow. He made certain to leave the last few drops for her, but, when he turned around to give her the bottle, he saw that The Rose had fallen asleep, curled up in the back seat like a baby.

V

There was a war on in March of 1943, but that was hard to tell in Lawrence, Florida. Apart from the blue-star flags—and a few gold-star flags—hanging in the windows of the bungalows, the little Gulf beach town, population 10,745, was enjoying a new prosperity. Lawrence had been hit badly by the Depression, but the booming war economy had shaken it up and given it new life. Oil, which had once taken a second place to coal, had become in wartime a precious and rationed commodity, and the soggy pools of tarry oil that had made Lawrence an unattractive place to live were now being pumped joyfully through tall steel rigs. Money was flowing like black gold throughout the tiny community. The Depression was finally over; happy days were here again.

Earlene Morrison met Randolph Raymond Foster in 1938, when she was a fourteen-year-old freshman at Lawrence Senior High School and he was a nineteen-year-old senior. It was love at first giggle for the tall, skinny, awkward boy and the short, plump, large-breasted girl. They decided to marry, even though Earlene was under age. There are some things that fourteen-year-old girls are too young to do, but Earlene had been doing them since she was twelve. Naturally, her parents refused permission, even though marriage at her age was not unheard of in that part of the world. The Morrisons based their disapproval on the fact that, at nineteen, Randy Raymond was still in high school, with no prospects of any job.

The young lovers ran away to a preacher, but were caught and brought back unwed. Over the course of the next three and a half years, Earlene shinnied down the drainpipe maybe six or seven times, but they never did manage to tie the knot.

When war was declared in December of 1941, things changed drastically for Earlene and Randy Raymond. He was drafted, and she dropped out in her senior year to enter the labor force, which was suddenly clamoring for women, since the men were going to war.

But Randy Raymond didn't go to war, he went to Brooklyn. The Navy was the lucky service that got him as its prize, and the Brooklyn Navy Yard was where he was sent. There, he helped to load ships, guard ships, paint and scrape ships—everything but sail in them. With Earlene earning good money at J. C. Penney and Randy Raymond sending home his service pay to be put into a savings account, marriage suddenly looked a great deal more feasible. Of course, there was always the chance that Randy Raymond might be shipped out to win the Battle of the Atlantic or to take on the Nips, but as the months progressed and he was still assigned to the scraping-rust-and-barnacles detail, it seemed less likely.

In late 1942, Randy Raymond came home on leave and he and Earlene went looking for a bungalow of their own, finding it about half a mile from the beach and well within the sight and sound of the derricks and the oil-pumping platforms. Also well within scent, because the oil stink filled the moisture-laden Gulf air. But the kids didn't mind; oil was a symbol of their new prosperity. The bungalow was, as Earlene kept putting it, "cute as an ole baby bunny," pink stucco with matching pink painted flamingos on the front "lawn," a tiny piece of grass about thirty feet square and choked with weeds.

79

The little house was just big enough for those two-and-baby-makes-three, which was just as well, because when Randy Raymond went back to the Navy Yard, he left a pregnant Earlene behind him.

But love stories should end happily, and an emergency Red Cross twenty-four-hour leave saw Earlene and Randy Raymond in front of the preacher at last, where they'd wanted to be for four years. So, a couple of weeks short of her eighteenth birthday and legal age, Earlene Morrison became Earlene Foster.

In March of 1943, Mary Rose Foster came kicking and yelling into the world, setting a pattern for all her future behavior.

Earlene was not about to let a J. C. Penney paycheck go begging, especially with a baby girl (they had really wanted a boy) to raise up and keep in pink ribbons. So, as soon as she was back on her feet, she wiggled into a tight girdle, put on her open-toed wedgies, spit on her black block of mascara, coated her lips with dark red Tangee lipstick, painted her nails with Chen Yu's Dragon Plum, checked her pancake makeup in the mirror, ratted her hair into a Ginger Rogers pageboy complete with snood, dabbed a little Evening in Paris behind each ear, dumped Mary Rose on Randy Raymond's mother's doorstep, and went on back to work.

Grandma Morrison wasn't a bad grandma, just a rather rattled one. Her idea of child-rearing was plenty of red pop—which is what they call cola down South—Nabisco wafers filled with imitation chocolate, and all the radio soap operas. She kept little Mary Rose starched and dressed in pink ruffles, since she did her ironing while listening to "Young Widder Brown" or "Our Gal Sunday," on the old Motorola radio. It seemed she did nothing but iron those pink ruffles for Mary Rose.

Mary Rose was left on her own a lot of the time, and she would wander out of the backyard and down through the little town. Drivers soon learned to watch out

80

for her, same as they watched out for the local dogs and cats.

Mary Rose Foster was a child with a mind of her own, and she purely did hate to be caged in. From her father she had inherited a skinny frame, and from her mother, short legs. Sometimes she appeared to be all fuzzy yellow hair and huge blue eyes and pink ruffles and nothing else. Randy Raymond's mother had been powerfully taken by cute, dimpled, sunny little Shirley Temple (she'd wanted Mary Rose to be named after her), and the old lady did her best to turn Mary Rose into a pretty darling like Shirley. Whenever she could catch hold of Mary Rose, which wasn't all that often, she'd get out the old rat-tail comb with the missing teeth and pull and tug and coax Mary Rose's stubborn wiry hair into Shirley Temple sausage curls. The little girl would howl and stamp her feet, but Mrs. Foster was bigger and stronger; besides, she controlled the supply of red pop and Nabisco. When Mary Rose finally made her escape good, she'd tear off down the street, huge satin bows tieing up her bobbing curls. But they never lasted. In an hour of Lawrence's humid weather, the bows would turn limp and the hair would return to its normal frizzy mess. She would never be a pretty darling.

On the other hand, it was Randy Raymond Foster's mother who got Mary Rose to singing. If Shirley could do it, why not a movie career for her granddaughter? At the age of two Mary Rose could sing "Animal Crackers in My Soup" and "If I Had One Wish to Make," and, inevitably, "On the Good Ship *Lollypop*." She had a loud, clear voice that stayed on the melody, but, alas, she lacked Shirley's bubbling personality, cute ways, and dimples. Mary Rose purely loathed and despised Shirley Temple, but she enjoyed singing, even if the cute songs were pains in the ass.

It wasn't that Earlene Foster didn't love her daughter. She did, in her own dimwitted way, without understanding anything of what motherhood was all about. On Friday nights, she'd pick Mary Rose up from her mother-in-law's house and bring her home to the pink stucco bungalow, which boasted a blue star in the window and a picture of Randy Raymond in a glass frame trimmed with American stars and stripes. In the photograph, Randy Raymond was wearing his sailor suit and looking very serious and grown-up. Earlene would set Mary Rose down on the sofa like a doll, and go into the kitchen to warm up a can of Campbell's tomato soup. That was Mary Rose's supper every night of the weekend, a can of Campbell's tomato soup, with a handful of saltines. To give her credit, Earlene did believe the meal was completely nourishing.

Earlene would spend every weekend polishing her fingernails and toenails, putting her hair up in metal curlers with wire closures, and talking to her girlfriends on her new telephone. She would also write to Randy Raymond on little flimsy pieces of paper called V-Mail. Somebody at the post office kept telling Earlene that you didn't need V-Mail for the Brooklyn Navy Yard, only for overseas, but you could never talk Earlene out of her V-Mail. It made her *feel* like a serviceman's brave bride.

On Saturday nights, Earlene went to the movies with Nancy Jean Bloomer, her best friend. This always left the problem of what to do with Mary Rose. They solved the problem by smuggling her into the Rialto Theater under Nancy Jean's voluminous raincoat, which was cut full to enclose Nancy Jean's voluminous body. The little girl's first memories were of black-and-white images flickering on a screen, of men's and women's faces so enlarged they loomed over the entire theater, scaring her. But she loved the musical comedies, even at the age of three. She had a phenomenal memory for a song, and would sing one of June Allyson's or Betty Hutton's numbers for her mother when she got home. Mary Rose liked June and Betty because they sang hot and jazzy;

Mary Rose didn't care for Alice Faye at all, with that taffy voice of hers and those dumb, slow ballads.

Best of all, Mary Rose loved Carmen Miranda. *Ay, ay ay ay, a chicka chicka boom chick.* That passion led to the first spanking Mary Rose ever received; it was the one she never forgot. One Saturday afternoon, she disappeared from home. When Earlene came back from the five-and-dime, where she'd gone to buy a bottle of leg makeup (silk stockings having become a casualty of the war with Japan, and nylon being used for parachutes), Earlene found her precious vanity table with its ruffled skirt an unholy mess. Powder and paint were spilled everywhere, and Earlene's newest twenty-five-cent lipstick had been worn down and broken off. The point of Earlene's eyebrow pencil had been broken too, and somebody had been at the bright blue eye shadow. Furious, Earlene went hunting for her daughter.

She found Mary Rose a few streets away, the center of delighted attention from the neighborhood kids, who were laughing fit to kill. She had made up her baby face outrageously, smearing it with lipstick and eyeshadow and drawing exaggerated brows. She looked like Halloween. Around her neck and her wrists she had wound strings of glittery beads—"My costume joo-la-ree!" shrieked Earlene—and on her head Mary Rose had managed to balance a bunch of bananas. And that was all. Beads, bananas, and makeup—Mary Rose hadn't bothered to put on anything else, not even her white cotton panties. Wiggling and shimmying her little bare ass, just like Carmen Miranda; and, at the top of her baby lungs, singing the latest Carmen Miranda hit. She was a scream, but Earlene Foster didn't stop to appreciate the humor.

Instead, yanking her daughter by the arm hard enough to pull it out of its socket, Earlene dragged the howling Mary Rose home, walloped her good, and scrubbed the makeup off with Octagon laundry soap. And all the while she scoured and spanked Mary Rose, Earlene was bright red with the shame the three-year-old had brought down on the family. She called on dear Jesus to forgive Mary Rose, but she acted like she doubted it would happen.

Mary Rose couldn't sit down with any measure of comfort for close to a week, and her cheeks ached where the scouring harsh yellow soap had abraded them.

No, they never did understand Mary Rose at all, not then and not a few weeks later when Randy Raymond came home from the service, the war having finally come to an end. Randy Raymond was far more interested in his young wife's big boobs and round behind than in his little daughter, who ought by rights to have been a son in the first place. But he did make Earlene quit her job to stay home and cook and sew, hoping to knock her up with a baby boy. No go.

So Mary Rose Foster grew up in a Gulf Coast town that had one industry—oil—and one set of standards—working-class. The older she grew, the more of a sore thumb she became, and the less she was understood. She was too vivid, too much larger than life, for the tiny little minds in this tiny little town. She loved bright colors, and the colors in Lawrence were all washed out in the sickly sunlight, fading to pale pinks and aquas. Whatever the Fosters' hopes or dreams were, they had never managed to achieve them. They stayed in the old bungalow year after year. The stucco cracked and was mended and cracked again. The flamingos on the front "lawn" chipped and faded. Randy Raymond raised a flagpole between them, and flew Old Glory on every legal holiday. On the other side of the lawn, Earlene put up a washline. The blue-star flag had come down from the window, and that was it. No other children, and no other changes, inside or out, except the ones in Mary Rose.

By the time she was twelve years old, her parents had bought a television set on time payments and had discovered a whole new world of indoor entertainment.

Mary Rose liked Uncle Miltie and Ed Wynn, but she gave the Mouseketeers the finger; they were too cutesy for her. All three Fosters agreed on their favorite show: "Your Hit Parade." Earlene would wipe the tears from her eyes when Gisele MacKenzie sang "Cherry Pink and Apple Blossom White," or Snooky Lanson delivered "Love Is a Many-splendored Thing." Mary Rose enjoyed the music, even though she felt instinctively that something was missing. Winds of change had brought word to her of something else—"Rock Around the Clock" and Bill Haley and the Comets—but the Fosters agreed that she was too young to go see a dirty movie like *The Blackboard Jungle*.

Even so, Mary Rose managed to clap her hands and snap her fingers in 1955. "Earth Angel" by the Penguins brought her to tears and sighs, but "Maybelline" by Chuck Berry was a revelation. Now, *that* was music. Mary Rose approved when her parents bought two 45 rpm records that were out of their usual sentimental mode: Teresa Brewer's "Let Me Go, Lover," and Rosemary Clooney singing "This Old House," toe-tappin' music.

The year 1956 was a crucial one for Mary Rose Foster in more ways than one. It was the Year of the Big Split—musically, that is. Earlene and Randy Raymond went down one road—Vic Damone singing "On the Street Where You Live," Bing Crosby and Grace Kelly in "True Love," and the one and only Doris Day with her big hit, *"Qué Sera, Sera."* Mary Rose, on the other hand, had discovered the Platters, Little Richard . . . and Elvis.

My lord-a-mercy, Elvis. Mary Rose begged for an Elvis Presley charm bracelet for her birthday, but she got a Pat Boone record instead. Cleverly, she rushed it down to the record store and traded it in on "Heartbreak Hotel." From then on, every penny she could scrounge, save, or scrape together went on 45s—"Don't Be Cruel,"

"Hound Dog," "Tutti Frutti," "Long Tall Sally," "Be-Bop-a-Lula," "Let the Good Times Roll," "The Great Pretender." Music fed her dreams, waking and sleeping, and rock 'n' roll was some dinner for her starving ears.

The year 1956 also brought another inheritance from Earlene to her daughter. Overnight, skinny short Mary Rose grew a huge set of knockers. She went from training bra to a C cup in what seemed like five minutes flat. No, flat is hardly the word.

Needless to say, this caused a good deal of excitement in Lawrence Junior High School. But it didn't have positive effects. For one thing, Mary Rose's tits were not cheerleader material. She refused to squeeze them into one of those pointy-tipped pushup bras that turned soft titties into cast-iron nose cones. Mary Rose let them bob and flop; it was more comfortable that way, and at first she rather enjoyed the sensation she was creating.

By the time she discovered that the other kids were laughing at her, she was too mad and too defiant to change. So, instead of their becoming objects of admiration or veneration, the way the other girls' budding breasts were adored, Mary Rose found that her abundance made her a laughing stock. It was a case of too much, too soon. How could a thirteen-year-old girl handle it? Defiantly. Cringing inside but grinning like a wolf, Mary Rose bobbed through the halls, letting 'em swing in the breeze. Yet her blue eyes looked neither to the left nor to the right.

By the time she was fourteen, Mary Rose Foster had given up all hope of ever looking like Suzy Parker or Natalie Wood, and had pulled their pictures down from her bedroom wall. Other girls seemed to do everything right. Their hair was silky and shiny and Toni'd into soft waves that bounced on their sweatered shoulders. They were taller than she, with long legs covered by the pleats of their skirts, and their modest, sharp-tipped breasts

86

poked out of the fronts of their pullovers just enough to tantalize. They didn't look cheap.

Mary Rose was considered by all to look cheap. Her frizzy hair would not take a combing and would never be silky. She wore bright red instead of regulation pastels. When she put on sweaters the boys in her class ogled and leered and slobbered openly and lewdly. There wasn't anybody else like Mary Rose Foster in all of Lawrence, Florida. Nobody decent, anyway. The girls in her class avoided her as though she were contagious, but the boys all asked her out. At least once.

It didn't take her long to discover that they all wanted the same thing, and it was this thing that made her popular. Hell, she didn't care. If a pimply-faced boy got off on poking his hands or his dick around underneath her sweater or her skirt, it was no skin off her ass. Let him. Inside, of course, she wanted desperately to be liked, approved of, wanted for herself and not for those huge and accommodating boobs or open thighs. But that never seemed to be in the offing, so Mary Rose took what she could get when she could get it. And she could get it often, although she never managed to snare a steady.

In 1958, the Fosters bought Mary Rose a copy of *Twixt Twelve and Twenty,* hoping that Pat Boone's pious advice to teenagers would have a calming effect on their wild and wayward daughter. Mary Rose took it to the bathroom with her every time she went. But it wasn't for reading on the pot. Instead, she'd pull out a few pages, put them to good use, and flush them away. Within three weeks, she'd finished the book.

During these years, Mary Rose went on singing, humming, doo-wopping to rock 'n' roll, even though nobody was listening to her. She loved to sing, and she loved the rhyms of r&b, jazz, rock, even folk. But there was always something missing for her. Even "Whole Lotta Shakin' Goin' On" by Jerry Lee Lewis didn't satisfy her fully.

But that was due to change. Satisfaction was on its way, and arrived on the scene in 1960.

Mary Rose was a wanderer—nothing could pin her to one place for long. Still, in all her seventeen years, she had never wandered as far as Darktown, which was what they called the southernmost tip of Lawrence, where all the colored folks lived. There was no earthly reason for a southern white girl to ever enter Darktown, which is why, one supposes, Mary Rose finally did.

One Sunday in summer, the heat drove her away from the Gulf and down the road in search of a breeze. The town was deader than a flounder and so damn hot the flies were dropping right out of the air and frying on the sidewalks. ZZZzzzzzz. Before she noticed it, she'd walked all the way into the fringes of Darktown. The little stucco bungalows and old frame houses had given way to shanties and sheds, with roofs of corrugated tin that broiled you in the summer and deafened you in the rainy season. She stopped, and was about to turn back, when a sound forced its way through the muggy, oily air and into her ears. Music. Singing.

Automatically, Mary Rose's feet began to move closer to the sound. It was rich, full, dark, deep, tuneful, earth-shattering. Mary Rose had never heard anything like it before. The words were coming clearer as she moved closer to the source of the music. The words spoke of Jesus and heaven and salvation. The singing was coming from the small, white-painted Abyssinian Baptist Church.

Mary Rose pushed open the church door, and gospel music washed over her and carried her away. For a moment, she thought she would faint.

There was a sudden rustling as forty or fifty faces turned in her direction, staring at this fuzzy-headed, yellow-haired white girl trembling in the doorway. But nobody stopped her as she took a hesitant step inside and stood with her back against the far wall, drinking in the singing, the hand-clapping, the gospel-shouting. Her soul, which had hungered and thirsted for seventeen years, was nourished, fed, and satisfied at last. She closed her eyes.

After that, Mary Rose went every week, always standing in the back with her eyes shut, listening. After a while, the colored folks became accustomed to seeing her there. On the third Sunday, Mary Rose put a dollar in the plate, and from then on she felt herself to be a member of the congregation. On the sixth Sunday, Mary Rose joined in one of the hymns, "I'm Goin' Home on the Mornin' Train." At first, she kept her voice down low, under that of the other singers, but soon it flew up and soared over their heads. Again, they turned to look. With her eyes closed and her face washed clean of makeup, Mary Rose looked like a pale young angel. Forty-five pairs of worn, calloused black hands clapped together as Mary Rose let it rip. "On That Rock," she sang, and "Jesus Is Real to Me," and "Jesus on the Main Line." Her soul was filled with the power and the glory, and her voice stretched and shouted, wailed and moaned as it had never done before.

"What Do You Think About Jesus?" sang Mary Rose, and the congregation answered, "He's All Right." And everybody smiled.

Mary Rose became their "blue-eyed soul sister," but, of course, nobody at home was to know about it. Nobody at school was to know about it. Only she and her soul brothers and sisters shared the knowledge of their love and of Mary Rose's music, and it was the sweetest secret she'd ever had.

As if the music weren't enough, Mary Rose made a friend that year, too. Her first friend. Is it necessary to say that he, too, was an outcast, a freak, someone beyond the pale of high-school society? His name was Arthur Pye, but the kids all called him "Cherry." That was because he was such a freak that nobody could imagine fucking him. And, indeed, there was a virginal air about him that went with his effeminacy. He wasn't just a pansy, Cherry was like an old-maid librarian, and he was the butt of everybody's jokes.

Yet he and Mary Rose became *simpático,* as he put it, and Mary Rose was let in on Cherry's dreams and ambitions. Which *were* pretty freaky, Mary Rose had to admit, never having met anybody quite like Cherry before. His dreams all seemed to revolve around a spotlight and a stage, on which he stood full center, wearing something dreamy. But he loved Mary Rose and admired her, and since he was the only man who had no interest in her tits (except to wish that they were his), she could relax with him and simply enjoy his company.

Together, they were outrageous, and each supported the other when the rest of the world came down with pointy-toe boots. Mary Rose confided in him about her Sundays with the colored folks, and he confided in her that he had swiped his mother's black garter belt and was wearing it this very minute.

It couldn't last. It was too good, too pure to last. But the ending was dramatic, traumatic, heartbreaking. One night, when Cherry's mother and father had gone to the drive-in to see Martin and Lewis, Mary Rose came over to hang out. There was beer in the icebox, cans and cans of it, and they got stoned on beer, high and giggling. They decided to have a little fun. Staging a lightning raid on Mama's dressing table, they grabbed up everything they could get their hands on and fled to Cherry's room. There, with rather unsteady hands, Mary Rose managed to paint Cherry's face. She glued on false eyelashes, extended the boy's brows with pencil, and filled the lid in with dark purple eyeshadow. Reddening his cheeks, she drew a Cupid's bow on his upper lip and heightened the color with bright pink lipstick. He was beautiful, more slender and beautiful than any girl Mary

Rose had ever seen. Transformed by the paint, Cherry swayed and bloomed and danced over to Mary Rose, throwing his arms around her and giving her a deep kiss of affection and gratitude.

"Arthur!" shrieked his mother from the bedroom doorway.

"You scummy little fairy! I'll break your ass!" howled his outraged father, making a grab for the boy. Mary Rose fled.

The next day, a garbled version of the story had been spread all over town by the neighbors. In this version, Cherry and Mary Rose had been "doing it" when they were caught by Cherry's parents. This did Cherry's reputation a lot of good, but it held little advantage for Mary Rose. Might as well have *been* doing it, thought Mary Rose gloomily. She had a right to sing the blues. Cherry was gone, gone for good, gone nobody knew where. He'd split during the night, taking only his father's wallet and his mother's silver-fox stole. He'd left no word for Mary Rose. So much for having a friend.

What the hell was she going to do with her life? If she stayed in this dumb town, she'd be a freak all her days. But where was she going to go? She held secret dreams of being a band singer, like Jo Stafford or Helen Forrest, or even Doris Day. She could picture herself with a gardenia in her hair, crooning dooodooodooodooo into a microphone, wearing a strapless formal. But when she opened her eyes, she knew it was hopeless. She wasn't tall enough or pretty enough and her tits were grotesque. But, worst of all, who wanted a white woman who sang like a nigger? And not even like Lena Horne, but Bessie Smith.

Still, she couldn't quite picture herself over a counter at J. C. Penney, like her mother before her, or working in the five-and-dime, or even selling records in the Disc Shoppe. Maybe slinging hash, in a low-cut uniform and a clean hanky pinned to one tit. Bet she'd earn big tips from the northern drivers in their diesel sixteen-wheelers, always sniffin' around southern poontang.

What about Betty Co-ed? College did not fit in with her future plans. Her grades were only one mark above miserable, and the Fosters had never laid aside a college fund for their only daughter. They knew better.

That left high school to finish and . . . maybe . . . singing.

Later, when she was The Rose, Mary Rose would skip over the years between 1960 and 1965 as though they didn't exist. They contained some of her darkest moments, lowest lows without any highest highs. She did get to sing some, in a beer joint called Monte's off the highway, but it was mostly bluegrass or c&w music, it was only on Saturday nights, and she had to wait on tables between sets. Hardly stardom. Other things happened in those years that she didn't like to think about, but all those black experiences proved to her that she was a freak, a misfit, different, somebody who hungered for color in a black-and-white world. She got plenty of attention, but she couldn't make a friend. Girls felt threatened by her; boys still wanted only one thing. Marriage was out of the question. Having watched her parents growing grayer and duller with every passing year, Mary Rose wanted none of that for herself. Besides, nobody asked her.

The only thing she prayed for was the key to the door of the outside world. And one day, early in 1965, that key arrived in the Foster mailbox, in the form of a postcard addressed to "The Rose, c/o Foster."

The card read: "Heaven is alive and well and is called San Francisco. If you are not here in three weeks, I'm going to fly down and get you. The gospel train is in the station; every sinner must get aboard. Hurry. There's just room for one more." The card was signed "CHERIE (Cherry Pye)."

It took Mary Rose three minutes to make up her mind and three weeks to hitchhike to San Francisco. On the way, she was obliged to fuck fourteen drivers and give eight of them blowjobs as well. But it was worth it. She arrived in the downtown area, Market Street, at three o'clock on a Thursday afternoon a week after her twenty-second birthday. The sky was blue and the air sweet and cool. The first thing she did was to call Cherry's phone number.

When he arrived to pick her up, accompanied by his entourage, Mary Rose blinked in surprise, then blinked again. Cherry, now Cherie, had let his hair grow to below his shoulders; over his jeans he wore a gossamer blouse; on his wrists were bracelets by the dozen. Around his shoulders was a rather ratty piece of fur, which Mary Rose vaguely recognized as his mother's former silver fox. The boys and girls with him had painted their faces with stars and flowers; all of them wore their hair long, and several of them had hair as proudly bushy and frizzy as a prince of Africa. Their smiles were dazzling in all their psychedelic glory.

"You are The Rose," said Cherie solemnly, handing her a long-stemmed red rose. "Here," and he held his hand out to her. In the palm was a sugar cube. "Eat this."

Wordlessly, Rose took the sugar with its microdot of LSD and swallowed it. The gypsy band scooped her up and carried her off, their tambourines going jang-a-lang-a-ling, to someplace they called "the Haight." As the acid hit her bloodstream, and strange new colors unfolded before her astounded eyes, The Rose knew that she was now a freak in a world of freaks, that the word *freak* held a new meaning, that she had come home at last.

VI

"Where are we?" asked Rose sleepily, her eyes only half open. The whining sound of the tires on metal plates had jolted her awake.

"This here's the Brooklyn Bridge, ma'am," said Houston Dyer, putting his chauffeur's cap back on. Rose caught only a glimpse of his face, which wasn't bad, but his hair was cut very short. That put her in mind of Billy Ray and his band of merry men, and she frowned unhappily at the recollection.

The long limo bumped over the rickety old bridge toward the lights of Manhattan, coming to rest on the other side of the island, where the all-night diners served the truckers. By now The Rose was hungry enough to eat her poke.

They were in the warehouse-and-trucks section of Manhattan, around Twelfth Avenue and Eighteenth Street, a place where all-night diners flourished, serving heavy, greasy food to the Diesel Dans who rode the turnpikes with their heavy loads. The smell of the hamburgers frying made Rose go faint with hunger, and she was in such a hurry to wolf down a burger that she wrenched a heel off one of her Joan Crawford opentoes. For one uncomfortable minute she hobbled after Dyer. Then, with a furious "Shit!" she tugged the broken shoe off her foot and hurled it away. Next the other one.

"Hell, I surely did love them shoes," she sighed regretfully as they vanished into the night. Dimly in the distance the shoes bounced off the bumper of a big semi parked outside the diner. On the bumper was pasted a sticker: "America. Love It or Leave It."

Barefoot, The Rose followed Dyer into the neon-lit diner. The counter was solid Formica. Vinyl booths banked with plastic philodendron lined the outside wall of the Pullman-shaped restaurant. Evidently a class operation. Ignoring the booths, Dyer and Rose plunked themselves down at the far end of the counter.

Dyer, with jungle instinct, had become aware of the bad vibes going down in this place as soon as his foot entered the door. It was a workingman's place; everybody in it was tired, rough and in no mood for anything but a sandwich and a cuppa java. He could see the hostile faces, many of them wearing caps with Nixon buttons on them, turned toward The Rose. Obviously, none of them were rock freaks or record buyers, and none of them knew who in the hell she was.

Dyer sneaked a look at The Rose. In her limp and sweaty finery, bare feet, and wearing broken, bedraggled feathers in her messy hair, she looked like some small escaped animal of a rare species. The young man pressed his lips together tightly and kept his ears wide open, while his eyes cut unobtrusively to all sides of him. Automatically, he gauged the number of men in the place and the distance to the door.

The waitress came over, pencil and pad in hand, her face impassive. But before she could ask for their order, the cook, his apron filthy with grease stains, a cigarette dangling from his lips, poked his head through the passthrough that separated the kitchen from the counter and snarled.

"We don't serve hippies."

"That's okay," said The Rose without rancor. "We don't eat 'em neither. Gimme a pig's foot and a bottle of

95

beer." It was a private joke with her, because it was a line from a real old Bessie Smith song.

Now the silence in the diner could be cut more easily than the home-made apple pie. It was a silence heavy with dislike and intolerance.

The waitress had been on her feet for eleven hours, and she'd never see forty again. Tired was her middle name, but she tried to be reasonable. The only thing in the world she couldn't find a use for was trouble. "Why don't you take something 'to go'?" she asked.

The hostile vibes in the place were washing over Rose now. And she responded according to her usual practice. Freak 'em out. Spit in their eye and charge 'em for the eyewash. "Suits the shit out of me," she said loudly.

Dyer leaned forward over the counter and spoke very quietly to the waitress. "What have you got that's ready? A couple dogs, a couple burgers, maybe. Anything that's ready."

Meanwhile, a fat, blue-jowled trucker was leering openly at The Rose's exposed breasts. Two stools away, he began to edge his bulk closer to her.

"Ain't you Paul Newman?" she asked him with cloying-sweet sarcasm.

Dyer's attennae were signaling to him madly. Danger. Danger. "Anything, anything, only just make it quick," he urged the waitress, one eye on Rose.

One of the truckers came up behind Dyer and muttered into his ear. "I'd haul ass if I were you, friend. Know what I mean?"

Dyer recognized the grudging friendliness behind the man's advice. "Yeah, I know what you mean," he nodded quietly. "Soon as we get our stuff."

But it was too late to head The Rose off. She was riled now, and defiant. Who the fuck did these pigs think they were, the King of England? Crummy cheap diner filled with crummy creeps staring at her, not even recognizing her! She planted her fists on her slender hips and

96

shouted over to Dyer, loud enough for everybody to dance to.

"I don't know about you, but I'm about ready to kick me some ass in here!"

Now even the men who had ignored her were staring at her, openly disgusted, shaking their heads and turning their lips down at the corners.

Dyer put a gentle hand on Rose's arm and moved her an inch toward the door.

The trucker who had been leering uttered a raucous laugh and yelled out, "That's right. Take the sloppy whore with ya."

Rose straightened up to her full five feet, one inch and brought her nose to within spitting distance of this smelly behemoth.

"Well, suck mah dick!" she sneered.

The trucker's face grew red with rage and he started up from his stool with doubled fists, ready to commit mayhem on the tiny girl who stood scowling in front of him.

Dyer took one step forward; his right hand moved so quickly it was a blur, but the chop landed square in the heavy man's kidney, doubling him over. But the trucker was too big to go down all the way, and he started to lumber to his feet again. This time Dyer used his left. Bending only the first joint of his fingers over, he aimed this semifist at the base of the man's skull, where the back of the head met the spine. Delivered any harder, it would have been a lethal blow, but Dyer merely tapped him there, and the beefy man fell unconscious, his face in his bowl of chili. He looked very peaceful.

Dyer put his hands up in the air to show that he carried no weapon. "Show's over, folks," he called genially. "Friend here's just gonna continue eating his chili and, believe me, we're on our way. Hearty appetite, everybody."

Smiling, he grabbed The Rose with one hand and the

take-out bag with the other, throwing a ten-dollar bill down on the counter. Before anybody could unboggle his eyes, make a move, or even ask "Who was that masked man?," Dyer had pulled The Rose out of the diner and was running with her toward the limo.

Both of them tumbled into the front seat, Dyer behind the wheel. They were out of breath from running, but as soon as the car door slammed, they burst into uncontrollable laughter.

"You're just about a tough motherfucker, ain't ya?" crackled Rose.

"You ain't so bad yourself," Dyer told her. "C'mon, let's get outta here. I think I busted my hand."

Footsteps sounded on the cobbled street behind the car, and Dyer floored it; the Caddy pulled out of there like a Thunderbird, heading uptown.

Rose had found herself a second wind; she wasn't tired anymore, she was having the time of her life. Tearing the greasy paper bag open, she spread it out on her lap like a linen tablecloth. She dug into the hamburgers greedily, tearing off large bites with her strong teeth and shoving pieces of the hot sandwich into Dyer's mouth. She divided the fries fairly equally—for her—counting off two for her and one for Dyer, dangling them in front of his nose before dropping them into his mouth. She was totally relaxed now, and wide awake. The long, heavy, wearing day forgotten, The Rose was ready to party.

Sitting beside Houston Dyer in the front seat, she kept sneaking looks at him. What she saw she liked. He had a strong profile, with a straight nose and a firm chin. She knew that, under the chauffeur's cap he was wearing, his hair was cut short, very short, unusual in this day and age for a young man.

How old was he? It was hard for her to tell. His cheeks were smooth, and his teeth very white. Young. But he had an air of maturity about him; he was really a take-charge guy who looked as though he had been around, seen and done things. Maybe not so young? Definitely more a man than a boy, but Rose believed he was still in his twenties.

It was the eyes that disturbed her. She could read eyes, her grandma always used to say that the eyes were the windows of the soul. But she had yet to see his. It was dark in the limo, and the shiny peak of his driver's hat covered his brow and shadowed his eyes so that they couldn't be seen. She found herself wanting to see his eyes, wanting to look through the windows to his soul. She felt comfortable with him, a feeling that was strange to The Rose. Comfortable and easy.

Music. Let's have us some music, liven this ole party up a little. Rose leaned over and switched on the dashboard radio, fetching up some middle-of-the-road music, mellow sounds. Before she could switch the station to something with a beat, the music faded out and an announcer's voice came over the air.

"News on the hour from station WHN. Government spokesmen reported today that enemy casualties continue to mount in heavy fighting north of Saigon. Three hundred and five Vietcong reported dead with no official count of the wounded. American losses were reported light—"

Dyer sneaked out one silent hand and turned the radio off.

Startled, Rose turned to look at him. Houston had his eyes fixed firmly on the street ahead of his lights; his mouth was set in a grim line. Tentatively, Rose turned the radio on again.

"—in Congress," read the news announcer, "the debate over the use of napalm and the strategy of defoliation continues. Charges were hurled that women and children are being burned to death—"

Again Dyer switched the radio off without a word.

This time Rose kept her hands in her lap, watching him curiously. He appeared strangely drained, his tall body slouching over the wheel.

The silence began to thicken, and Rose broke it.

"Houston?" she said softly.

"Yeah?"

"Lemme buy you a drink."

The bar was west of Hudson Street, down a snaky series of right turns. Dyer could never have found it himself without the help of an Indian guide, a geodesic survey map, and a gyrocompass. But Rose knew exactly where it was, and led him expertly through red lights and illegal turns until they reached a dim tenement doorway on the western fringes of Greenwich Village. A dimming, sputtering neon sign proclaimed "77 Club," but if it weren't for the limos and fancy cars double-parked outside, Houston would have had grave doubts. It was a derelict street of crumbling tenements, fire escapes, doorways furnished with half-conscious winos lying in their own puke.

Rose hopped out of the car squealing with joy, straight into the arms of a huge black bouncer who covered her face with kisses, lifting her two feet off the ground.

"Rose, baby! Where you been, girl?"

"George!! Am I glad to see you."

With a flourish, the bouncer threw open the club door and waved them inside. "Show's just starting, Rose. The girls will be real charged up when they see you."

The cigarette smoke was so thick and the music so loud that Houston took a minute to get his bearings. It was definitely a night spot, an after-hours joint. Popular, too, to judge from the fact that every table seemed to be filled. Many of the customers were in evening clothes, as though they'd come from a hundred-dollar-a-plate dinner uptown.

There was a small stage at one end of the shabby room, and a runway leading from it down to the audience. On the runway a strapping . . . person . . . six-two without the silver lamé high-heel slippers and six-five with them . . . was lip-synching to a Peggy Lee record. The hair on this person's chest was playing peek-a-boo with the sweetheart neckline of the evening gown this person was wearing. There was a long black wig, askew a little, and a mile of mink fur eyelashes.

Houston blinked—maybe from the smoke—and looked around the room. On the wall were framed portraits of Joe Dallesandro, Judy Garland, and Marlene Dietrich, as well as posters for *All About Eve* and *Some Like It Hot*. There was a huge black-light poster of Nico and the Velvet Underground and one from last year, advertising The Rose in concert in Los Angeles. When Dyer saw the hostesses circulating among the tables, hustling drinks, he began to get the idea. They were all drag queens in full evening regalia, swishin' and sashayin' and carryin' on for the general public and because they loved it.

By now Rose was being smothered in little cries and kissy-face by a red-haired man even taller than the bouncer. This was the owner, incredibly named Bruce, an old friend of Rose's, a loyal fan, and a fag who knew a stellar attraction for his club when he saw one. The Rose's presence here tonight would ensure him turnaway business for months to come.

"Rose, you look stupendous!" enthused Bruce with a hug. Then he turned his attention to Dyer, who'd removed his cap, exposing his short haircut. "Well, darling . . . who's the young Republican?" Bruce purred in The Rose's direction, appreciating Houston's size and physique.

Rose switched her hips at him saucily, rolling her eyes in her best Mae West manner. "Dream it, but don't scheme it, Bruce. This man saved my life *twice* in one night!"

101

"Mouth to mouth, no doubt," returned Bruce, leading them to a table with a Reserved sign on it. Bruce always kept this one for visiting celebrities; it rarely went empty. "Some girls get all the breaks." As he pulled her chair out for The Rose to sit, he put his hennaed head close to her ear and whispered, "I've got a nickel bag. No lactose. No quinine. You can run *this* horse all the way to Aqueduct and win."

Rose shook her head firmly. "Uh-uh. Mama don't ride that horse no more." She turned to Houston Dyer. "What are you drinking?"

"Tequila."

"Bring a bottle and two glasses, Bruce, willya?"

"How daring!" camped the owner archly, and flounced off.

Rose leaned back in her chair, grinning around her with delight. The noise, the music, the female impersonators, all made her happy and excited. She found the atmosphere uninhibited and cheerful—exactly the opposite of that pig diner. Now she was in her element.

"Freak City, Houston!" she chortled. "I love it! Come on, relax! See how the other half lives. You know, I once lived right over this place. No foolin', right upstairs; I wouldn't shit ya." She pointed above her head. "I never left the room. We just shot horse for eight months. I weighed eighty-seven pounds and could hardly remember my name. But I knew every single word to 'My Heart Belongs to Daddy.' Including all the verses." She was high now, coasting along on sheer nervous energy, and her eyes never left Dyer's face. Her speech was becoming more and more rapid. "Did you ever shoot heroin?" she asked, without waiting for an answer. "Why do you wear your hair like that? What are you thinking?"

Dyer grinned at her slowly. "I'm thinking we should set up a date with Miss Peggy Lee up there and that goon from the diner."

102

Rose gave a shout of laughter. "Houston, I hate your hair, but I love your head. What else are you thinking?"

"I think I think too much," grinned Houston.

"That's why I drink," nodded Rose, and grabbed the bottle with an exaggerated gesture. She poured two glasses full to the brim, and picked hers up for a long, thirsty gulp. When she lowered it, she saw that Dyer's was still sitting on the table untouched.

"Hey, it's legal," she told him, pushing the glass in his direction.

With sudden determination, Houston Dyer picked up the brimming glass and belted more than half of it down. Rose broke into delighted applause, and leaned over the table to fill his glass up again. She felt a glow that arose from something other than the liquor, a kind of warm peacefulness.

Now, for the first time since they'd met so precipitously, Rose was able to look into Houston Dyer's face and see his eyes. They were large eyes, set wide apart in a broad brow, and a deep brown in color. They were serious eyes, serious and a little sad. There was so much contrast in this man; he appeared to be paradoxical. He was silent and slow to speak; when he spoke it was in the soft drawl of his Texas birthplace. Yet he moved with quiet . . . authority . . . yes, that was the only word for it. Authority. As though he knew exactly where he was going and how to get there. He had no nervous mannerisms; he was quiet as a resting cat; yet, when he swung into action, it was immediate, swift, and deadly. And he was not yet thirty; although the planes of his handsome face were sharpened by outdoor life, there was still a boy's vulnerability around the mouth. The more Rose looked at him, the more she liked looking at him. He was one helluva hunk, tall, muscular, handsome . . . and something beyond that. Rose lived in a world of panicky, high-strung, hedonistic people who were always

103

teetering on the edge of some deep crevasse. Many of them had fallen in and been lost. But Houston Dyer had the calm and depth of a mountain lake.

"Get your life story ready," she told him. "I'm getting curious."

He flashed her one of his grins. They had connected, and both of them were on that high that two people get when they feel truly together.

At that moment, the band broke into a blaring fanfare, and the young, gay master of ceremonies grabbed the microphone.

"Thank you very much, ladies and gentlemen, thank you very much," he began to scattered applause.

"And now, ladies and gentlemen, before bringing on the featured attraction of our late show, the lady you've all come here to see tonight, let me introduce a very special guest. She's here with us tonight, direct from doing her own sold-out show, a concert where she killed thousands of people . . . and they're not buried yet. . . . May we have a spot, please?"

With a pleased groan, Rose blinked as the pin spot was directed at her table, finding her golden head. She and Dyer blinked, and she flashed him a proud yet embarrassed smile.

"The one and only *Rose!*" yelled the MC, and the place went bananas. Cheers and whistles and stomps, and the heavy scraping of chairs as the patrons got to their feet to get a closer glimpse of the legendary singer. Rose stood up to let them get a good look at her, raising her arms in the V-for-Victory-and-Vietnam peace signal. This made the crowd go wilder than ever.

Houston sat back in his chair, out of the spotlight, watching her grin and groove and glow for the people. Two hours ago, she was the most exhausted, tore-up person he'd ever seen, a limp, baby girl. Now she was a radiant woman, every nerve alive and tingling in the warmth of the affection she was getting from the crowd.

"And honey . . ." the MC was leaning hard into the mike, talking straight at Rose, ". . . have we got a surprise for you! Hit it, boys."

The spot swung back to the runway, and the band broke into the first bars of "Fire Down Below," one of The Rose's great numbers. Out onto the runway swaggered a six-foot-three transvestite squeezed into satin jeans with Rose patches. Over his hugely padded bra was a sheer, tie-dyed blouse; there were rings on all his fingers, and bracelets halfway up the muscular arms. He came out strutting, shimmying, shaking his ass. On his head was a giant wig of blond frizz.

Grabbing the mike with a suggestive gesture, the singer placed his legs wide apart, thrust his pelvis forward lewdly, and shouted at the audience, *"Hiya, motherfuckers!!!!!"* He was The Rose to the life, only twice as big.

The customers went out of their minds, screaming and applauding and craning their heads to see how Rose was taking this. She was beating the table feebly with one hand as tears of hysterical laughter kept her doubled over. This was rich, rich! God, I am going to piss in my pants, right in front of all these people. Let me die, Lord. I've never laughed so hard in all my life.

Then the transvestite broke into "Fire Down Below," a down and dirty, heavily suggestive song about the energies a woman possesses below her waist, and Rose wiped the tears from her eyes. He was good, shit, he was good. He'd not only caught the nuances of her singing, he also had a damn good voice, rough and raunchy like hers. She was stunned and flattered by the faithfulness of his impersonation, and she knew suddenly there was only one thing to do. She would pay him tribute like he was paying her. Dues time.

She ran to the runway and scrambled up. A delighted MC handed her his own microphone, and Rose joined in. There were two Roses up there now, a big one and a little one, two big voices joining in the song, making history right there before your eyes. The audience responded with blanket hysteria as the two of them got down, wiggling and growling, shouting and grooving, hips shaking. What a sister act! Nothing like this had been seen on any stage before.

The girls waiting in the wings broke free and ran into the runway to join the fun. One impersonator came out as Barbra Streisand, in a heavy bubble-cut hairdo and false nose. Another was Mae West, huge tits above a big bustle and an ostrich-trimmed picture hat topping the whole mélange. They broke into the song; who didn't know "Fire Down Below"? It was the anthem of every hot-to-trot lady, gentleman, or—in this case—both at once. The tiny stage and runway were filled with the steamy heat of the song. In the center of all that camp was the tiny figure of Rose, sparking a million volts and jolts of sheer personal electricity. And all for Houston Dyer.

She was singing directly at him now, turned on out of her mind, showing him everything she had. And he was responding to her, giving her one of his slow, broad smiles. All of this was new to him, this show-biz excitement and camp-sleaze atmosphere, but he was beginning to relax and take it all in stride. The wiry, jumpy little body of The Rose was having its effect on him, too. He could feel the space between them crackling with her excitement, and his own physical awareness of her was heightening with each minute. Small as she was, she was dominating that stage, crowding out those outrageous drag queens with the overwhelming force of that personality.

Kindled into flame, The Rose was cooking with all her heat. She crooked her finger at Dyer and beckoned to him.

"Hey, come on up here!" she shouted.

Dyer looked around him, then pointed to his chest and raised his eyebrows in an elaborate "Who, me?"

"Yeah, you!" The Rose yelled happily. "I'm talkin' to you! Git on up here!" Sweat was pouring off her body as she danced on to the music.

Dyer shook his head shyly, and grabbed tight to the arms of his chair, gluing his big body into his seat. No way! Rose laughed and poured herself off the stage, shimmying her way through the tables, boogeying on down. When she reached Dyer it was the irresistible force meeting the immovable object.

The immovable object lost. Rose's energy was too much for Houston's shyness. He drained his tumbler of tequila abruptly, to fuel his courage, then stood up resolutely. Something told him that this was only the beginning, that he was going to have to play by a different set of rules from now on, and that it might just be worth it.

Half dancing, half escorting, Rose managed to get Dyer through the clapping, yelling crowd and onto the stage, where he found himself face to face with a trio of big men wearing dresses and wigs. Well, there was a first time for everything.

The little band had reached a fever pitch and were laying down some mean riffs, with a strong dance beat. Although Dyer had never been world famous as a fantastic light-tripper, the music was working on his feet and in his soul. With a Texas whoop, he began to stomp his feet in something between a hoedown and the hully-gully. He waved his arms around and raised the dust on the stage into a fearful cloud. Rose chortled in delight. Outtasight, this dude was something else!

Now they were dancing face to face, sweating and grinning at each other, each of them completely caught up in the music and the animal presence of the other. Having reached a fever pitch of excitement, they sustained it by continual eye contact, and the occasional brushing of hand against body as they danced.

"Are you trying to get into my bloomers, sonny?" Rose demanded, shouting over the music.

"Yes, ma'am, workin' on it," Houston replied seriously.

Rose threw her head back in a long yell of laughter. She felt warm and happy, safe, protected, admired, relaxed. The longest day of her life was coming, God only knew how but thank You kindly, to a satisfactory conclusion. She wriggled closer to Dyer, so that she could talk directly into his ear, above the merriment and the madness of the crazy queens, the driving music, the screaming, adoring, grooving fans.

Her voice, hoarse from singing at top volume, croaked happily in Dyer's ear. "You brown-eyed motherfucker, where ya been all my life?" she demanded joyously.

From The Rose, that was poetry.

Nothing but the best for The Rose. Houston Dyer was the best. The Plaza Hotel was the best. So it was to the entrance of the Plaza Hotel that the Cadillac pulled up, weaving somewhat unsteadily up the curving driveway.

The night doorman had been on shift since midnight, five hours ago. He was due to be relieved at seven. It had been a quiet evening, a soft summer night filled with fragrant breezes wafting in from the Plaza's backyard, Central Park. He watched curiously as a long black limousine wobbled down Fifth and Fifty-ninth, and turned into the driveway slowly, its whitewalls scraping the curbstones. The car drifted to a stop, and a young driver in a chauffeur's cap stepped out smartly and opened the passenger door with a flourish.

"Ever polite," The Rose remarked graciously.

"The way my momma taught me," said Dyer. He held out his arm for The Rose to take.

"Which momma was that, son?" asked The Rose, stepping out of the limo.

The doorman blinked and blinked again. His back

108

stiffened automatically, a silent physical protest. Emerging from the ordinary, respectable Cadillac limousine was the most extraordinary sight that the doorman's eyes had rested on in ages. It was a child . . . no, a young woman, now that he could see her . . . ah . . . bosoms. The girl was barefoot, and feathers of some indeterminate kind appeared to be sticking in her hair. Had she been sleeping in the aviary in Central Park Zoo? She appeared to be a gypsy, but why would a gypsy be riding in a limousine? Yet her tattered and stained clothes were certainly a gypsy costume. Or worse. The doorman closed his eyes in pain; it had been such a quiet evening. Couldn't they have waited only a couple of hours more? Ryan was on the day shift; why couldn't they go away and come back when Ryan was on the door?

Jesus, Mary, and Joseph, the driver was leading the gypsy up the steps as though she were a princess of some kind. A foreign dignitary? Was he going to have to deal with this? The doorman closed his eyes again, wincing. The Plaza Hotel was no place for gypsies, not even gypsy princesses.

Rose stopped on the steps, looking up in admiration at the baroque façade of the grand old hotel, with all its flags flying in the morning breeze. The canopy, with its intertwined P's, gave her a thrill of luxury.

"I'm rich, you know," she told Dyer. "I could buy this place if I wanted to."

"You like being rich?" asked Dyer curiously.

Rose grinned and nodded her head like a six-year-old. "There's a rumor going around that being rich is a drag. I don't know who started it, but I know he didn't have a dime. I *looove* having bread. Were you ever rich?"

Dyer thought the question over seriously. "A couple of years ago," he answered slowly, "I went down the Salmon River in Idaho. Y'know, in one of them little rubber rafts? I didn't see another soul for six days. I felt like I owned the whole thing." He smiled, savoring the wealth of the memory, the wild white water, the rugged banks, the leaping fish, the green calm silent stillness that brought the peace to his soul.

Rose stared at him with boundless curiosity. Alone for six days! With nobody to talk to, nobody to sleep with, nobody to groove on, yell at, drink with, tickle, pinch, lick, fuck. It was inconceivable. She shrugged her slender shoulders.

"I haven't been alone in about three hundred years," she marveled.

They continued up the steps and the doorman braced himself for a heavy eviction. Instead, he found himself staring at a twenty-dollar bill, being dangled at him by the tall young man in the chauffeur's cap. The doorman smiled and touched his cap, as doormen do to visiting royalty in all the best hotels.

Screw it, the doorman thought, making the twenty disappear like magic. Let them handle it at the desk.

But a twenty at the desk worked its enchantment, too. With a precious hotel-suite key in hand, Rose and Houston—without luggage—went up in the elevator of the most famous hotel in the world to work out their destiny.

VII

There is no sensation in the world that is comparable to going to bed with somebody for the first time. There is only one first time for each new lover, one occasion on which the body is totally unfamiliar territory and must be explored. Later, when lovers know each other's contours, likes, dislikes, passions, and preferences, the sex can become better, transcendant, more and more pleasing. But it can never be that trembling, insecure, "Am I doing it right?" and "Will he like this?" feeling that you get when you look and smell and touch and taste another's body for the very first time. You may forget the last time you slept in somebody's arms, but not the first.

We are with Rose and Houston and it is for them the first time with each other. Both are young; in both the drives, the fires, the juices of life run strong. Her experience with strangers is greater than his, yet, oddly, he is in command. His command is total, yet it is not tyrannical. He takes his time, despite her furious push toward climax. He takes his time to stroke and kiss, to tease and pet and gentle her down; she responds at last by—as he intends and as is unusual for her—relaxing. Totally relaxing into his arms and his strength and his warmth, so that when he enters her at last, his lips and tongue on her breasts, it is an act so inevitable that they feel as though they are entering each other, each of them experiencing what the other feels. This is new to Rose, and she is close to withdrawing from it. It is almost too much. But before she can adjust to the strangeness of the sensation, it changes into the familiar rushing, burning, hurry-before-it's-too-late feeling that carries them both up and over and leaves them gasping like sea creatures stranded on the shore as the waves recede.

Fulfilled, they sleep, but Rose wakes soon. An hour or two, perhaps a little longer. She lies in the dark, adjusting her sight to her surroundings, remembering slowly where she was, where she is, who lies sleeping beside her. She is sated, yet hungry at the same time. Hungry not for the fierce clutch of anonymous sex, but for the body of the man in the bed, the man with a name, with long, smooth muscle, large, gentle hands, a mouth both strong and soft. She wants Houston Dyer. She wants him all to herself.

She touches him gently, wonderingly, reluctant to wake him. He sleeps soundly and silently. As he does everything, secure and patient. She runs her hand along his body, only the lightest touch of fingertips along his skin. She bends to taste him, then tastes him more deeply, more voraciously still, until he wakens to find her face buried in his belly and his passions aroused. He moves to pull her up, to make love to her in his turn, but she wants none of it. Rose wants only to make love to him, to feel *his* pleasure, *his* climax. And he lets her, his strong fingers wound in her golden hair.

Afterward, they sleep again; and this time it is Houston who wakes her, curled behind her, already inside her. She wakes up groaning with passion. In her sleep she had begun to move to his rhythm, and when she wakes, she is halfway to the top and climbing fast. They come together, she sobbing, he laughing, and fall asleep again tangled in the sheets and in each other.

They are awake now. The late-afternoon sun comes creeping in the western window and throws bars of light

112

across the messy bed. Room service has been and gone; crumbs and bits of food have stained the sheets. The pillows and blankets hit the floor hours ago and sleep there quietly. A bottle of whiskey is mostly gone; ice has melted in puddles on the expensively gilded night tables. They are full and happy. They are waiting for the fullness to go away, so that the hunger will return and they can make love again. And yet again.

Rose doesn't want to leave this room. The Plaza has become her new home, and Houston Dyer her new protection. On his chest she has laid her head to sleep, and no harm came to her. Almost, almost, she trusts him.

"Do I ball like I sing?" she asked suddenly, coquettishly.

Houston laughed out loud. "Lady, you sure are something," he told her.

Why am I embarrassed? Why do I feel suddenly naked in soul as well as body? She didn't know but all at once she felt like a girl, not a woman, a girl of little experience. She wanted him to see her at her best.

"You sure are something," he repeated, marveling.

"Mister, so are you," she said softly. She wrapped a sheet around herself and headed for a mirror. "Do you think I'm sexy?" she asked him tentatively. When she heard no reply, she whipped around anxiously. "Hey, The Rose wants to know."

Dyer rolled over onto his naked belly and regarded her good-naturedly. "Anybody who talks about themselves in the third person is in trouble."

The Rose raised one eyebrow. "You don't mess around, do you?"

Houston Dyer shook his head. "I don't have the time."

Rose ran across the room and jumped into the large bed, pillowing her head next to Houston's. "You got time for me?" she asked softly. "You want to go steady?" She held her breath, waiting for his answer.

"Well, what the hell," he drawled, "I'll just stop into the nearest five-and-dime and buy a box of them chocolate-covered cherries for you."

"God, do you remember them?" giggled Rose. "They wrap 'em all up in gold with lots of cracked hearts all over it. Looks real classy. Yeah, an' all the boys and girls gave each other boxes on Valentine's Day." She stopped, caught up in the pain of her memories. Recollections of all the lonely Valentine's Days, and the chocolate-covered cherries that were never for her. "Shoot," she said sadly, in a voice not much louder than a whisper, "I wish I'd known you in high school."

Dyer reached over and touched her gently, but Rose jerked herself away.

"I don't need charity from trash like you," she sniffed.

Laughing, he moved to envelop her; Rose pulled herself out of the compass of his arms.

"I hate mushy love-stuff," she growled. "Wake me up when the killing starts."

But Dyer wouldn't let go of her; she could feel the strength of his arms flowing like neon through her skin and into her body. She wanted it so badly she couldn't let herself have it. It made her too soft, too vulnerable. She was The Rose; she hadn't been born to just be a man's woman. But, oh, she wanted it so bad! She could feel her body turning to his automatically; her breasts ached for his kisses.

She had to do it. Had to tell him something so bad that he'd turn from her, reject her, leave her as others had done. She needed his rejection to reinforce her own self-loathing. Leaning toward him, she whispered into his ear.

"I'll tell you something so weird about me you won't even believe it."

Dyer felt a chill. She was The Rose; he'd heard stor-

ies about her. Everybody had. One of the most noto-
rious was that she used to stick a tab of acid up her
snatch so that anybody who ate her pussy would go away
tripping.

"Oh, yes I will," he said softly.

"Oh, no you won't."

"Bet I will." He laughed into her face, and Rose
tried to smile back. Suddenly, she wanted to stop herself, to take back her words, but it was too late. She was
going downhill and the brakes had failed.

"Once in high school," she said slowly, trying to
keep her words and voice casual, "I got drunk and took
on the whole football team." She stopped, out of breath,
her heart in her mouth, waiting for the worst.

It wasn't so much her words as the pain behind them
that told Houston Dyer how awful her experience had
been. For a minute he was tempted to put on his pants
and get the hell out of there. This woman was trouble
with a capital R-for-Rose; he knew it. Her need was so
naked, and her inability to deal with that need would lead
to deepshit trouble.

But he wasn't a man for running away. Except
once . . .

"You always tell Christmas stories like that?" he
asked her wryly.

"You're shocked, aren't you?" demanded Rose.

"No," lied Dyer.

"I woke up in the morning on the fifty-yard line."

"I'd hate to tell you the places I've woke up," replied Houston equably.

Rose relaxed against his shoulder. The trial was over,
and somehow she'd been judged . . . if not innocent, at
least not so very guilty. A great wave of relief washed
over her. Staring up at the ceiling, she spoke softly, not
so much to the man holding her as to herself.

"I've waited all my life to go back to that place, like

115

a star. Hometown applause. The thought of it is what gets me up in the morning and puts me down at night. They're gonna push and shove to get a view of the one 'n' only Rose. And she'll toss it in their teeth."

"Toss what?"

Rose turned to look at him. "Herself. Rich and famous. Me. The Rose."

She reached for him, to pull his face to hers in a long kiss. But, before their lips met, the telephone rang, startling them and breaking them apart.

Who the hell knew they were here? Was the management about to evict them because of the beer cans on the oriental rug and the grease stains that had somehow wandered onto the gold brocade draperies?

It rang again. Rose picked it up.

"Yes?" She listened for a minute, and her face crumpled like paper, an expression of sheer panic clouding her large blue eyes. "Jesus . . . I'm sorry. I'll be there as soon as I can. I was wrong! I was *wrong!*"

Dyer heard a click at the other end, and Rose set the receiver back on its cradle with a trembling hand.

"I was supposed to be at a recording session," she whimpered like a frightened child. "Oh, God, am I gonna get it."

"Who the fuck was that?" demanded Houston. He hated seeing her like this, so defenseless, so terrified.

"Rudge. My manager. Rudge."

"How in hell did he find us?"

"Are you kidding?" Rose dashed naked from the bed and ran to pick up her scattered clothing. "There ain't no place on this green earth of God's that you can hide from Rudge Campbell, does he want to find you."

"Do I look awful?" asked Rose, not waiting for an answer. It was her standard question in moments of panic.

They stood outside Jimi Hendrix's Electric Lady-

116

land recording studios on Eighth Street, the main drag of Greenwich Village. Rose's panic, which had subsided in the limo on the way down, was now rising again to choke her.

"You look fine," Dyer assured her. But in fact she did look awful. She was pale as writing paper, and the dark kohl makeup around her eyes stood out like rings on a 'coon. She kept twisting the rings on her small hands, and Houston took both her hands in his to make her stop. He smiled at her reassuringly as they entered the building, but Rose didn't seem to notice.

The recording studio was dark, empty of everybody except the man who sat with his costly boots propped up on the huge custom-built console, his arms folded.

Rose snapped on the light and looked around her, bewildered. Microphones stood around unplugged; the keyboards were covered and locked; the musicians gone.

"Where is everybody?"

"I sent them all home," said Rudge without moving. His voice came to them from the control booth.

Rose ran across the studio, careless of the coils of electric cable lying in wait to trip her up. She threw open the door of the control booth and burst inside.

"Where were you?" demanded Rudge, looking coldly at her bare, dirty feet and disheveled clothing.

"Rudge, this is Houston Dyer. Houston, Rudge Campbell," said Rose as calmly as she could.

"Howdy," Houston said pleasantly, holding out his hand. "Nice to meet you, sir."

Rudge ignored the outstretched hand. He didn't take his slitted green eyes off Rose. "Terrific, fucking terrific," he snarled. "Keep everybody waiting for hours and what do we get in return? A fucking cowboy! They said you'd never show up. I said, she'll show, and guess what? She shows all right, and not *one* hour late, not *two* hours late, but five fucking hours and three thou-

117

sand dollars late. I should have my head examined!" Rudge snapped open his crocodile case and swept a handful of tape reels inside, preparing to go.

Houston Dyer took a step forward. His voice was level, but his hands were balled into fists. "Hey, mister, these are real live human beings you're talking to here," he protested.

Rudge turned to him as though noticing him for the first time.

"Listen, sonny, me and this woman go back to when you were still in high school whacking off before sixth period. I'm in business with her. I talk to her any way I want because Miss Me-Gimme-Mine over there treats *me* any way *she* wants. So you butt out!"

Rose, who had been standing to one side with her fingers pressed against her mouth, now spoke up feebly to Rudge.

"C'mon. Don't be talkin' trash to him," she whined.

"My mistake," said Rudge crisply, in impeccable British. A sure sign he was furious. "I thought we had an appointment to make some money." He stalked out of the control booth, slamming the door behind him.

"Jesus!" exclaimed Dyer after Rudge had gone.

Rose leaned weakly against one of the tall Ampex eight-track master recorders. "It's only a performance, man," she shrugged. "That's what it's all about." But her face was still deeply troubled.

Dyer shook his head, completely and angrily at sea. "I don't under*stand* you people!"

Rose spread her small hands out, palms up. "Look, we're into money like everybody else," she explained. "The style is different, is all."

"I don't like his style," said Dyer stiffly.

"You shut up!" exploded Rose suddenly, her face working on the edge of tears. "Rudge is a fucking magician and he don't need no help from a piece of meat in a chauffeur's cap!"

118

The words hung between them, carved out of fire. A piece of meat in a chauffeur's cap. Oh, God, I want to cut my tongue out, thought Rose. She quivered under the long, hard look Dyer gave her. As he turned and walked through the door and out of the studio, Rose lifted one silent hand to stop him. But he didn't glance at her again.

The limousine was parked at the curb, and Dyer slipped behind the wheel. He looked up angrily as Rose yanked open the passenger door of the front seat.

"Close the door. I gotta go," he told her curtly.

"No! I won't let you!" she yelled.

"He's right about you," Dyer barked.

"I want some Chinese!" screamed Rose, tumbling onto the seat.

"Miss Me-Gimme-Mine!"

"NOW!" ordered Rose. She was frantic, unable to bear the thought of losing him so suddenly. She reached for the wheel, crowding Dyer, squeezing herself almost on top of him. The car leaped and lurched forward, then shuddered to a stop as Dyer regained control of the wheel.

"That ain't gonna work."

"Yes, it will," insisted Rose. " 'Cause you ain't goin' anywhere without me."

"Get out!" snapped Houston.

"Never," said Rose very quietly. She sat back and folded her arms.

"I said, 'Get out!' "

Rose stuck her lower lip out defiantly. "Make me."

But Dyer wasn't about to argue with her; he was turned off by her trashy attack on him. All he wanted was out of this situation, so he pushed open the driver's door and catapulted himself out of the limo.

His move caught The Rose by surprise, and Houston was halfway down the busy, traffic-choked street by the time she could scramble out of the car and run after him. Cars came at her from both directions; the drivers honking their horns and shouting obscenities and profanities at her. But she ignored them, running in front of their bumpers, weaving in and out between them, making them screech to a halt and stall. She was desperate to catch up to Dyer.

As she ran in front of a Ford wagon, the driver leaned loudly on his horn, scaring her half to death.

"Piss off!" she shrieked at him and at the world in general.

"Up yours!" yelled the driver.

"Hey . lady!" hollered a cab driver behind him. "You can't leave that big car parked like that in the middle of traffic. Hey, come back! Lady, it's against the law!"

She turned and gave them all the finger. When Rose turned back, it was just in time to catch sight of Dyer turning into a doorway.

Desperately, she pushed her way across the street and ran after him. She'd lost sight of him now. Where the fuck had he got to? Her bare feet burned on the pavement. Somebody must have dropped a lighted cigarette butt. Shit!

Why was she chasing him like this? She was The Rose and he was nothing but a long drink of water, a Texas shitkicker. Sure, he was a good lay, a great lay, but so what? There was a whole forest of stiff dicks out there all ready and waiting to get into The Rose. Starfuckers all.

Because he was different, that's why. He wasn't a starfucker; she knew that instinctively. He couldn't give a shit about stardom, fame, success, money—all that jazz that she got off on. Houston Dyer had a quiet strength she needed more than anything in the world. She *had* to find him; she *had* to lie in his arms again.

Rose, panting, reached the doorway she'd seen Houston vanish into. She looked up. There was a sign over the door.

She pushed both doors open at once, the two scratched and dented doors with the porthole windows in them. She came through like no one had ever entered—like Gangbusters—and stomped right past the bespectacled man standing there at the counter with his pile of towels and open, astonished mouth. She was halfway through the second set of doors when he said, in a louder, stronger voice than he'd used in some thirty years, "Hey lady, you can't go in there!"

But she could.

And she did.

The locker room boy, leisurely propped up in a broken red leather chair near the door, looked up from his copy of *Penthouse*. Perhaps because he'd been staring at various sets of mammaries for the past half hour or so, or maybe because The Rose had such an eye-catching pair of knockers, he looked directly at her breasts, a vision lifted from the very pages in his lap. His eyes widened. He sat up straight. The magazine fell to the damp floor.

"Hey." Rose called to him, "you seen a guy come in here?"

He couldn't believe it. Here's this chick with electric hair and the biggest tits he'd ever seen and bracelets clanging all over her arms and tight tight velvet pants on top of crazy bare feet—here's this chick standing in the locker room of a male Turkish bath asking him if he saw a *guy* come in there. "There's only *guys* in here, lay-dee." He drew it out. "What guy?"

Her blue eyes quickly took in the microphone on the little desk shoved next to him in the corner. She grabbed it, flicked the black switch with her thumb, and stuck her head down to it. She knew all about micro-

121

phones; she was going to use this one like she'd never used one in her life. "Houston Dyer," she screeched, as nasal as possible, shrill, ear-shattering, *"Houston Dyer, please report to The Rose."* That ought to knock the shorts off him, she thought. Then she added, *"You're wanted up front, Houston Dyer."*

She giggled to herself at the double meaning. The boy grabbed the mike and yanked it away from her. The Rose turned and shook her head, like a dog who'd just come in from the rain, gaining strength, mustering up guts. And with a sly smile on her face, for as mad as she was, the situation was totally ridiculous. In her path were men. Fat men. Middle-aged to one-step-from-the-grave men. Bald men. Red-faced men. Pot-bellied and flabby and smoking cigars, desperately trying to cover their hairy privates with towels, some covering their faces, some trying to shove their fat selves into their skinny lockers. She charged through them, a clothed Lady Godiva with her mane of hair flowing in the harsh fluorescent light riding a path through the naked townsfolk—how's that for a switch?—and all the way muttering, "Dyer, Dyer, Dyer." They scattered before her right and left, diving into the swimming pool.

"Hey," an elderly gentleman who had the guts to take a stand said, "fer Chrissake!"

"That's all right, man," The Rose said out of the corner of her mouth, "I've seen worse."

They scattered as she moved on through the rows and rows of lockers. One of the few decent-looking guys in the place shot her a leer, and she shot him a finger right back. Her eyes combed every nook and tiled cranny. "Dyer!" she yelled. No one admitted to it. "Dyer, c'mon outta there!" No one came out of anywhere. The walls were of sweating greenish tile, the kind of green you only find on hospital walls and toilet stalls, and men backed up against them, frozen. What was this crazy broad doing?

She kicked open a door and looked inside a room, but it was empty except for a pile of weights and those machines where you stand and pull on straps like you're kneading saltwater taffy in Atlantic City. When she turned around and screamed, *"Dyer!"* again, an owlish sort of man stepped up in front of her. She looked at him as if to say yeah, what can I do for you?

"Can I help you, madam? My name's Dyer. I'm George Dyer."

The Rose looked him up and down. Beads of sweat all over his scrawny body. Even his spectacles had sweat on them. Then she looked down—with the whole room riveted to the scene—and lifted up the front of his towel. Her eyes lowered in disappointment. She dropped the towel. "Wrong Dyer," she cackled, and pushed past him.

The room echoed with the laughter of his pals as George Dyer stood there red-faced from head to toe.

Rose found another door and kicked it open. A gust of steam hit her in the face. She stepped back and the door swung shut, but she wiped a peephole in the glass porthole and checked out the inhabitants. And there he was. Well, he wasn't hard to find, his body being some fifty steps up the ladder of success. He was just sitting down on the long wooden bench, ready to take some steam. Good. That's just what she was going to give him.

She shoved through the doors and planted herself in the center of the schvitz room, hands smack on her ass, pelvis forward, eyes glaring straight at Dyer, ready to do battle. The rack of men facing her—some sitting bare naked, others with their legs spread sufficiently enough to show this unannounced visitor all the family jewels—reacted with anger. "Hey, for God's sake!" one character shouted.

"Jeezus Christ!" another sputtered.

"Ohhhhh," a young man, embarrassed to hell, moaned.

"Shit, what next?" another voice muttered.

But Rose couldn't give a damn. "Everybody out," she ordered. "No more 'Drop-the-soap.'"

The room cleared in a moment. She never once took her eyes off Dyer, half lying so he slatted the bench in his white towel with Luxor stamped on it in fading block letters. "If I don't get a kind word in the next ten seconds, I'm gonna do something terrible."

He faced her. Eyes locked. Horns locked.

She reached down hesitatingly, then stopped herself and began the motion again; this time she was confident, fighting. She crossed her arms and reached for the hem of the long flowered blouse she had on, threatening in that gesture to pull it over her head.

Dyer didn't move a muscle. He dared her with his silence, with his set jaw, sitting quietly there in the steam.

"One . . ." She clenched her fingers on the hem. "Two . . ." Come on, you fucker, come on, I dare you, I swear I'll do it, I'll take it off and I'll show these— "Three . . ." Goddamn you! She began to lift the material up to her face.

And then he broke. "At ease, at ease," he said, curiously, at ease himself. "Take it easy, Rose."

She dropped the hem, dropped the long blouse, which was already starting to cling to her body with sweat. The feather boa around her neck was starting to look like a chicken caught out in a thunderstorm. She smiled. She shrugged. And then she moved toward him, lifted her leg, and climbed up the bleacher like slabs of wooden planks to sit next to him. Matter-of-factly.

He knew she had something to say. He waited, leaning back, propping himself up with his elbows, curiously enjoying the steam as he saw her begin to calm down. "Jeezus, dogshit, I got a big mouth." She leaned back and shook her head and wiped the perspiration from her forehead. "It's nice in here," she added.

He looked around. It was?

She took a deep breath, drawing in the heated, humid air, and then let it out slowly, closing her eyes as she did so, her breasts, heaving, then falling, the length of her body relaxing, resting, calming out. "I'd . . . I'd love to go away someplace and lay out awhile an' do nothin'."

"Where?"

"Anywhere." She thought about it. She looked up and saw the big spotlight in the center of the ceiling. "Out in the sun, in the woods . . ." They were on the top rung of the bleachers. "On top of a mountain." Her eyes were tight, fantasizing.

"No Chinese restaurants up there," he said.

But there was no reply. She sat there, humming a little something he didn't recognize, shaking her head suddenly, opening her eyes again, licking the sweat from her upper lip, crossing her sticky feet. "Why do you wanna walk out on me?" she asked him after a while.

He chewed the side of his lip for a moment. "It isn't *you*," he tried to explain, "it's your life—"

Her head jerked toward him.

"It's like . . . like a grenade range." Then he closed *his* eyes and he said, "And it's me."

"Mmmm. I love mysteries, they're my favorite thing." And she waited for an answer, for she'd been just a touch sarcastic, hoping it would bring it out of him. She was desperate to find out about this man, discover him. He had a secret; she was convinced. "C'mon," she finally said, laughing a bit, "I told you about the football team."

And he let her have it. "I'm in the Army. I'm a master sergeant. I just got back from six years overseas." He sat up and put his hands between his knees.

She gulped and thought she was going to laugh out loud, but immediately her brain told her he wasn't kidding, and it wasn't difficult to believe, not at all. And no laughter.

"Now I'm absent without leave," he said, and his voice took on a note of strain. "I was due back at Fort Campbell, Kentucky, three weeks ago."

"Aw, that ain't nuthin'. I once kept twenty thousand people waiting in the Cow Palace for days. Just give 'em their money back."

A soft smile graced his strong face. "It doesn't work that way in the Airborne. Did you ever hear of the Screaming Eagles?"

"Sounds tough."

"Yeah."

She looked at him, with honest concern. "You're thinking about walkin' out on the Army for good, aren't you?"

Dyer nodded his wet head. "Yeah."

She had the answer and it was simple: "Then walk. I got a cousin in Canada. Jerry. He walked." Fact is, she thought, he ran.

"It's all I *know*," he explained, opening like he'd never opened to anyone before. "I've been in since I was seventeen."

"Seventeen!?" Jesus Christ. He was younger than she'd thought. Three years younger than she was.

"I joined on my birthday. Hot food, a roof over my head, socks lined up in a row. It's a beautiful thing." He meant it.

"Were you in the war?" she asked softly.

"A lot."

"What happened?"

"I—" He opened his mouth to speak but nothing happened. He was sweating but his tongue was dry as the Gobi. He turned his head away and lowered his head, then he dropped it all the way back and let out the resistance. "I can't do it anymore."

She heard the pain in that statement, the agony in his voice. She reached out and ran her hand over his short Army-cut hair, down over his ear, down over his

126

cheek. He did not move. She let her hand rest on his shoulder. "Don't go back," she said. "I'll take care of you."

He turned to her and smiled, feeling more in that one moment than he'd felt in his lifetime.

And Rose, clothes glued to her body, the feathers around the back of her head drooping so much now you couldn't even see her wild hair, just stared into his big, telling eyes. She could not smile. She could not even fall into his arms. For she was paralyzed, unmoving, but certainly not unmoved. He had shared something with her, something deep and personal and—what was the word?—precious. And no one had ever done that before. No one had stirred her. Oh, they had stirred her, stirred her mind and stirred her pussy and stirred her anger and frustration; Christ, they'd put her through a mixmaster, through a goddamn blender, and she'd come out cold, come out mush, come out dead. This was unique, and this was special. This was just about the first time anyone had . . . had *touched* her.

Tears welled up in her eyes, but she didn't realize it and he couldn't see them because tears were falling down the walls in this damn inferno of hissing hot water, and just as he was about to say something to her, the doors opened and in burst a burly, fully clothed—uniformed, no less—New York City police officer, arms folded, face to match. Behind him was the man from the towel desk and the locker-room boy. And behind them was the other Dyer and the assorted fatsos who'd been so outraged—and fascinated. "Okay, lady, let's go," the cop barked. "The party's over."

Rose looked at Dyer. Dyer looked at Rose. She gave him a grin and turned to her audience and cracked, "Damn, just when I was startin' to have a good time!"

They dragged her down the steps of the Seventeenth Precinct, having wrapped her up in a blanket like some

127

Indian papoose in an early John Ford Western, barefoot and looking none too happy. Fun at first, freaking out "the boys," as she called the customers when the police pulled her out of the Luxor, kicking and shouting how their wives were going to lock them all out in the cold once the pictures broke in the papers in the morning, but it was draggy now. Dyer walked by himself, but Rudge and Dennis held onto her as though she would bolt and take flight any second. Three policemen and a detective provided escort, one of them fumbling in his pockets to pull out a pen to go with his autograph book. "Please?" he asked her, holding it out in front of her nose when they got down to where they'd moved the limousine.

Looking like she was born to do it (after she freed her arms from the strangulation of the ugly green police blanket), she snatched the book and signed her name. As she did, she abruptly announced, "Rudge, we're canceling our bookings after the Florida date."

Rudge wasn't amused. "Here we go again. What's wrong now?"

She tossed the book back to the cop. "It's everything. It's my life—" She stopped and tossed Dyer a strong set of vibes. "It's like a grenade range."

Dyer let his mouth move into an understanding grin. "Maybe I better wait across the street." He put his hands in his pockets and moseyed his way across the street to the parked Caddy.

"You know this guy for ten minutes," Rudge growled, looking off after the sauntering Texan, "and because he hasn't picked your pocket—yet—or told you you look like Petunia Pig, you think he's the White Knight!" Rudge, that lousy cocksucker, really could go for the jugular.

She pushed the blanket off her shoulders and faced up to him. "After Florida, we're going away together, 'n' that's that." A cop picked up the mound of green wool and folded it.

128

"Lay off for a year, and they'll bury you in the remainder racks." Rudge's face was set in a glare of pure hatred.

"I'll take my chances."

Rudge was seething. He nodded to the tall body leaning against the black car across the street. "How does *he* feel about this?"

"He doesn't know about it yet." And she didn't wait for a reaction; she just walked away, toward Dyer, and then they got into the car and drove away.

Rudge stood watching until the car was out of sight. Then he kicked a flattened beer can that had been lying on the curb. It flipped into the air like a frisbee, but dropped quickly to the dirty, hard pavement. It clanked. Like his spirits.

There are times and places when New York City is the most beautiful, enchanted spot on the planet. A warm summer evening on the Promenade in Brooklyn Heights is one of them, especially if you're beginning to fall in love. From the Promenade you can see the skyline of lower Manhattan stretched out ahead of you like a diamond bracelet, lights winking, the spires of Wall Street pushing their way into the night sky.

Rose and Dyer walked slowly, side by side, as she told him her plan.

"Are you crazy?!" demanded Houston. "You can't leave!" He looked seriously into her face, lit by the gentle streetlights. "You've got your whole career—"

Rose cut him off. "You stay with me until I do my concert back home and then I'll go anywhere with you. Into the woods, on top of a mountain. Out of state. Out of sight." She promised this freely, smiling.

"Out of the country?" asked Dyer carefully.

"Outta the world!!" caroled Rose joyously, flinging her arms wide. She felt as though a great weight had been removed from her shoulders.

"You're outta your mind!" joked Houston.

Rose cocked her head up at him, enjoying his height and his calm good looks. "Yeah? Whatta ya gonna do about it?" she teased him.

For answer, Houston Dyer caught her up in his arms and kissed her hard on the mouth.

VIII

By the time World War II ended, Reg Callahan's education—if not his schooling—was complete. He didn't see any bloody reason to sit for stupid examinations and go on to a higher school when there was plenty of lolly to be made in postwar London. And there was; lots and lots of money was floating around, just waiting to be picked up by anybody smart and quick and not overly honest. Reg, although only in his early teens, fit that description to a T.

London after the war was every bit as bleak and dreary as it had been during the war. Almost everything was still on the ration—food, clothing, coal for fuel, petrol. The only thing missing was Jerry. There were no more air raids, only a lot of ruins and bomb sites, craters that would stand untouched for years, a depressed and depressing monument to the Blitz and to Britain's savaged and crushed economy. All hail the victor! It would take Britain years longer to get on her feet than Germany or Japan.

From 1939 to 1945, private automobiles had been put up on blocks and covered with tarpaulins. Even if you had a motor car, you couldn't get petrol, or tires, or spare parts, unless you were high up in government circles, or had political or economic pull. Some "wide boys" of Reg's young acquaintance formed a ring for

131

stealing these unused cars right out of their garages and cannibalizing them for spare parts. For every three or four cars they managed to make off with, they could turn out one perfect automobile, maybe even two. It wasn't so easy to pull off a theft; after all, you couldn't *drive* the bloody things away. It required getting the vehicle off the blocks and into a large van and away safely. But the boys were strong and resourceful. Reg, who had an artist's instinct and who hated heavy work, supplied the new paint job that disguised the finished product.

A car in running order, with four fairly sound tires, could be sold on the black market for eight or nine hundred nicker. Eight hundred quid was a fortune, even when divided by four and a half. The half share was Reg's, because he wasn't cut in on hazardous-duty pay. After all, he never actually came along on the burglaries. Even so, by the time Reg Callahan was fifteen years old he had over eleven hundred pounds in a postal savings account. That sum represented four times what his father earned in a year on the docks.

Reg had been living away from home for two years. He had rented a bed-sitter, complete with a shilling-meter gas fire, in Camden Town. London in 1950 had become a much more interesting place to live, and Rudge needed to be on his own to enjoy it.

At seventeen, he wore Teddy-boy clothes and slayed the prettiest girls with his wide green eyes and his wide lapels. Some years back, he'd discovered sex, and he practiced it just as his mother practiced Roman Catholicism—every day and twice on Sundays. His greatest passion was still money, but beautiful women ran money close second.

He'd discovered another passion, too. Music. Bebop, that outrageous form of jazz, had come from Greenwich Village to London Town. Eerie, wailing music played by blacks wearing small goatees, berets, and sunglasses

132

All the bebop musicians were either colored or trying their best to appear colored, and they were the very epitome of cool cats to young Reg. He would sit in the coffee houses of Soho, making faces over his tiny cup of bitter espresso, listening with quiet joy to the mellow yet titillating sounds of the saxophone, trumpet, drums, vibes. Bop—it was the sound of Mingus, or Charlie "Bird" Parker. It changed your head around, making you smile, feel warm.

But there must be good money in music, and Reg was impelled to find the way to it. He had never been entirely comfortable working in the automotive black market. It was not so much that he dreaded the risk as that he despised it as unnecessary.

His first thought was to take his savings out of the post office and open a coffee house of his own. But where was the profit in that? It dribbled in with sticky cups and sixpenny buns, in pence, not pounds. Reg wanted pounds, and thousands of them. Why should he lay out capital, hire wog waiters, hang about the place for hours on end making certain he wasn't being shorted at the till? Nah, that was okay for Greeks and Italians and other foreign muck, not for a clever English boy like Reg Calahan.

His second thought was the good one: Why not represent a musician? Agents, they called them. Or, better yet, managers. If you rep an artist, you can work out of your pocket. All you need is a handful of twopenny pieces for the telephone. And you've made yourself 10 percent, if you're smart and lucky. Rep two artists, and you've made 10 per cent times two. Manage three, and you've earned yourself an office.

Within a year, Reg had his office. It was one dingy room in Museum Street, up two winding flights of night-dark stairs. On the ground floor was a grimy tea shop where Reg received his telephone messages; all it took was four shillings a week to an accommodating waitress. A very accommodating waitress.

Painted on the door of this office was *Rudge Camp bell Associates Ltd*. There were no "associates," neithe had he registered his "limited" partnership in any legal o official way. Nor were there any partners, silent or vocal The name came about this way.

Once the lease was signed, the painter came, with hi little pots of gold leaf and black, and his thin Japanese brushes, to do the sign on the glass door.

"Wot name, then?"

Reg hadn't given it any thought. "Oh, Reg Callahan No 'g' in Callahan." But, as the sign painter had nodded and unscrewed the little bottle of black paint to make the outlines, Reg had one of his famous flashes. "Reg Calla han" had served its purpose. It was time to go on. New life, new business—that required a new name. It called for a celebration of the future, and a total desertion o the past.

" 'Ere," he said suddenly. " 'Alf a mo. Make tha . . ." His cat eyes narrowed in thought. "Make tha Rudge Campbell Associates Limited."

"It'll cost yer more than 'Reg Callahan,' " warned the sign painter.

" 'Ow much more?"

"Three bob."

"Make it two and six and abbreviate 'Limited,' " said Rudge Campbell.

The Rose's jet knifed through the sky. Houstor Dyer sat next to Rose at the rear of the plane, watching the guys in the band passing the reefer around. Whenever the joint was offered to him, he shook his head. He wanted to stay straight to keep an eye on Rose; she was fading fast. Also, a tug of amusement appeared at the corners o his lips. These stoned-out potheads thought they were toking on good shit. If they only had a taste of what was smoked over in 'Nam, they'd lose their fuckin' minds Dyer was certain they'd never even seen a Thai stick.

Brad had taken a 'poon out of his jeans pocket and was blowing a soft blues into it. The wail of the harmonica music created a strange sense of longing in Houston; he couldn't put a name to it, but it was painful. The Greeks had a word for it, as they had a word for everything. The word was "nostalgia," which meant the pain of yearning for home. Dyer was very far from home, even if he wasn't sure anymore where home was. The Army? Texas? Rose's bed? The conflicts were rising strongly in him, and he knew he had to deal with them sooner or later.

Meanwhile, The Rose was not in such hot shape. They had finished the album in two twelve-hour sessions; the overtime costs had been staggering, but the album was good. While they were in New York, The Rose had stayed reasonably sober. She went from the Electric Ladyland studios to Dyer's bed without a stop in between. She sang and made love, made love and sang.

But once they'd hit the road, she had become morose and despondent, dependent less on Dyer and more on the brandy. Now she sat gloomily at the plane window, raising the bottle to her lips with depressing regularity. Houston, who believed in minding as much of his own business as humanly possible, sat silent and kept one eye on her. He was there; when Rose needed him, all she had to do was turn her head and ask.

Although he was getting deeper and deeper into this relationship with Rose, Houston knew that he was marking time in his own life; he didn't plan to stay on the road with a rock 'n' roll band forever. Rose's stud. Fuck *that!* Soon he would have to come to a decision about where he was going to light. Wherever it was, he intended to take Rose with him. She was still promising him that the hometown concert would be her last. Well, soon enough they'd see.

A shadow fell over him, and Houston looked up to find Rudge Campbell leaning over his chair, beckoning

135

to him silently. He stood, and followed Rudge to the front of the plane, where two chairs faced each other over a small round table. Rose didn't bother to turn her head to watch them go; she kept her eyes fixed on the clouds outside the window.

Dyer sat down in one of the chairs, and Rudge took the other, smiling pleasantly. But there was something of the reptile about that cold smile of Campbell's, Dyer decided. It went with that expensive imitation-cowboy shit he wore—the silver and turquoise Navajo jewelry and the large wardrobe of custom-fitted boots from Nevada, all of them of weird, reptilian skins like cobra or iguana. He wouldn't give you a sackful of crap for one of Rudge Campbell's smiles.

"Smoke?" asked Rudge pleasantly, reaching into his Levi's jacket's studded pocket.

Dyer shook his head.

There were two coffee cups on the table between them. Rudge produced a bottle of Jack Daniel's and sloshed a generous amount into both cups, pushing one toward Dyer. Both men lifted their cups in a toast.

"Sippin' whiskey," remarked Rudge.

"Lynchburg, Tennessee," toasted Dyer. It was the home of Jack Daniel's.

"Population five hundred and seventeen," added Rudge.

Dyer laughed. "Everybody wants to be a shitkicker."

Rudge took a sip of the whiskey, his eyes watching Houston over the rim of the cup.

"You and Rose are really getting along," he observed pleasantly.

Dyer smiled and said nothing.

"She trusts you," said Campbell.

"You, too," granted Houston.

Rudge grinned and shrugged. "Aw, no. I'm like a parent. Who trusts their parents nowadays?"

Again, Dyer could think of nothing useful to say. He was waiting to see what Rudge was getting at in so circular a fashion. It had to be something. Rudge was never this friendly. Usually, he looked at Dyer as if he'd just stepped in it with new boots.

Rudge smiled again, brilliantly. He was a handsome son-of-a-bitch; Dyer had to give him that. His beard was more gray than black, but his hair was thick, springy with life, and made a dark, curly frame for those cat eyes. It was the smile he mistrusted—sudden, bright, cold, and quick to disappear.

"I'm glad she's got a friend at last," continued Rudge. "I've seen the studs come and go. I always hoped that one might stick." He looked sharply at Dyer, to see if the barb had sunk in deep, but Dyer didn't even blink. Smoothly, Rudge went on. "Be good for her to have somebody to take the weight off her, you know. Give her an anchor."

Dyer watched him carefully, saying nothing.

"Do you think she's drinking too much?" asked Rudge solicitously. "Do you know she's up to a quart a day?"

"I hadn't noticed," Houston lied.

Rudge shrugged slightly, agreeable. "Maybe that's what she needs. Someone who won't notice. Do you think I nag her too much?"

"I think you do what you got to do," said Dyer, giving nothing away.

"It's just the old frying pan and the fire, you know," went on Campbell, with a small sigh. "She had a hundred-dollar-a-day habit when I found her. She was singing in a coffee house in Christopher Street. And shooting up in an alley between sets."

Dyer could see Rudge's gambit now; Dyer sat silent and waited.

"One Christmas, they busted her at Macy's. Grand larceny. She had eleven watches up her arm and a pair

137

of diamond earrings in her underwear. I had to use all my juice to get her off. Pathetic." He shook his head sadly at the memory. "Well, she's clean now. But I am worried about the booze. I hope it stays just booze. She's not doin' any pills, is she?" He glanced slyly at Houston.

"I ain't been watchin'," lied Dyer curtly.

Rudge flashed him another stunning smile, all teeth and sympathy. "Keep an eye on her for me, will you?"

The son-of-a-bitch. The slimy, cunning bastard. What a tricky, deceiving mother he was. Laying it all out there, stabbing Rose in the back, just to scare me off and get rid of me. Other men. Booze. Pills. Smack. Theft. And all under the pious guise of parental concern. You had to admire the gall of the man; he made a hyena look stupid. Dyer shook his head.

From the back of the plane, Danny struck a riff on his guitar, low and bluesy, funky and primitive.

"You ever been on the road with a rock 'n' roll band?" asked Rudge. "You're gonna love it."

Rose had been staring out the windows at the clouds. They were beautiful—heavy formations of bounteous white reflecting the sunlight from below, casting the light back up in tones of red, pink, and darkening purple. Suddenly she turned from the window, tears streaming down her face.

"Where am I?" she shrieked, close to hysteria. "I don't know where I am! I *never* know where I am! All these fuckin' clouds look alike!" Her shrieks gave way to low moans and she passed out, her head hitting the back of her seat, her mouth open.

Rudge Campbell raised his coffee cup to Houston Dyer in another toast. "Welcome to rock 'n' roll," he purred.

By the time that the 1960s had arrived, bringing prosperity to London, which became "mod" and swinging like a pendulum do, Rudge Campbell had acquired associates. He owned a small piece of a recording company, a smaller piece of a music newspaper, *Pop Toppers,* and even a morsel of a music-publishing firm. He also had eight pop artists in his managerial stable. One was a poof with a high, greased black pompadour who swished his arse around like Elvis but who sang like Frankie Avalon. It was an unfortunate combination, and most of the poof's bookings were in Sydney and Melbourne. Rudge also had a pair of Brenda Lee sound-alikes. While he hadn't exactly achieved his dream of untold wealth, he was quite comfortably fixed, thank you very much.

But comfortably fixed meant uncomfortable to Campbell. If he wasn't stinking rich, he wasn't anything. Except maybe bored. True, he never went cold or hungry; true, he never would be reduced to eating fish again; true, he could work shorter hours, but none of that was what he really wanted. He craved a challenge; Rudge wanted life and excitement and money coming in from north, south, east, and west; money spilling out of his pockets and his mattress and even his ears.

R&b—rhythm & blues—had given the music business a shot in the arm for a while, but there was something new in the air. Something was definitely cooking: rock 'n' roll. It was hot, raunchy, uncivilized, electric, and it would blow everything else away. From the moment Rudge heard the first lowdown riffs, he knew he was onto it. Rock 'n' roll; it would change the musical habits of millions, would sell a new group of artists and a new group of records. Rudge was as certain of that as he was that this new music would somehow make him a millionaire. He had to get in on the ground floor, while the rest of the world was still laughing.

When Rudge heard that a group of four Liverpool boys were setting the Cavern Club on fire, he hopped into a taxi and headed for Euston Station. Too late. A Jewish boy named Brian Epstein had gotten to the Beatles first.

Rudge had an early chance at the Rolling Stones,

139

but on the day he sat mulling over their grotty image, they were snapped up by other management. It was Rudge's first and last real mistake. He was still known to break out in a slight rash whenever he heard "Jumpin' Jack Flash."

By early '67, Rudge's little group of artists had expanded to include a long-haired folk-singing lady who believed she was Joan Baez. When she wasn't writing and singing long, complicated, and plaintive songs about the lovers who'd left her, she was out marching to ban the bomb. He was also managing two rock 'n' roll bands who'd nosed their noisy way into the charts, close to the bottom: the Rocket Launchers and the Pee Bodies. He was also dicking around with a third group, Jimmy and the Peace Makers, but their sound was too derivative.

For years, Rudge had been trying to get the Who away from its management. It was his favorite group. Although he never gained ground, he never lost hope. He'd become thick with Keith Moon, and often they would go out pub-crawling together. Keith was especially fond of the Thameside taverns, and the old familiar smell of the slimy river mud stirred mixed feelings under the rainbow patches of Campbell's denim jacket. He was thirty-four years old now, and still had a long way to go for his first million pounds. Sometimes he got discouraged.

"Goin' to the States next month," Keith told Rudge one April evening, as they leaned over the embankment and shared a quiet joint.

"Oh, yes? A tour?"

"No, the Who is playin' something called Monterey Pop. In California."

"Monterey Pop?" queried Rudge lazily, only mildly interested.

"Yes. It's a big outdoor concert, goes on for days. They've signed up some pretty big groups for it. Not the Beatles. Nor the Stones. But Eric Burdon's going over with the Animals. And a lot of those new American bands. The Jefferson Airplane; maybe the Grateful Dead. Country Joe and the Fish. They say Otis Redding will be there. Ought to be pretty good, y' know. California's not half bad. Sunnier than Spain even."

Rudge's brain had come awake and was ticking away madly. He was experiencing another of his famous flashes, the kind that had changed the course of his life before. He kept seeing a vision of dollar bills instead of pound notes. Bright green, crisp, highly desirable dollar bills. His instincts were telling him that they were about to float into his grasp.

"New talent, you say?"

"Pots ot it," replied Keith lazily, toking deeply and passing the j back to Rudge. "Great, lolloping gobs of bright new talent. Why? You interested, mate?"

"I might be."

"Come with us, then." Moon smiled beatifically at his friend. "Plenty of room on the plane. They say the birds in California are prettier than anywhere else in the world. All tanned and long legs and bikinis. Natural blondes. Healthy teeth. It's all that orange juice."

Rudge's eyes narrowed. "I just might at that. Might even be worth me while. Never know, do yer?"

But Rudge did know. Somewhere inside, he knew. His future lay across an ocean and a continent. Six thousand miles away. Now all he had to do was go and find it.

They were singing on the street when the Family Dog found them and invited them inside, into the Avalon Ballroom. They were surprised to find out that they were part of something called "acid rock," but it made sense. They all dropped acid and they played rock 'n' roll. Rose handled most of the vocals, backed up sometimes by Lonnie. The band was often terrible, stoned out, spacey, too loud. They drowned out Rose, who was forced to shout over her own backup band. Not that it *was* hers; she was just their singing chick, and she'd been everybody's old lady at one time or another. Now she was Lonnie's.

But, bad as they often were, they had something —a likable, friendly, puppy-dog quality that made the spaced-out audience respond to them. They weren't stars, would never, could never be stars. They were family. *You* could sing and play as well as they could.

When they'd played on the street, they'd pull down maybe thirty dollars in a good day. Not enough for the six of them to live well on, just enough to get by. Whitey, Danny, Dennis, Norton, Lonnie, and The Rose shared a large communal pad on Fillmore; it was loose, and they ate a lot of rice. Brown rice. Brown rice and Mallomars. Grass was practically free, and acid cost maybe a buck a hit. For windowpane, clear light, sunshine. Rose loved the names—they carried her into a new world of sensation and experience. New sounds, new colors, new feelings. She *related,* man. She was relating for the first time in her life and she was digging on it.

Rose would get dressed up in old feathers and old laces, bits of worn finery, funky glitter, rhinestones, face paint. She felt free; she was stared at, but with a kind of admiration. Others were dressing like that, too. Cherie had formed a drag mime troupe that one day would become the nucleus of the Cockettes. She saw him often.

And she was balling, freely, happily. She'd balled half of straight San Francisco, and all the guys in the band. They had grooved on her big tits; nobody found them grotesque. Now she had settled on Lonnie. He was her old man, and she was happy with him. San Francisco was just the best place on earth, and she could never believe that life held any more happiness than singing, Lonnie, acid, and the psychedelic freak show that was going on around her daily and into which she fit like a thumb in a mitten. For the first time in her life, Rose felt beautiful and wanted.

The easy sexual life in the Haight had freaked her a little at first. She was accustomed to sex; she'd fucked a lot of guys back home—even the whole football team. But she never thought about that anymore. She liked to fuck, liked to suck, but she was used to thinking that she was evil, unhealthy, sinful, and cheap. Here, everything was free and blissed-out. Here, nobody took sex as anything heavy. It was just a friendly thing to do with somebody you liked. No hassles. Back home, it was something you did with guys you *didn't* like. In the communes and apartments in the old houses of the Haight-Ashbury, you'd crawl into a bedroll or a sleeping bag with somebody who you'd smoked some hash with, somebody whose face or eyes or beard turned you on, and you'd make it and that was cool. Sometimes it lasted one night; sometimes a week, sometimes longer. But it was always done with dignity and respect and no hassles. Rose liked that.

The frizzy hair that was her secret shame back home, along with her big titties, here were considered beautiful, alive, touchable, and kissable. Rose, thrilled, let it grow long and free and decorated it with flowers and feathers. She learned that she had a sense of style, and for the first time in her life, she gave it free rein.

The singing bothered her a little; something was missing. Rock 'n' roll was the greatest, but she missed the blues, and she remembered the gospel shouting at the old Abyssinian Baptist Church in Darktown. She missed that, too. But rock, heavy and driving rock, was what everybody wanted to hear, and Rose knew she was luckier than most, because the band did get gigs.

"Monterey? Where's that?" Rose asked with her mouth full of Mallomar. She licked the gloppy chocolate off her fingers.

"It's down the coast. It's going to be a big festival,

143

the biggest yet. Country Joe is going; Gracie and the Airplane are gonna be there; Canned Heat; Big Brother and the Holding Company. . . ."

"Janis? She gonna sing at Monterey?"

"Yeah," said Lonnie. "Also Jimi Hendrix and the Mamas and the Papas and the Who are coming over from England—"

"The Who? I want to go!" clamored Rose.

"That's what I'm trying to tell you," said Lonnie patiently. "We *are* going. We're gonna sing there. We've been invited."

Rose's heart stopped beating for a second in eternity, and she fought to catch her breath. "We're gonna sing? In front of Gracie and Janis and Jimi and Keith—"

"And Cass and Michie and Art Garfunkel and Paul Simon and Otis Redding—"

"Otis REDDING?!" hollered Rose. "You're shitting me! We're playing the same gig as Otis Redding and those other cats?"

"Mama, sweet hot fudge, you never do listen to a word I say, do you? It's the Monterey International Festival 1967, it's two weeks away, we've been invited down, and you'd better get that little ass of yours moving if you want to get any part of a new set together by then."

"Lonnie, I swear to the good Lord Jesus that I'm gonna pass out right this minute."

"Well, don't fall on the Mallomars. Your tits will crush 'em to death."

IX

The St. Louis concert started off badly. The kids holding tickets had been told by the cops in advance that there would be no dancing in the aisles on pain of instant eviction from the auditorium. For the first two numbers, The Rose had worked herself up to a real high, yet she felt nothing kinetic flowing her way across the stage-lights. They were sitting on their asses like mummies. Rose needed to see her audience on its feet boogeying. She began to tremble with anxiety, and the third number went to pieces. Rose forgot the lyrics, came in too soon after the band's solo, and slammed the mike back so hard on its stand that the connector snapped.

"Get it together, mama! What's wrong with you to-night? You were cooking there for a while, but now you're in little pieces." Dennis pulled her to the side of the stage, his face a mask of concern.

"Don't you see them out there, staring at me like I was some kind of exhibit? Why the fuck are we playin' this shitty gig, if they don' wanna hear me sing?"

"Honey, what do you want them to do? Can't you hear them clappin' their hands and yellin' for you?"

"I see them sitting on their asses! Why the fuck don't they move it around? Do they think I'm workin' up there all by myself? I gotta see a little action, man! A little life, a little movement! Find out what the hell is goin' on."

145

In a minute Dennis had returned with the news that the kids didn't dare to dance—that they were afraid of being thrown out of the concert hall.

The Rose uttered a wild whoop of mingled rage and indignation and stomped back onto the stage, her tits bouncing, hair flying. Striding down to the edge, she grabbed the mike and yelled into it. It was broken, and she tossed it away.

"Can you hear me?" she yelled to the crowd without a microphone.

"YEEEAAAAHHHHHH!" the kids hollered back.

"If you ain't dancin', ah mus' be doin' somethin' *wrong!* Am ah doin' somethin' wrong?"

"NNNOOOOOOOOOOOOOO!" the kids hollered back.

"Well, then, why ain't you-all dancin'?" She was so down-home now, you could butter the mush in her mouth. "Tell you whut," she yelled. "Gonna give you all your money back. We cain't have us no play-party heah 'less you-all dance."

At the words "money back," the promoters turned pale and turned on Rudge in a flying wedge. Was she crazy? Had she any idea? . . . Panicked, Rudge sent for the chief of police.

Up on the stage, the band took a break to retune their instruments, while an engineer worked on the broken mike getting an earful of screeching feedback and loud boos from the audience. The Rose stood there, eyes sparkling, toe tapping, hands on hips, waiting for all hell to break loose, waiting for word.

It came within two minutes. Dennis ran onto the stage and whispered into her ear. With a loud "WA-hooo!" The Rose grabbed the mike out of the engineer's hands. It was working.

"Got a little message for you-all. Chief o' police here's a good frien' a mine, and he say that if you-all don't git off you asses and stomp you feet, he's gonna send you all home without supper."

"AAALLLLLL *RIGHT!*" With the roar of a lion, the audience was on its feet, screaming, bopping, yelling, when the band broke into "Fire Down Below." The Rose grabbed the mike and began to wail into it; now she was down on her knees, low, low, low, letting them have it all, soul as well as body. She rolled over on her belly and took a good look.

They were dancing. Some were standing on their seats, waving their arms in the air and their asses from side to side. Others had crowded into the aisles and were shakin' in place. Others had moved to the back and were stomping up a storm. But there wasn't a body in the house not moving to the music. The Rose could see long hair flying and hear the thump of feet keeping the beat. She smiled and went on singing. Now she was satisfied.

After the concert came the obligatory backstage private party for the local big wigs—the record distributors for the area, disc jockeys, newspaper people, security staff—anybody and everybody whom Rudge thought deserved a closer look at The Rose. They set up tables backstage with a spread, every eatable, drinkable morsel of which had been negotiated and hondeled back and forth between Rudge and the promoter weeks in advance. X number of bottles of white wine, Y number of red, so many pounds of cold cuts, so many loaves of bread, and so forth. A rock 'n' roll tour is expensive to mount; the costs incurred by a traveling band are staggering, and Rudge cut those costs to the smallest ha'penny whenever and wherever he could. He hadn't been a barrow boy in London's East End without learning something.

The Rose, clinging to Houston, was being hemmed in on all sides and pressed by local fans and well-wishers, people who wanted merely to get close to a celebrity so they could go home and brag that they'd met a superstar.

147

It was Rudge's job to sort these people out into important and not-important-enough, to send the first group in the direction of Rose and the second group away, and keep the tourist action flowing without bottlenecks. Those who were most useful to the operation he escorted over to her personally.

"An' this here's Chief Morrison, Rose. He gave us a little extra protection tonight," Rudy told her with a significant nod that meant "be polite."

"You've got a mighty generous manager," said the chief with a greedy smile.

Rose didn't return the smile. "I've heard ol' Rudgie called everything, but that's the first time anyone called him generous. Next?" she barked at Rudge.

Rudge gave her a quick dirty look and pushed a younger man forward. The man was loaded down with American Indian jewelry that must have weighed at least ten pounds. Huge nuggets of turquoise set in silver hung around his throat, on his wrists and fingers—everywhere but in his nose. He was wearing a tight-cut suit of polyester denim, the kind that had the creases stitched in permanently. His toupee was cut with full sideburns and was far too long in back. He was the walking embodiment of what "hip" meant in St. Louis.

Rudge urged him forward with a hand on his shoulder and a large, brilliant smile, his cobra best.

"Say hello to Don Frank, who's been handling midwestern distribution," he instructed Rose.

The rack jobber didn't wait for his hello but instantly pounced on Rose. "Honey, you were sensational tonight. My God, you knocked me out. I wet my pants—"

"Don't you wanna go home and change?" The Rose asked sarcastically.

"I think Rose is getting tired," said Dyer protectively.

"Don's a *very* good friend of ours," hissed Rudge, his eyes enraged slits.

148

"Rack jobbers rule," recited Don nervously.

The Rose shook her head decisively. "They ain't gonna rule me." She turned to Houston. "I wanna go home."

"I didn't mean to upset you, Rose," babbled Don.

Rose took a deep breath. "That's okay, man. I know you been doin' a good job." But her smile was wan, and her voice lacked conviction. She was so tired she couldn't tell one of these hayseeds from the other. And she no longer cared.

Rudge put one hand on Dyer's arm and pulled him away, into a relatively quiet corner of the noisy backstage party. As he passed the rack jobber, he told him, "See me tomorrow. We're not leaving till late. I've got a little something for you." His friendly smile disappeared and the tone of his voice changed the instant he turned on Houston Dyer. "You don't belong here! Don't you *ever* tell her 'tired'! She's got obligations and responsibilities. These people are *important* to us!"

"The lady needs to rest," insisted Dyer stubbornly.

"When *I* tell her to!" Rudge snarled. "When she's finished her business. We got a partnership here."

Rose, seeing Rudge and Houston together, took a good guess that Campbell was reading Dyer's beads. She pushed her way through the hangers-on and would-be starfuckers, holding them away from her at arm's length as she shoved through the crowds to get to Dyer's side.

"I'm tired. I'll see you on the plane, Rudge." She looked up at her lover. "Take me to bed."

The road was a series of Holiday Inns and Formica coffee shops, but Rose and Dyer were making the best of it. Every room they stayed in had a king-size bed and a big color TV, and bed was all they cared about. They'd switch on the set, order up ice, glasses, and a bottle, and climb under the covers to make love while the TV set played. Most of the beds they slept in had Magic Fingers, where you put a quarter in the slot and the bed began to

149

rock 'n' roll; the vibrations under the mattress turne
Rose on, so Houston kept his jeans pockets heavy wit
quarters.

Being with her man every day and every night, th
same man, a real man and not some funky, space
groupie, worked a change on Rose. She was more im
patient that ever—wanting this tour to be over so th.
she could quit the gigging and spend all her time wit
Houston. She was still promising him that she would g
away with him, anywhere he wanted. At the same tim
she was even more dynamite on the stage. It was as if th
power of his love lent her new strength; she sang as nev
before, reaching out to her audience, insisting they r
spond. She wanted every drop of love she could ge
Houston's affections made her hungry for more and mor
And the audience did respond, pouring out such admira
tion over the stage that Rose could take a bath in it.

Sometimes at night, when they had made love an
were resting up so they could do it again, Rose would e:
press her fears about her hometown concert. Agai
and again she'd tell Houston how strange and freaky sh
had been to the people of Lawrence, Florida. She wa
sure they didn't want her, wouldn't recognize he
wouldn't care, wouldn't come to hear her sing. Again an
again Dyer would explain, patiently, lovingly, how impo
tant she was, how good, how brightly her star shon
Sometimes he didn't understand her at all. Up on the stag
she was confidence itself, pouring out her talent, insistin
on recognition and acknowledgment and getting them. O
the stage, she was often so frightened and insecure, cling
ing to him, needing him.

That's why he stayed with her. She needed hin
Dyer hated the rock 'n' roll business—and it was ju:
that, a mercenary business, run by sharks and people
by barracudas. If Rose didn't need him so much, wasn
leaning on him so hard, he would have split, long ag
Houston's idea was Wyoming or Idaho. He wanted

cabin, mountains, pine trees, deep cold lake waters. He thought he'd hunt out a cabin for just the two of them, where Rose could join him after the tour was over, after the hometown concert. He dreamed of getting it all ready, chopping the wood for the winter, welcoming her with a big fire on the fireplace and a pot of coffee on the stove. But Rose couldn't let him go, not even for a week. She got panicky when she couldn't find him, and once she even followed him into the john when he had to take a leak, because she was too nervous to let him out of her sight.

So Houston stayed around, even though Rudge hated him and trashed him whenever he thought he could get away with it. Dyer kept his temper, because he knew that losing it would make trouble for Rose.

But Houston Dyer was getting nervous, too. He was, after all, AWOL and traveling around with the biggest star in rock 'n' roll wasn't exactly the same as slipping anonymously into Canada one dark night. The spotlight seemed always to be on The Rose, and it always caught Dyer, blinking at her side.

Houston had had enough of killing. He'd seen so much wanton death and mutilation, such desolation in Nam that he had turned his back on death, seeking life. The Rose was life personified—she had immortal zest, immortal gusto. She tore at life like she made love—fully, deeply, joyfully, taking huge bites and slurping sucks. Squeezing the juice out of the fruit and throwing the peel away. He loved that about her—her vitality and electricity, the way she moved and laughed. Even her depressions were exciting, total and black. And fifteen minutes later she was laughing again. How could he resist her? How could he turn his back on her? He couldn't.

But he was counting the days until the tour ended, until the damn hometown concert was over, and Rose belonged to him, not to the readers of *Rolling Stone,* or anyone else with the price of an album or a concert ticket.

Nights after a concert, it would take Rose hours to unwind, to go from "The" Rose to just plain Rose. She'd come off the stage hot and exhausted, wanting to make love right away, turned on by the applause and the cries of "Rose!" "Rose!" and "More More MORE!!!" She'd run off the stage and into Houston's arms and they'd barely make it to the dressing room, where Rose would lock the door, or shove something against it if the door didn't lock. It would take her at least three minutes to peel herself out of her skin-tight jeans, but Houston would be hot and waiting for her, and she'd wrap her legs around his hips while he fucked her standing up, or lower herself onto his body if there happened to be a comfortable chair in her dressing room. These were short fucks, boiling and furious, quick, sharp releases, after which Rose would get her jeans back on and open the dressing room door to Rudge, who was invariably standing outside, knocking angrily.

The two of them would talk business for half an hour, while Dyer, bored, thought of other things. Then they'd make an appearance backstage for the inevitable party, and split for their hotel room, the television set and bed.

It was on these nights that they exchanged the stories of their lives. Houston's was short and simple—a Texas kid from a dusty town; his father a telephone lineman; his brother killed early in a truck accident; his mother old before her time. The Army at seventeen. The story stopped there. No way could he ever tell her about the atrocities of Vietnam, about the napalmed children and the civilian massacres. He wondered if the war would ever end, or if the country he'd loved and had served would ever turn away in horror and shame from her involvement in the torment of Southeast Asia.

The Rose told him mostly funny stories. When she related the tale of her first spanking and got out of bed naked to take off Carmen Miranda, Houston laughed so much he choked on a Colonel Sanders chicken bone and she had to thump his back hard until he spit it up. She told him about Cherry Pye and the early days in San Francisco, when the word "hippie" was just coming into use, and "flower power" and about the first Be-in, where she sat on the grass and sang. She told him about gigging on the street corners with the guys, people throwing them quarters, dimes, even nickels, and about the first gig they played at the Avalon Ballroom, where the audience sat cross-legged on the floor and drank organic orange juice, ate brown rice, and smoked pot.

Houston asked her one night how she'd ever teamed up with Rudge Campbell. And she told him.

For a week, they'd been putting a short set together; they'd been allotted fourteen minutes onstage. They knew that the big groups, like the Airplane, and Big Brother, would be bringing their own light shows, and would have powerful amplifiers and speakers with them. They had small amps, shitty, but all they could afford. And Rose was close to hysteria trying to decide what to wear. Monterey Pop was nearer to the big time than they had ever been, and they had no decent equipment, not even an engineer. Dennis doubled on drums as the only technical person in the group.

The Rose had combed every charity thrift shop in San Francisco until she found what she was looking for. It was a bias-cut black dress from the 1940s. It sported a peplum over the tush, and a side-wrapped pleat, and a beaded rosette at one shoulder. In the same store she found open-toed old black wedgies with ankle straps, a little hat with a veil, and a fake gardenia. The whole outfit came to $8.75, including the gardenia, and she carried it back to the pad and unwrapped it with trembling hands. Getting out the battered old ironing board and an ancient iron left behind by a previous tenant, The Rose sponged the dress carefully and pressed it, careful not to melt the

153

beading. She slipped it on over her head and managed to get the zipper halfway up the back, as high as she could reach. She strapped on the shoes and tucked the gardenia behind one ear. She was now a gin-u-wine band singer.

"Rose," said Cherie solemnly, walking around her three times slowly before he zipped the rest of the dress closed, "you look like an albino Billie Holliday."

"Is that good?" asked Rose, with her heart in her mouth.

"Is that *good*? Honey-chile, it's faaaaaaaabulous! Only one thing, though." Cherie cocked his head to one side, tapping his teeth with a long red fingernail.

"What's that?"

"That fake gardenia is Tacksville. Trash City. Honey, what you need is a *real* flower, and Sister Cherie pledges it to you. It will be her little good-luck token on The Day."

"Oh, wow! Thanks, Cherie. You're the greatest."

"No, Rose, you are." Cherie's voice dropped to its normal male register and he looked at her very seriously. "You are going to be a very, very big star, honeybuns. I wouldn't say it if it weren't so. You know I never lie to you."

"You really think so?"

"Honey, I know so. I believe it with all my heart. Now, I'm not going to give you any crap about being humble when you reach the top. Git it while you can, and git all of it that's going, but remember, Rose, remember to share it with your friends, and remember karma. Selfishness and cruelty are bad karma, and you'll have to pay for it in your next life. When you are sitting up there on a silk pillow counting your millions, remember, think back, never forget that you owe the universe a debt you have to pay back. You gotta keep passing that good karma along, Rose, circulating goodness back into the world."

154

When Cherry talked like that he was very serious indeed; he'd recently been living with an Indian boy and had just given up eating meat. Well, dead meat, anyway.

When the guys in the band saw her outfit, they shit a cupcake.

"What *is* this act? The Andrews Sisters?" asked Dennis incredulously.

"Are we supposed to wear tuxedos?" Danny drawled sarcastically.

"Now, wait a minute, don't you go hittin' on Rose," said Lonnie loyally. "She may look funny, but she's got style. They'll look twice, and that's what we're after, isn't it? With the low-watt amps and speakers we've got, and no lights, how the hell are we gonna stand out on a stage with groups like Canned Heat? Let them stare; then they'll listen. Rose always knows what she's doing."

But later, when they were tucked up together in the bedroll, Lonnie turned to her and asked her earnestly, "Uh . . . Rose . . . do you know what you're doin'?"

At which Rose had one of the best and longest laughs of her life. Wiping the tears of hilarity from her eyes, she confessed, "Nope."

"Well, I think you look dynamite," whispered Lonnie.

"Thanks, papa. I think *you* do, too."

On The Day, they got up around five in the morning to drive down Highway 1 to the Peninsula. Dennis had borrowed a VW van, battered on the outside, but with good brakes and a well-tuned motor. Dayglo daisies were pasted all over the doors and the hood, and peace symbols on the roof (in case of enemy helicopters). But it held the drums, and the amps, and a borrowed keyboard, and the guitars, and the six of them. And two cases of beer.

As they were pulling away from the curb, Cherie

155

came whooping around the corner, clutching the silver fox to his shoulders and waving a transparent box. In it were six ice cubes and a fresh red rose.

"It's beautiful," said Rose, opening the box to sniff the heavy fragrance.

"Keep the box closed and the ice cubes will keep it fresh. I hope. Anyway, good luck, lady, and kill the people."

The drive down the Pacific Highway was beautiful and perilous, with Dennis at the wheel chugalugging beer and the old van rattling along at sixty miles an hour on the winding turns. Below them, the ocean beat on the rocks; seals barked and gulls wheeled and mewed. The Rose sat on the van floor, on a rolled-up piece of carpet, drinking beer and smoking hash to calm her terror. This was the most important gig of her life, and she was convinced that, one way or another, she'd fuck it up. Stoned and paranoid, she was oblivious to the breathtaking scenery outside the van windows. Her stomach was clenched into a knot the size of a lumberjack's fist, and, for the first time in her life, she wished she was back home in Lawrence, Florida.

And then they were there, among the kites and the balloons, the iridescent bubbles, the tinkling glass wind chimes and the music of the Monterey festival. The seats were filling up, and hippies and freaks were camping out on the grounds, passing joints and mellowing out. Dogs were barking and children were running around naked, laughing in the sunshine. Lovers painted each other's bodies with symbols of the sun, and the third eye, and cosmic rays. It was going to be a memorable gathering.

They found a parking space for the van, and left The Rose to guard the instruments while they signed up and were assigned their places in the concert. They were scheduled after Eric Burdon and the Animals, but before Country Joe and the Fish. A hard act to follow, and a

156

hard act to precede. But how could they expect anything better? Nobody had ever heard of The Rose, and their fourteen minutes would give the audience a chance to go to the bathroom or buy hot dogs. They weren't fooling themselves.

After the instruments were unloaded and carted into the musicians' tent, The Rose dressed quickly in her 1940s drag, drawing curious stares from the other female singers in the women's dressing tent. Her hands were cold as she clasped the rhinestone bracelets around her wrists and picked up the rose, still in its box. She wouldn't take it out until they were ready to go onstage; that way, it had a chance of keeping fresh. Roses wilted so quickly.

Rose was still a little spacey from the strong hashish, but she didn't forget to check her bag to see if the bottle of cherry brandy was still there and still intact. It was. Carrying her bag and her precious flower, she went backstage to watch the other acts and listen to the music.

The Mamas and the Papas were on, their voices blending harmoniously in "California Dreaming." Sweet, warm voices—Michelle's soprano and Cass's alto weaving around each other like holly and ivy, while John and Denny lent the group masculine strength. It was so pretty that tears came into Rose's eyes as she listened, and they rolled down her cheeks at the melodic interplay between Art Garfunkel and Paul Simon. It was going to be the best music festival ever held anywhere.

Rose remained blissed out until the Jefferson Airplane took the stage. It was the sight of Gracie Slick that brought back her panic. Gracie was so breautiful, unearthly beautiful in a flowing tie-dyed caftan. Her long white face was a pale, classic oval, and her hair was black satin. She looked like she had gone to all the best schools in the East, which she had, and Rose felt totally outclassed. And Slick's voice! It rose in a long rock cadenza, entwining around Marty Balin's. God, they had their act so together! How the hell was she ever going to match

157

that? Rose felt the muscles in her stomach begin to cramp again, and she looked around for a bathroom. Great! She was going to have to do her number from the potty! Wonderful!

"Nervous?" asked a voice nearby.

"Yeah, kinda," The Rose replied, turning. One of the young stage technicians was eyeing her sympathetically. He saw the dark circles of perspiration staining the armpits of her dress, and he could tell the palms of her hands were clammy.

"Here." The boy dug into his jeans and came up with a couple of dark pink capsules. "These'll even you out."

"What are they?"

"Reds. Secs." At Rose's blank look, he added, "Seconals. They'll calm your stomach nerves."

"Thanks. Hey, man, thanks a lot." Rose accepted the capsules, unscrewed the cap of the brandy, and washed the reds down with a long swig. The heat of the brandy warmed her little belly and she felt instantly better.

The Airplane played a long set, drawing wild applause from their following. They were, at that time, the top San Francisco group, and were beginning to be widely known all over the country. Singing and playing with style and confidence, they were sparked by the incredible vocal range of Gracie Slick, whose voice rose from cool to hot and back to cool again without a break.

Rose shook her head in admiration. If only she could possess one particle of Gracie's beauty and self-confidence, she thought mournfully. She took another drink.

When Big Brother and the Holding Company brought their instruments out, Rose took another nervous pull at the bottle. She knew Janis Joplin, and the girl was good, real, real good. Big Brother was not yet as well known as the Jefferson Airplane, but they were getting

158

there. Janis was a belter, like Rose; low down and bluesy, like Rose; southern, like Rose. She felt a kinship with the other girl, and she'd always believed that Janis would someday be a star.

Janis was not a pretty girl; she was pudgy, and her face was pitted with old acne scars. But she had the biggest, sweetest smile, that you forgot her flaws and often found her beautiful. Today she was wearing a beaded pant suit and a pair of backless mules, and she appeared nervous, a sharp contrast to the cool dignity of Slick.

By now the reds were working together with the brandy and the hash, and Rose was feeling low-key, a little dim, maybe. It was getting hard to concentrate on the music, but she stood backstage watching; she was kinda fading innnnnn and outtttt, innnnnn and outtttt. Minutes went by and Rose lost all her orientation; she had no idea where she was or what she was doing there.

It wasn't until she heard Janis's voice, moaning . . . "Wo, wo, wo, wo-oh, rock it to me, sock it to me. . . ."

Rose woke up. She shook her head and blinked. It was the noisy audience that had penetrated her high with their cheering, stamping, and yelling. Up on the stage, Janis Joplin was halfway through "Ball and Chain." Sweat was pouring off her like rainwater, and she was bouncing up and down on her backless mules as she moaned and wailed and shouted and killed them dead. She was terrific! Sensational! A star! Janis was becoming a star, right there, right now, right in front of Rose's eyes.

Panic gripped Rose, and she wanted to crawl away and hide. Nothing could persuade her to follow Joplin onto that stage. The audience was screaming with one voice for more, more of Janis, more of the star they'd just created.

"Far fuckin' out! Isn't she great?" Lonnie put his hand on Rose's shoulder.

"Yeah, great," croaked Rose. It was all she could do to get the two words out. Her stomach was hurting again, and she opened the brandy bottle and tilted it back, letting the liquid pour down her throat, burning and comforting. Her dreams had turned to ashes. They were coming true for somebody else. The new queen of rock 'n' roll, only it wasn't her.

"Hey, mama! Cool out! You don't need that stuff now. We go on soon. Set after the next one."

Didn't need it? That's how much *he* knew.

Whitey and Danny joined them, holding their guitars. Their eyes glittered with excitement and hash; they were high and happy. Rose felt completely out of synch with them; they were total strangers. What would she be doing on a stage with these dudes? For that matter, what would she be doing on a stage at all? She watched Janis Joplin, sweaty and triumphant, taking her bows and making her thank-yous, motioning the boys in her backup band to stand up for the people. There was a radiance about Joplin now that Rose recognized; it was starshine. Rose had never felt as lonely in her life as she did right this very minute. All around her, the guys in her own band were high and bopping, ready to go on. It didn't matter to them that Janis Joplin had just copped the prize The Rose had been hoping for. They thought there was room at the top. The Rose knew that there was only one winner in any race, and she'd just been scratched at the post.

She stood dully, not listening to Eric Burdon's heavy rock set. She was very, very, far away from everything. The reds and the brandy had made her eyelids heavy, and she felt like the top of her head had floated away. Nothing seemed to matter, because nothing good could come of this day.

"C'mon, mama. It's us. Let's go." Lonnie gave her a squeeze, and the boys came out on the stage to their introduction, and to a polite hand from the audience, which had been spoiled on superstars that day and were waiting for the next stellar attraction. This obviously wasn't going to be it.

Rose followed the boys out listlessly and stood in front of the microphone as they plugged in their amps and tuned up their axes. She made no effort to reach out to the audience, which was squirming around, getting up to take a leak, stretching. Rose just stared at them, not seeing them.

Dennis laid down the beat on the drums, and the guitars picked it up and handed it to The Rose. She opened her mouth and sang; she did it automatically. It was a hard rocking number, an old r&b standard, "Jelly Roll," and a favorite of The Rose's. She'd sung it a hundred times or more, but never as badly as this. Her brain was in a fog; everything moved in slooow motion, and she was half a beat behind the band and trying to catch up. Sensing that something was wrong, she felt panic descend on her. She took a step backward, and her high wedgie twisted under her ankle, sending her almost sprawling. The shock of it sent adrenalin rushing through her system, clearing some of the mist away from her brain, and she finished the song with a little more sparkle.

The audience applauded politely, but they weren't impressed. Obviously they were accustomed to better.

Trembling, Rose walked over to the keyboard, where she'd left her bag and her bottle. Her mouth was so dry that sand fleas could live in it. As she reached for the bottle, her eye fell on the box containing the rose. The ice cubes had melted, but the flower was still fresh, glistening with moisture. Rose opened the box and a rush of heavy fragrance met her nostrils. She heard Cherry's voice in her ears.

"You are going to be a very, very big star, honeybuns. I wouldn't say it if it weren't so."

Her fingers shaking, Rose pinned the rose in her yellow hair. Then she picked up a tambourine and went

161

back to the mike. As the boys broke into their next number, she smacked the tambourine hard with the heel of
her hand, then banged it against her hip. The sudden
noise of it seemed to wake the audience up, and they became less restless, fixing their attention on the girl up on
the stage.

It was a bluesy number, something old from Ma
Rainey that The Rose loved, backed by a hard-driving
beat. Rose planted her feet firmly on the stage and began
to move the rest of her as she sang. Her breasts bounced,
her hips shook to the tempo, and the tambourine kept
time with her. The song came out loud, raw, and raucous,
sexy and dirty, mean and lowdown, as Rose played it
for laughs. Her eyes began to sparkle as her pelvis swiveled shamefully. What the fuck! she seemed to be telling
them. Live it up! Love whoever you can whenever you
can. Life is too short to do anything but stay high and
ball. It was an infectious message, and the audience was
obviously enjoying it, because they began to clap their
hands along with Rose's energy.

When the song was over, the set was finished. They
got a good hand this time, with some warmth and enthusiasm behind it, but Rose's heart was still in her
shoes. Warmth and enthusiasm you could roll up and
stick where the moon don't shine. What she wanted was
the outpouring of total love and acceptance that they'd
given Janis. She wanted to hear those cheers and pleas
for more. Shit. She'd fucked up; just like she knew she
would. Morosely, she evaded the guys, who were packing
up their instruments, and went off with the bottle to be
alone.

"Hey! Wait a minute! Hey! Hold on a tick, can't
you?"

Who me? The Rose turned. A tall, lean, dark-
haired man with a short beard was chasing her across the
grass. What the fuck?

"Me? Ya mean me?"

"Yes, I mean you." He came up beside her, slightly out of breath. "My name's Rudge. Rudge Campbell."

A Limey. He had a Limey accent and was wearing a suit of Edwardian cut with a velvet collar. Carnaby Street. Winkle-picker shoes. He looked oddly out of place in the strong California sunshine. Rose squinted up at him, wishing she'd brought her sunglasses. He was good-looking, about thirty maybe, and had green eyes like a cat's. But there was nothing of the domestic pet about this Rudge Campbell. He looked more like a jungle animal.

"What's yours?"

"My what?"

"Your name. What's your name?"

"Rose. Why?" There was something about him that triggered her paranoia. Or maybe it was her high wearing off. Maybe she was just coming down.

"Rose what?"

"*The* Rose. That's my name. The Rose. I only need one name, right?"

"Right," said the Limey. "Listen, I want a word with you. Ever heard of Janni Meredith? Lyle Christmas? Stella Grace? The Rocket Launchers? The Pee Bodies?"

"Sure, I heard of 'em. What are ya, a record salesman?"

"No." The Limey flashed her a brilliant smile. "I manage them," he told her. "I own them, I think for them, I feed them, bath them, and dress them. I made them stars. I can make you a star." His arrogance was total.

Rose shook her head and turned away. This fast-talking Limey with the cold eyes was the last thing she needed.

"I don't wanna be no fuckin' star, man," she lied despondently. "Split and stop shittin' me."

"I'm not shitting you," replied the Englishman. "I'm in dead earnest. Look, I want to hear you sing."

163

Rose's eyes narrowed impatiently. "I thought you just heard me sing," she said suspiciously. She was tired and thirsty, and her high had vanished totally, leaving her low and dispirited. She wanted to be alone, away from this British bullshit artist.

"I heard you *try* to sing. Now I want to hear you *really* sing. Come on. Give, lady," he snapped.

Rose's eyes opened wide. "Out here?" She waved her hands around at the blue sky, the kites, the frisbees, the cooking fires, the campers.

"Yes, here. Here and now. Do you know 'Mean Ole Lover Man'?"

He touched a nerve. It was one of Rose's all-time favorites. "Uhhh, yeah," she conceded.

"Well, then, girl, let's have it, shall we?"

Rose looked hard at Campbell, but he was watching her seriously. He appeared to mean business. With a small shrug, she opened her mouth and let the song out slowly, then more surely, as it poured out of her belly and not her head. Campbell's eyes narrowed as he listened in silence until she'd finished the song.

"Good," he told her crisply and without emotion. "You have real talent. Are you under management?"

His words took Rose totally by surprise. Managed by an Englishman? "Uhhh, no," she said hesitantly.

"You are now. RC Associates Ltd. I'll set up a New York office, with a small branch in Los Angeles, and—"

"Hey, man, whoa! Not so fast. First, I gotta talk to the guys. We don't sign no papers until we talk everything over."

"What 'we'?" spat Rudge scornfully. "There is no 'we' from now on. It's you I want, not that third-rate collection of amateurs in your backup. They're ruining your sound. I'm signing *you,* The Rose, not them."

"What the fuck are you talking about?" demanded

164

The Rose hotly. "Those are my men; that's my band; they're my main guys—"

"They're a disaster and you know it," Rudge Campbell snapped, his green eyes chips of steel. "They're not fit to hold instruments. We'll get you a new band, the best, one that—"

Now it was The Rose's turn to interrupt. What the hell kind of fink did he take her for? "You Limey scumbag, I wouldn't sign with you if you threw in Buckingham Palace and the fuckin' Queen! Not if you could get the Beatles to back me! Nobody's gonna trash my band, not you or ten more like you!" She balled her small hands into fists, and her eyes were slits of fury. "You can take your fuckin' contract, roll it up small, and shove it up your royal Limey ass." With those words she turned and lurched away on her wobbly wedgies. God, she needed a drink! He'd left a bad taste in her mouth, that green-eyed cocksucker.

"An' that's how we met," said Rose, reaching for a chocolate-covered cherry.

"But if that's how you met, then how the hell did you ever get together?" asked Houston.

Rose pulled his head close to hers and let some of the creamy insides of the chocolate dribble onto Dyer's tongue.

"Oh, man, that's the longest, saddest song I ever sang," sighed Rose. "I don't wanna sing it tonight, baby. I just wanna lay back and let the good times roll. Whaddya say?"

"I say," said Houston, reaching for the breast nearest to him, "I say amen to that."

165

X

The rain was vying with the boredom to see which could drive them all asiatic first. The worst thing about St. Louis is waiting to get out of it, and they'd been waiting for over two hours now. The St. Louis Municipal Airport had been socked in by a sudden gale, with heavy rains and driving winds, and everything that flew had been grounded. If they'd known in advance, they could have hung out at the Holiday Inn, staying stoned and watching TV. Instead, the band was stuck here at the airport, sitting in this depressing coffee lounge, with its institutional green walls, cracking acoustical-tile ceiling, eye-aching fluorescent fixtures, and weak coffee. Over everything, hanging like a funeral pall, was the monotonous whine of the Muzak, artificial sound that bore the same relation to music as cream soda does to champagne.

The guys were sitting at a long table in the center of the room, chewing on hamburgers and greasy french fries, and playing an endless variation of the old match game, for quarters. Rose and Houston had snagged a corner table by the window. They could hear the rain and the high winds howling outside, but the glass was so misted up, they couldn't see anything. It looked like they'd be here for hours more. Almost more than flesh and blood could stand.

Rose fished around in her poke and came up with

an organic pharmacy—a bottle of honey, two lemons, some protein powder in a can, and her giant bottle of multipurpose vitamins. Taking a knife from the table, she cut the lemons and began to squeeze them into a glass. Dennis, his hair wet from the rain, a rubber poncho over his denims, came in to make his announcement.

"It's gonna be a while till it lifts," he told them to a chorus of groans.

"Can't we wait on the plane?" asked Rose plaintively.

Dennis cocked his head to one side and thought a minute. "I'll see what I can do," he said, vanishing out the restaurant door.

"Lemme see your tongue," said Rose to Dyer.

Houston put one hand up in protest. "Hey, come on—"

"Lemme see it!" ordered Rose, who wouldn't be denied.

Reluctantly, Dyer stuck his tongue out and Rose inspected it closely, not liking what she found. Vitamin deficiencies showed up in the mouth first, and you could always tell by the color of a person's tongue. She had finished mixing her concoction of pills, protein powder, lemon juice, and honey, and was pushing the glass over to Dyer.

"Take some of this."

Houston shook his head and made a face. Rose's brows drew together in a tiny thundercloud.

"Drink it!"

Wincing, Houston picked up the glass and swallowed some of its contents. It tasted even worse than he'd feared.

"You need B-1, minerals, and iron," lectured Rose serenely. "I'll get you straightened out when we go away."

"I feel like I just drank St. Louis' sewer system," complained Dyer. But he had to smile; Rose in a maternal mood was a hoot. Also sweet and oddly touching.

167

Rose laughed at Dyer's reaction, then her attention was pulled away from him to the bar at the far side of the room. Two servicemen in uniform, surrounded by empty beer bottles, had grown louder and were yelling for service. A waitress carrying a tray approached them suspiciously. On the tray was a bowl of eggs, still in their shell.

"Who asked for the raw eggs?" the waitress' face reflected her incredulity.

"A dozen raw eggs! Over here!" bawled one of the soldiers. They were young, maybe eighteen or nineteen, no more, and their hair was clipped so short that circles of white skin showed around their ears, and their scalps glistened pink under the stiff haircuts. Their cheeks glistened the same shade of pink.

"An' a dozen raw beers!" chimed in the second soldier.

"Look what the Army's done to them sweet dudes," exclaimed Rose, and Dyer sensed from experience that she had something on her mind.

"Leave 'em alone, Rose," he said quietly. The sight of the two boys had set up conflicts in him that he didn't want to deal with. He knew these kids well, had seen thousands just like them, green kids fresh out of high school, with no idea of what they were getting into.

"Hey, Colonel!" Rose called over.

The soldiers, who were pretty drunk by now, wheeled around unsteadily.

"You talkin' t' me?" asked the larger one.

"Yeah, I'm talkin' t' you," The Rose answered affably. "You eat them eggs, you're gonna line your veins with fat," she warned them.

The tall soldier turned to the smaller one. "You hear that, Tiny? We're gonna line our veins with fat." They guffawed and, simultaneously, both of them cracked an egg and let it drain into their open mouths.

"What's your name, friend?" hollered Rose, glad of anything to break the monotony of the waiting and the rain.

"My name's Mal. Malcolm Johnson. He's Tiny. Me 'n' Tiny graduated one-two from basic, one-two from advanced, one-two from jump school. . . ."

Rose found herself warming to this Mal. There was a sweet, innocent openness to him that she found entirely disarming. "Very good. Where are you going now?"

It was Tiny who chimed in, hating to be left out. "Back to camp for a few days, and then to 'Nam."

"You like the Airborne?" Rose asked Mal, but once more it was Tiny who answered. Once he started rapping, he found it hard to stop. "Me 'n' Mal kin wipe out a squad of slopes in ten seconds flat," he bragged. It was the beer talking.

Houston shut his eyes as the ugly memories washed over him; he wished Rose hadn't picked up on these kids and started up this conversation.

"How about you, Mal? You like the Airborne, too?" Rose sounded genuinely interested, but once more, Tiny rushed the ball.

"All me 'n' Mal want t' do is kick us a little ass." He lumbered off the bar stool and began belting out the Airborne song at the top of his powerful young lungs. The sound reached the ten-thousand-decibel level, waking up the band and every other passenger in the place.

"DOWN from heaven came eleven. . . ." Tiny roared, and Mal chimed in dutifully. With a gleeful giggle, Rose got up and joined them at the bar, yelling out the words in her best marching style.

"Shout Geronimo . . . GERONIMO. . . ." the trio wailed, to the puzzled stares of the rest of the world. As they broke into another chorus, Dennis, water streaming off his poncho, threw open a side door.

"Everybody this way!" he announced. He'd cleared

169

it for them to wait the storm out in the comfort of their private plane.

Half an hour later they were still on the ground, but Rose was stretched out luxuriously across two seats while Mal, stoned on the smoke the band had plied him with, was rubbing the kinks out of Rose's back and shoulders. He had a great pair of hands for massage.

"Lord," he told her, "these knots feel like they've been in there a thousand years."

"They have. They have," groaned Rose.

"You need a sledgehammer to get 'em out," Mal observed, kneading more deeply. Rose shut her eyes, feeling some of her tensions draining away under the tall boy's fingers.

Tiny suddenly loomed up from the back of the plane. The rain had slowed, and the winds were dying down. Planes were taxiing into position on the runways, preparing for takeoff.

"Hey, c'mon, Mal, we got to go," urged Tiny.

Mal ignored him as he bent over Rose, working on her neck and shoulder muscles. Little groans of pleasure mixed with pain emerged from Rose's lips, as the knots in her muscles were loosened.

"Mal, y'ought to open up a school," she advised him happily.

"Feels good, huh?" Mal smiled down at Rose, content just to be of help.

"Hey, c'mon, man," said Tiny nervously. "If we miss our plane we're goin' to get our ass in a sling."

"I'd love to have my ass in a sling," grinned Rose. "I'm so tired o' shakin' it." She stretched like a cat, almost purring with relaxation.

Tiny looked around him anxiously, belching a little from all the beer. "I'll see you, soldier," he said at last. "It's gonna be your ass." With this warning, he lurched down the aisle to the plane door and out of his friend's life. Mal continued working on Rose; Vietnam and the eleven-down-from-heaven no longer played the major role in his universe.

"You could learn this," he said earnestly to Dyer, who sat watching him through half-closed eyes. "You just got to push all the way in. You got to feel the muscles under you. Work 'em. You could relax her at the end of the day. I'd do it for my gal if I had one."

"There goes your buddy," remarked Dyer sleepily.

Mal looked out the plane window. He could see Tiny, tottering drunkenly, disappearing in the distance on his way to the terminal.

"I'll catch up with him," he answered calmly. Then he turned his attention back to Rose, working the heels of his hands down over her spine.

"You missed your calling, Mal," Rose told him happily. "You're all doctor. You were born to heal."

"You think so?" Mal's young face shone earnestly. "Truth is I always wanted to be a vet. I delivered a calf once. She was a breech, but somehow I got her switched around an' she came out good as new. A feller from the 4-H saw what I did, and said I ought to be a vet. Said I had the hands for it."

"What happened?" Rose wanted to know.

"Couldn't afford ag. school," shrugged Mal.

Rose picked up her poke and fished around in the bottom of it for her money. "How much is it?" she asked him.

"What?" Mal thought he musta heard wrong.

"How much to go to ag. school?" asked Rose, her hand closing on her wad of bills. She came up with several thousand dollars in her hand.

Mal's eyes widened as he pushed her hand away. "Oh, I couldn't let you do that," he protested strongly. "No way."

Rose studied him thoughtfully. He was tall and very

171

muscular, but there was still a babyish quality in his face, an innocence.

"You don't really want to kick ass, do you, Mal?" she asked him shrewdly.

Mal shook his head. "No," he mumbled. Killing was terrifying to him; he was incapable of shedding anyone's blood, and would rather be killed himself than raise his M-1 against another human being. Dyer recognized the breed. Mal's kind was invariably killed.

"Do you want to come with us?" asked Rose gently. "We'll take care of you, won't we, Houston?"

Houston kept his mouth shut and his eyes fixed on Mal.

"I can take care of myself," mumbled Mal awkwardly. He wasn't certain where to find the words. He looked around him, at the drifts of marijuana smoke circling the heads of the musicians, at the peaceful camaraderie among the guys, at Rose, whose yellow, frizzy head had already become precious to him. He had already decided that there was no more beautiful, generous, or good person in the world than this small-boned little singer with the big tits and the big smile. He loved her already, with a love that went deeper than sexual attraction. What he wanted was to be allowed to follow her, to protect her. "I . . . I . . ." he stammered. "I just want to fool around for a little while . . ." his voice trailed off, uncertain.

But Rose understood. She pulled his head down and kissed him very gently on the forehead. Mal's eyes filled with tears and a few of them rained down on Rose's face. Were they his or hers?

Into this tender moment stepped Rudge Campbell in boots made of the matched skins of diamondback rattlers.

"Who's this?" Rudge was not in a friendly mood.

"Rudge, I'd like you to meet Mal," said Rose, remembering her manners. "Mal is going to be traveling with us as my masseur and bodyguard," she added grandly.

Rudge gave Mal the old up-and-down, dismissing him almost instantly. "This troupe gets bigger every day," he snarled at Rose, but he was looking at Houston Dyer.

In the years to come, Rudge's and Rose's memories of their meeting would be seen through different-colored panes of glass. In fact the same, in feeling worlds apart.

Monterey Pop, 1967. Rudge looked around him with amusement. Beads and hair, bubbles, balloons, frisbees, kites, peace signs. Tie-dye and batik, spangles and sequins, sandals and T-shirts. Banners and macramé and woven symbols of the Eye of God. Bizarre makeup and bare feet and headbands. Love and flower power and good vibes and the dope and the music. He couldn't take any of this seriously except the music.

The magnificent California landscape was dotted with tents and sleeping bags, the motorcycles of the police department and Hell's Angels. The grounds were occupied by hippies and long-haired freaks selling handcrafts or brewing herbal tea or pots of franks and beans over their little cooking fires. Babies ran naked, and dogs were underfoot. Rudge shook his head at these vivid Americans dressed like Arabs or East Indians or red Indians, skipping through the California sunlight in dayglo paint, children of twenty. He wanted to laugh out loud.

But the music was something else again. Wearing an identification badge that permitted him backstage, Rudge stood in a tangle of heavy wires that led to the amplifiers. Most of the groups had brought sound equipment of their own, and the wiring had to be changed again and again, almost with every act. Above his head and behind him, a light show was being projected onto a triple screen—the psychedelic shapes and colors melding and

173

blending, separating to become sharp and clear, then turning into images imposed and superimposed and triply imposed, vanishing, reappearing. The Monterey International Festival 1967 was definitely impressive.

Rudge stood motionless at the side of the apron, letting the music and the voices wash over him. The Mamas and the Papas, joining in their uncanny harmonies. Canned Heat, their ferocious rhythms. "Slow down, you move too fast," sang two slight, small, intense Jewish boys to their acoustic guitars. And there was Gracie Slick, darkly, aristocratically beautiful in a caftan and long, flowing jet hair. What he wouldn't give to manage the Jefferson Airplane.

And a group new to him. Big Brother and the Holding Company. A singer named Janis Joplin, plump, dough-faced, dynamite. "OOOOOOhhhhh, wo wo wo wo," and Rudge was electrified. This dumpy little girl just had to open her mouth and everybody in the place was standing up. "Ball and Chain"; Rudge had never heard anything quite like it. A hurried question as they came off the stage. They'd been signed; Grossman had gotten there first. Bugger all!

After Eric Burdon had left the stage, a new group wandered onto it as though they didn't belong there. Five longhairs with the usual setup. Keyboard, drums, guitars. As they set up and plugged in their amps, their singer came aboard. She was dressed like Patty Andrews, and she was stoned out of her mind. She trickled over to the microphone in those ludicrous wedgies and stood gaping at the audience. She was a short, skinny little chickie in a dress too big for her, except across the boobs, where it stretched too tightly. Her bright yellow hair was a frizzy mass. Now the girl put out one tentative hand and touched the microphone as though she'd never seen one before in her life. Terrific; she was so loaded she was practically catatonic. Rudge turned to leave, but a coil of wire had tangled around his buckled leather winkle-pickers, and he stooped to free his foot.

The band struck up a long riff, loud and uneven, and the girl began to sing. It was "Jelly Roll," a standard, and this group had no special arrangement of it. The first thing that struck Rudge was that the band was too loud. For some reason, he wanted to hear more of the girl, and they weren't backing her up, they were drowning her out. Even so, she managed to get some feeling into the song, high though she was. The audience was restless, having sat through several hours of A-1 prime music-making. And whoever these amateurs were, they were definitely not prime.

Sensing the crowd's restlessness, the girl took a step backward, as though struck a blow in the face. She stumbled on her clumsy wedgie and nearly fell. A small gasp came up from the audience, but the blond girl, smiling uncertainly, regained her balance and came back to the microphone. All at once, Rudge felt himself drawn to her plight, and he decided to stay. She finished the song, to polite and feeble applause.

He saw her approach the amp nearest to him, and he got a good look at her face. She was far from conventionally pretty, but there was an air about her that drew the eye to her. She had presence, and without it there's no such thing as a star. Rudge watched as the girl took a rose out of a transparent box and fixed it in her hair, picked up a tambourine, and returned to the center of the stage. Now he was definitely curious.

Once again, the band laid down the rhythm line, and once again, it was all wrong. It muddied her tempo. She raised one arm high and shook her tambourine, then beat it hard with the heel of her hand, setting a different rhythm, one that the band was forced to follow. Then she broke into song. This time her eyes sparkled and she grinned as she sang, and Rudge decided that pretty wasn't

175

where it was at. This girl was beautiful in a way that belonged to her alone.

She sang an old song that Rudge knew from years ago, a blues that Ma Rainey had made famous. Now he understood why the band was so wrong for her; they were only rock 'n' roll, while she was something more. She was rock 'n' soul. She was really getting into the song now. Her tiny body was shaking in tune with the music. Her hips swiveled and her large tits bounced under the sleazy black dress. She was making the audience see and hear and *feel* the down and dirty sexiness of the song, infecting them with her warmth and her humor. Two round bright spots of color burned in her cheeks as she tried to outshout the band. The audience was waking up and shaking the feathers out of its brain, and this tiny girl was doing it. Rudge sensed an energy here—dynamic, kinetic, one hundred pounds of the force of nature. Wherever the band and the girl came together, it was accidental, but magical. Rudge wanted to chuck them all off the stage, to let the girl sing by herself so that he could really hear her.

The audience was having a good time now, rocking in their seats as she brayed out the lowdown lyrics, nasty and brassy, shaking her little round ass and her tits at them. When the number rose to a screaming climax, she turned around and gave her behind one final wiggle and a thump with the tambourine, getting a good laugh along with a generous hand.

They liked her; the audience definitely wound up liking her. She had *made* them change their minds. She had forced them to like her through sheer energy and personality. Rudge felt a surge of excitement run through his arteries, making the blood pump faster. With the right backup and, especially, with the right management, this girl could become a star. A big one. He had to talk to her, but she had run off the other side of the stage and had vanished.

As Country Joe and the Fish surged on, Rudge went off looking for the blonde. He didn't even know her name or the name of her group, but he soon spotted her moving across the grass behind the stage. She walked uncertainly, but whether it was her clumsy ankle-strap wedgies or something else, Rudge couldn't tell. She certainly *looked* loaded. Booze? Pills? Smoke? Snort? A combination of all of them?

"Hey! Wait a minute! Hey, hold on a tick, can't you?" He ran after her, shouting.

After he had convinced her to sing for him, Rudge felt a shiver run through him, and he sensed he was in the presence of a great deal of money. He was almost never wrong about these things.

This voice had everything—a sexy growl, a clear pitch, a good range, but it also possessed something above and beyond those technicalities. A something that defied being described in words. It possessed a power, an electricity that *communicated*. It was a voice that reached deep inside you and pulled hard at everything that made you tick and run and feel. Unmistakably, this girl was a musical genius and a potential gold mine.

Easy, old boy. Not too eager. By the time Rose had finished the song, Rudge had his excitement under careful control. "Good," he told her crisply, his emotion suppressed. "You have real talent. Are you under management?"

His words seemed to take her by surprise. "Uhhh, no."

"You are now. RC Associates Ltd. I'll set up a New York office, with a small branch in Los Angeles, and—"

"Hey, man, whoa!" grinned the girl, shaking her head. "Not so fast. First, I gotta talk to the guys. We don't sign no papers until we talk everything over."

Rage boiled up in Rudge Campbell's blood, and his face darkened. "What 'we'?" he spat scornfully. "There

177

is no 'we' from now on. It's *you* I want, not that third-rate collection of amateurs in your backup. They're ruining your sound. I'm signing *you*, The Rose, not them."

The girl's face flushed bright red with anger, and her voice choked with emotion. "What the fuck are you talking about?" she demanded hotly. "Those are my men; that's *my* band; they're my main guys—"

"They're a disaster and you know it," snapped Rudge angrily, realizing that he'd made the wrong move too suddenly. She was probably balling all of them. "They're not fit to hold instruments. We'll get you a new band, the best, one that—"

"You Limey scumbag," yelled Rose, "I wouldn't sign with you if you threw in Buckingham Palace and the fuckin' Queen! Not even if you could get the Beatles to back me! Nobody's gonna trash my band, not you or ten more like you! You can take your fuckin' contract, roll it up small, and shove it up your royal Limey ass!"

With these words, she turned and stalked off with as much dignity as she could muster on those wobbly wedgies.

Bloody fucking hell! Rudge raised one hand to stop her, but pulled it back. Stupid bloody cunt! Dumb twat! Someday she would come crawling to *him,* begging him to sign her up. And he'd spit in her face.

But, inside, Rudge knew he wouldn't spit in her face. He'd sign her, all right, and make her the biggest star there was. But first he'd make her crawl. *And* pay; she'd never get through paying. With interest.

He was furious, not so much at this little blond girl and her fierce loyalty and independence as he was at himself. He'd mucked the whole thing up, moved too fast, showed all his cards. Next time, he'd know better. And there would be a next time. As soon as he'd told her that he was going to open a New York office, Rudge realized that it was the truth. His destiny would be here, in America. America was the future, Europe the past.

178

First, he'd go home and wind up his affairs there. He could raise a tidy sum on the contracts he held, enough to rent decent office space in New York. He'd do bloody well without that frizzy-haired, big-mouthed cunt. The Rose! What a laugh. But he laughs best who laughs last, and he intended the last laugh to be his.

Still, all the way across the continental United States and then across the Atlantic Ocean toward London, Rudge could hear The Rose's crystalline voice in his ears. He felt a strange sense of loss and, oddly, he thought he could smell the mud of the Thames at low tide.

—

XI

There had never been an audience like the one that greeted The Rose in Memphis. If she was hot, they were hotter; like one pair of hands and one mouth, they reached for her greedily, feeding on the sight and sound of her. And Rose responded, writhing on the stage with unfaked passion while they screamed and yelled for more. She moaned and pumped her hips as though fucking all of them at the same time, then leaped to her feet to deliver the climax of her song on so high an upsurge of energy that it carried her and the audience away to heaven. When she finished, a tidal wave of applause shook the auditorium, applause so deafening it became something you could touch as well as hear.

They rushed the stage. Like one wild animal, clawing for prey, they rushed forward at The Rose. At once, the security guards formed a circle around her, but there weren't enough of them to keep the mob at bay. The kids lunged up and over the stage, clambering over one another in their attempts to get to The Rose, to touch her, feel her presence with their own hands. Rose shut her eyes and screamed as the first one touched her. Then she felt a strong pair of arms encircling her waist, lifting her up off the floor, carrying her out. The arms were familiar; so was the man-scent. She dared to open one eye. Houston was carrying her off the stage, to safety.

Behind her, she could hear bedlam, pandemonium, Mongol hordes of screaming kids swooping down. I did that. Me, she thought proudly. I drove 'em crazy tonight. The thought of the near riot she'd started warmed her, causing her female juices to flow. She buried her face in Houston's neck, feeling the strength and power of his arms and shoulders. God, she was so turned on, so hot.

"Fuck me!" she half whispered, half moaned to her lover. "Fuck me to death!"

Dyer, too, was burning with sexual energy. He had watched his lady dominating the stage, strutting and yowling like a she-cat in heat. He'd watched what she could do to thousands of people all at the same time, and he was as turned on as she, almost not believing that this incredible woman was all his. Holding her tightly, he ran to the dressing room with her and set her down, kicking the door shut and locking it. Instantly, they were at each other like barnyard animals in rut, tearing at each other's clothes while their mouths and tongues joined in deep kisses.

Suddenly, Rose went rigid in Dyer's arms, staring over his shoulder. He turned. They were not alone.

A girl—young, slim, dark—was sitting quietly in a corner of the dressing room, watching them. The ashtray at her side bore silent witness to the length of her wait; it was overflowing with lipsticked cigarette butts.

Rose touched Dyer lightly on the shoulder and slipped out of his arms. Her face wore a look that Houston had not seen before—wonder mingled with fascination. The girl stood; she was several inches taller than Rose. Holding her slender arms out in an embrace, she took one step closer to Rose. A moment's hesitation, no longer than a heartbeat, and Rose moved into her arms. They hugged and the dark-haired girl turned her lips to Rose's. At the last minute, Rose's head moved away, and the girl's lips brushed only Rose's cheeks.

Dyer stood watching them, his brown eyes moody and darker than ever. Something about this girl made all his nerve endings jangle. He kept silent, as he usually did in the presence of an unknown threat.

"How have you been, Sarah?" asked Rose throatily.

The girl smiled, a wry half smile that was as attractive as it was rueful. "Living and partly living," she replied. Her voice was husky and dark; it went with her short, curly cap of hair.

Rose shook her head slightly, as though to clear it of a misty dream, then turned quietly to Houston. "Houston, this is Sarah—would you believe it?—Willingham. Sarah, this is Houston Dyer."

The girl called Sarah gave Dyer a quick, sardonic glance. "Looks more like Galveston to me, honey," she said, making Rose laugh. Open war had been declared.

Rose bent over the sink in her hotel bathroom, enjoying the scent of the shampoo and the luxury of Sarah's long fingers massaging her scalp. She'd forgotten just how capable Sarah's hands had always been for inducing pleasure.

"Watch out for the soap, mama, you're gettin' it into my eyes," Rose laughed.

At once, Sarah cupped Rose's brow, lifting it slightly from the basin so that the rinse water flowed backward, out of Rose's face and away from her eyes.

Steam was everywhere; all the mirrors in the large, high-ceilinged, old-fashioned bathroom were misted over by the hot breath of the scalding rinse water. Rose wore her comfortable old terry-cloth robe, but Sarah was still dressed in her Jax suit.

The suit was of denim, bleached out to the softness of velvet, the jeans cut close to her small bottom and thin thighs, flaring below the knee into wide-bottomed bells. The jacket fitted Sarah like a second skin, and was zipped up only part way to the neck, exposing the tops of her delicate, tanned breasts. Rhinestones of dazzling whiteness outlined the yoke, collar, cuffs, and pockets of the jacket, and made a deep hem of dazzle on the bottoms of the jeans. Rose had checked out the outfit with a little gasp of pleasure. Her experienced eye informed her that it must have cost at least five hundred bucks, probably more, and that it had been made exclusively for Sarah.

Exclusive. That was the word for Sarah, the perfect word to describe how she had always held herself aloof from the crowds around Rose, from the crowds around anybody. She had saved herself for the exclusive use of The Rose in those days.

And now? Now her hands were rinsing the sweet-scented shampoo from Rose's golden hair, moving more and more slowly, making wide circles on Rose's head, on her neck, her shoulders, her back. Now she leaned her cheek against Rose's back and folded her arms around Rose's body.

Abruptly, Rose straightened up and pulled herself away from the girl's embrace.

"You're gonna get me all fucked up again, Sarah," she said softly, sadly.

"Rudge told me you *were* fucked up," said Sarah quietly, her brown eyes never leaving Rose's blue ones.

Rose laughed lightly and shook her head. "I love the way you say 'fuck,'" she told her. "Sounds like white gloves and tea at the Ritz."

Sarah looked steadily at Rose. "I missed you." As always, her words were direct. Sarah had always scorned pretense, preferring to demand whatever she wanted. And she usually got it, whatever, whoever it was.

Rose returned Sarah's look, assessing her. Sarah had changed; she was thinner, for one thing—if that were possible, for Sarah had always been pared down to her delicate bones, shadowy as the gossamer of a moth's wing. Perhaps it was her new haircut, which suited her small, pointed face and high cheekbones. At a time when girls were letting their hair grow as long as nature permitted, and ironing it straight, Sarah had had hers shorn close to the head, where it curled softly all over her shapely skull. She looked like some small, woolly animal, fragile yet strong.

Memories came back in a rush, overpowering Rose with their sweet pungency. She recalled exactly how Sarah looked when she first laid eyes on her . . . how many light-years ago? Only a little over a year? It seemed impossible.

Yet it was so clear. Rose's first album had just gone platinum, and the executives at Atlantic Records had flung a gigantic party in honor of their newest superstar and money-maker. They had rented Arthur's for the night, Sybil Burton's hot discothèque, and had filled it with the classiest acts in Fun City. Andy Warhol brought Viva; Baby Jane Holzer was bugalooing in white go-go boots; Mary Quant was dancing with Truman Capote, and Paul and Linda were expected at any minute. The Rose, center of all this attention, was having the time of her life. She was resplendent in a crushed velvet turban from a Third Avenue thrift shop. It went with her plastic necklaces, and the glass rings on her fingers.

Suddenly, she became conscious that someone was staring at her from across the dance floor. She stared back. A tall, cool, needle-slender girl had come in with three flaming faggots who were flying on a hallucinogenic cloud. The girl moved like the eye of a storm, silent, dark, watchful. She was watching The Rose.

Her hair was long in those days, with deep bangs that covered her forehead and met her black eyebrows. She was wearing a futuristic Rudi Gernreich dress of simple black wool, with a miniskirt so short it barely covered her pelvis. Her thighs and legs were very long and very slender, and were covered by a tight-fitting pair of black suede boots that came up almost to the hem of her skirt. Her breasts were so tiny they almost weren't there.

184

Suddenly, The Rose felt like a cow, a fat, dowdy cow with dangling udders. She felt so tacky and shabby she wanted to die, right now, right here where she was the guest of honor. No, what she really wanted was to be immediately and magically turned into that cool, dark princess in the Rudi Gernreich dress. That princess who was now approaching her until they stood face to face in the shrill mob of partygoers.

"I like your music very much," the girl said in a low voice, close to Rose's ear. The voice was husky, yet flat, a cultured, educated voice.

"Thanks." The dazzled Rose couldn't think of a goddamn thing to say.

"My name is Sarah Willingham."

"Are you in the music business?" Rose had to raise her voice to be heard over the noisy crowd.

The girl's dark head went back and her long hair rippled like black wheat as she laughed. "Oh, no, I'm not in *any* business."

"What do you do?" asked The Rose.

"I play. I have a good time." She took a step closer to The Rose; Rose could smell the heavy sandalwood of her perfume. "Have you ever had a good time?" asked Sarah.

The Rose thought a minute, then shook her curly head. "I guess not."

Sarah's eyes looked deeply into hers; they were large and oval and faintly oriental, dark brown with slanted outer corners masked by long, heavy, black lashes.

"Let me show you a good time," she offered.

And that was the beginning.

Late winter in New York, before the first signs of spring arrive and disappear into the onrush of summer heat. There was dirty, gray snow underfoot, but Sarah and Rose never traveled anywhere on foot. They always went in Sarah's Rolls-Royce, a 1952 Silver Cloud. And they went everywhere—to every art gallery opening, including the large, barnlike lofts and galleries of lower Manhattan, which was now being called by its new name, SoHo. Sarah loved art, and collected modern paintings that Rose couldn't comprehend or appreciate. Some of them looked like comic strips, complete with dialogue in balloons over the characters' heads. Others looked like designs, with straight, hard edges. Now Sarah was getting into something she called photorealism, but Rose said, "Why not just spend your money on a picture postcard?" Which always made Sarah double up, yelping with laughter.

They didn't only go to art openings; they also went to Park Avenue parties. There, Sarah introduced Rose to Lady Cocaine. Rose had been clean for over a year, but she still wore long sleeves to cover the fading tracks where the needles had gone in. She was wary of coke at first. But Sarah laughed at her. Using a tiny gold spoon, Sarah would snort up two and two, emerging from the ladies' room with her face flushed and dazzling, her eyes so bright you had to shield your face. So Rose had tried cocaine, and the white powerhouse knocked her for a loop. She loved it, loved going, as she called it, "snowblind," and making long, endless, passionate love.

They didn't only go to parties; they also ran away from winter. Sarah would lease a private plane, and they headed down to Jamaica for the weekend. They would land at Montego Bay, and an ancient but perfect Mercedes would pick them up at the airport and ferry them into the mountains high above the Caribbean, where the bougainvillea and the croton ringed the beautiful house with plants thirty feet high, where they could swim naked in the gem of an inlaid swimming pool and spend the long, hot nights high on strong Jamaican grass, rum and pineapple juice, and each other.

They didn't only run away from winter; they also ran toward it. Sarah also had an old farmhouse in the

Berkshires. It was deep in snow this time of year. They would take the train to Great Barrington and drive in the station wagon down the back roads, groceries piled high on the seat behind them. They would light a fire in the fireplace, set the coffee pot on the stove, and give themselves up to the joys of being cozy when the snowdrifts piled high against the house.

Sarah was an orphan, but a very rich one. She had inherited some of her trust funds on her twentieth birthday, and her guardian had resigned on her twenty-first, handing over the rest of the money into Sarah's eager keeping.

"I intend," she told Rose, "to spend it all. And that won't be easy, since it seems to come in faster than I can pour it out."

"Why do you want to spend it *all?*" puzzled Rose. "What about your children? Won't they get any?"

"Children?" scoffed Sarah. "What children? For children, you have to go to bed with men. And I don't go to bed with men."

It was true. Sarah was an ardent disciple of Sappho, and it wasn't long before she had initiated Rose into the mystical erotic arts of Lesbos.

It was different, Rose had to admit that.

"Better," insisted Sarah.

"Different," said The Rose thoughtfully. "I mean, I really dig it. But I dig cock, too. A lot."

"Pig," said Sarah affectionately. "You want it all."

"Fuckin' A," said The Rose.

"Isn't this enough for you?" whispered Sarah, reaching out with her fingers and her tongue, burying herself in the warm, moist body of The Rose, lapping the dew from her petals.

"Fuckin' A," said The Rose in a strangled voice, giving in.

If Rudge Campbell hated any one person on the face of the earth, it was Sarah Willingham. The dyke

187

cunt! He would have gladly torn out her heart and eaten it. But for the moment, his hands were tied. Rose was cutting her second album in a studio on Eighth Street, so they were tied to New York at present. He had to admit that Rose was looking sensational, developing more of a flair and a sense of her own style under Sarah's tutoring. Also, Rose was in excellent spirits and excellent voice. The album should have been finished by now, but they were still missing one song, one dynamite hit that could be released as a single. Because of all the money to be made on royalties, Rudge had one of the songwriters under his own company's management working on it, and the *putz* was taking his sweet old time, while Rose was out partying all night with her new lover.

Spring brought a new deepening of the relationship. Some of the haste went out of it, to be replaced by a feeling of growth and of lasting. Rose and Sarah explored new depths of emotion together, coming toward each other as friends as well as lovers. Sometimes, Rose actually believed she was in love. It was a relationship of more dimension than she'd ever had with a man. Sarah was not only her lover, she was also her sister, sometimes her mother. Sitting in the large library of Sarah's duplex overlooking Central Park, late at night, after they'd been dancing at the Electric Circus downtown, they would look out the tall windows and watch the street lights glowing. And they'd talk. Rose could tell Sarah anything.

She told her about the best and the worst moments of her life. About growing up freaky in an ugly, humdrum little town. About splitting for California and teaming up with the guys. About Monterey and how she'd met up with Rudge, and walked off on him when he'd trashed her band.

"Then what happened?" Sarah had wanted to know.

"Well, then it got really bad, man. First, Lonnie split. Without a word. I mean, I was his old lady an' all,

188

and he just split on me. Walked out and never looked back. Hell, that was a real bummer."

"And then?" Sarah's eyes glowed warm with sympathy.

"Then it got worse. You know my friend Cherie, Cherry Pye? Well he was my best friend in the world, and some creep fed him bad acid and he freaked out and jumped off a roof on Castro Street."

"Jesus!" breathed Sarah. "Was he killed?"

"No," said The Rose softly, her face mournful. "I wish he had been. He broke damn near every bone in his body, and shattered his skull. He's a vegetable, a drooling vegetable. Can't eat or even take a crap for himself. They keep him locked up. God, Sarah, he was the prettiest thing you ever saw in your life. And could he dance! Now he just sits in one place and dribbles, and the nurse says that someday he's just going to choke to death on his own spit."

"Ah, baby, that's so terrible." Sarah's voice was as soft as a kitten's kiss, and her gentle fingers rubbed at Rose's aching neck. "Then what happened?"

"Well, then it got worse yet. The band broke up. I couldn't sing anymore, not after Cherry got . . . hurt. And I picked up a new old man who was a junkie, though I didn't know it at first. I was down all the time, and he got me to snortin' heroin. Then I started chippin', you know, skin-poppin', and before you could say 'addict' I was on the needle, ridin' the horse. Josh, that was my old man, he got hepatitis off a dirty needle in somebody else's pad and he sort of hung around for a while, sick all the time and hurtin' and vomitin' an' shootin' up. Then he died."

"You poor baby. Ah, Rose, Rose."

"You know, I'm not sure how I got to New York. I was with some kids and they decided to hitchhike East, and I guess I went along for the ride. I had a pretty big habit by then, thirty–forty dollars a day at the old street prices, and I guess . . . I guess I just earned money however I could."

"How, Rose?"

"Sometimes I hooked, but more often I stole, 'cause it was faster. I was good at it too. Did all the big Fifth Avenue stores. I had this old black coat, see, and I sewed big pockets on the inside and I'd go into a store and make out like I was 'just looking, thanks,' and . . . whoosh . . . into the pockets."

"Didn't you ever get caught?"

"Yeah, three times, as a matter of fact."

"What happened?"

"The first time, they let me off because I had no previous record. The second time, they sent me up for three months to a 'correctional facility.' "

"Jail?" Sarah's mouth formed a horrified "O."

"Jail," nodded The Rose. "I came out of there hating bull dykes and with a hundred-dollar-a-day habit. There were two things that everybody and anybody could score for in that joint: sex and heroin."

"And the third time?"

"The third time Rudge got me off. But it cost him plenty. And he never lets me forget it."

"Rudge. I'd forgotten about Rudge. How did you meet him again?"

"Well, after I came out, I touched bottom so hard my ass still shows scrapes. I was living in a crash pad over a drag joint in the West Village, and we were shooting up all day and all night. Never left the apartment. There were four of us, two girls and two guys. The guys would go out and pick up johns and bring them back to us. And we'd blow them or fuck them . . . anything they wanted. Then the guys would grab the bread and go out and score the smack. See, we were so skinny by that time that we could pass for fifteen or even fourteen. Even these were smaller, a lot smaller." Rose held her breasts

190

in her hands and weighed them thoughtfully, her eyes dark blue with the horror of her memories. "So the johns thought they were getting baby nookie. Hell, we didn't care about anything. As long as we could stay high."

"And?" asked Sarah breathlessly. She was as fascinated as she was repelled.

"And," continued The Rose, "one of the fags downstairs in the drag joint was fuckin' a guy who owned a coffee house on Christopher Street. And they were lookin' for a girl singer. A folkie, you know, 'All my trials, Lord, will soon be over.' Hell, I could sing that shit in my sleep. And there was something inside me that never let go, not even when my ass was in the gutter. All that time, I knew I'd come back up. I figured if I could get only one deep breath of air, maybe I'd start breathing again. So I went over there and I got the job. And one night Rudge comes in. An' he sees me, an' he remembers me, and now he's got me right where he wants me. He makes me promise to kick, and to straighten up, and, you know, vitamins and the whole bit. An' he tells me he's gonna make me a star, but only if I sign the contract and he gets half of everything, 50–50 partners. And I gotta live clean from then on."

"And you did!" Sarah clapped her hands like a child when a terrifying fairy tale ends happily.

"Well, yes, eventually, I did. But it took a little doing, and a lot of patience on Rudge's part. An' I have to hand it to him: He stuck by me, even when I backslid almost all the way back to jail. I got busted for boosting in Macy's." Rose laughed. "But that was the last time. Now I got charge accounts at Macy's and every other store I ever stole from. What a hoot."

"And that's how you became a star."

"Yeah, but there's somethin' else I forgot to tell ya. The best part."

"Tell me, tell me at once!" commanded Sarah.

"Well, there I was, this junkie and all, and Rudge

191

Campbell dictating terms like it was unconditional surrender time, an' me having to say 'Yes, Rudge' to everything, right? So he whips out this pen and hands me the contract, and I say to him, 'I'll sign under one condition.' And he gives me one of those panther looks of his, like he's going to snap your spine with his teeth, an' he says, 'And what condition is that, may I know?' And I say, 'I want my band back. All of them except Lonnie, 'cause I don't know where the fuck he is. But I want Dennis and Whitey and Norton and Danny or I don't sing.' "

"And?"

"And he flies to San Francisco and sure enough a week later he's back with the guys. *My* guys. My old band. And he tells them, 'You blow one false note and you go back to California. I'm paying to hear this girl sing, and I want you backing her up, not drowning her out.' "

"And?"

"And that's it. We're all in it together. Sometimes Rudge looks at all of us and you can hear his teeth grinding. But I think he's pretty resigned to the band now. Besides, we finally did learn to cook together."

Silence fell as Rose finished her story. Sarah, whose life had been an escalating series of material attainments, sat looking out of her library window, reflecting on what Rose had told her, a horror story of rejection, addiction, death, and degradation. And yet, out of all of the horror Rose had emerged stronger and more independent than ever, the phoenix of life triumphing over the ashes of death. Sarah had never met anybody so remarkable or courageous in her life. With a small cry, she turned and threw her arms around Rose, bursting into tears.

"Hey, man," laughed Rose, pushing the girl away slightly. "What the fuck is this? It's *my* life, and *you're* cryin' over it? Hell, I'm not sheddin' any tears, and neither should you. It's all behind me, Sarah," she told the sobbing girl more gently. "It's over. Now I'm on top, an' I'm gonna stay there. Besides, Rudge would bust my ass if I didn't."

Heaven knows that Rudge would have busted her ass with a shovel. The album was finished now—Atlantic was all excited about it and the company executives were planning a huge advertising campaign. It was time to tour, to become a traveling band again. The Rose was a monster attraction now, and Rudge could dictate terms for the promoters to swallow. A nationwide tour, coinciding with the release of a major album—every rock 'n' roll manager's dream. One would sell the other, and money would flow in from all sides.

But Rose didn't want to leave New York. She was happy, comfortable, and in love. She had everything she had always dreamed of—success, fame, luxury, and somebody to keep her happy in bed. Why give up comfort for a grueling stint on the road, with bad food, no rest, and a depressing series of Ramadas and Holiday Inns? And the road was no place for a spoiled princess like Sarah.

"Sarah?" screamed Rudge. "Who the fuck said anything about Sarah? If you're into chicks, Rose, there'll be chicks by the thousands waiting at every stage entrance, just begging to be allowed to lick your pussy." He tugged almost angrily at the fringes of his buckskin jacket; Rudge was almost complete now in his metamorphosis from Londoner to Texan.

"You got a fuckin' filthy mind, you know that, Rudge?" Rose yelled back. "It's not like that . . . I mean, it's not *only* that. Sarah loves me, and I love her. I mean, she really loves me, man."

It was Rose's insistence on Sarah's devotion that gave Rudge the idea that Rose's insecurities were at work again, tearing at the fabric of the relationship. Rose never could understand how anybody could want her or love her. Up on the stage was different—there, she was The Rose, the one they'd paid their money to see. She could do anything with them—make them laugh, or cry, or get

193

up and boogey until their legs dropped off. There, *she* was in control. Offstage, she felt smaller, homelier, and very vulnerable.

Anywhere there was a vulnerable spot, there is where Rudge Campbell struck.

He began by inviting Sarah to lunch at the Four Seasons. It was a new experience for him, too, since he usually spent the lunch hour attached to a telephone, getting greasy crumbs all over the receiver. He wore a suit and tie for the occasion, and he dropped the shit-kicker image long enough to be Prince Philip.

Sarah, of course, turned up in old Levi's and Frye boots, and the *maître d'* fell all over himself getting the princess properly seated.

Rudge instantly changed his tactics, realizing that subtlety from him would be totally unsuccessful.

" 'Ere, you don' wanna go on tour with a rock 'n' roll band," he told her.

"Why not?" Sarah replied coolly. "It sounds like fun."

"Fun?" Rudge's eyebrows disappeared into his thick thatch of curly hair. "About as much fun as dismemberment. The Rose will be hyper all the time, onstage and off. She'll be the most impossible, big-mouth bitch cunt you'd ever not want to see—demanding, selfish, greedy, bad-mannered, exhausted, and stoned."

"Then she'll certainly need me," said Sarah primly.

"That's where you're wrong, entirely wrong. I hate to put it bluntly, girl, but what The Rose will need . . . is cock. Men. A different one every night, sometimes two."

Sarah stiffened in her chair, and her face turned pale under the tan she wore all year 'round. "That might have been true once. It's not true anymore." She bit each separate word off close, staring at Rudge with loathing.

But Rudge was shaking his head, allowing a sympathetic expression to work its way over his features. "I

194

wish you were right. I think you're good for her. She's never looked or felt this good in her life." Or sung this bad, he added mentally. A raunchy singer like The Rose has no business getting comfortable. It's misery and pain that bring out the best in her. Takes an irritated oyster to produce a pearl. Although Rose on her worst day was more worth listening to than a thousand other "stars." Still he, Rudge, knew the difference, and comfort was too much of a luxury for The Rose. Keep her miserable, and she'll be happy.

"Of course I'm good for her," said Sarah, pushing her salad around on her plate with her fork. "I take care of her."

I take care of her, cunt! thought Rudge savagely. Instead, he said, " 'Course you do. That's why I don't want to see you unhappy. But Rose on the road is a different person. She's hungry all the time, and not for affection. For a kind of . . . brutality . . . for coarse, raw sex. For men. Look at me, Sarah, look at my eyes. I'm tellin' y' the truth. I've seen her. It's like she wants to relive every bad moment of her past. . . ." He had the satisfaction of seeing Sarah shiver, and he knew he'd touched a nerve.

"She comes off that stage so horny she'd fuck a lightstand if it was thick enough. She wants to be knocked down and stepped on, hurt and humiliated, used. Can you do that for her, Sarah?"

The girl dropped her eyes. "No," she said so quietly he had to read her lips.

"Do you want to see that, Sarah? Night after night? Do you want to be the one who gets to do her nails and zip up her jeans? An' somebody else zips them down? Is that what you want?"

"No." The girl's full lips were trembling; tears were forming under the thick lashes.

"Well, then . . ." Rudge spread his hands out, palms

195

up, in the familiar gesture of innocence. "Well, then . . ."

"But we love each other!" Sarah burst out, slamming her fork down on the table.

"That's why you don't want to spoil it, right?" Rudge gave her the same wide smile he used to give the Islington ladies when he'd short-changed them at the age of eight. "It's only a six-week tour, baby. She'll come back. And she'll have it all out of her system, all those bad vibes and the hostility. She'll be the old Rose you know."

"No!" protested Sarah suddenly. "It doesn't have to be that way! She's different now . . . we have each other."

"It's not enough for her!" snapped Rudge. "You want to find out for yourself, come along. Watch her on the plane. She goes into the back with one of the guys . . . *any* one . . . maybe even all of them . . . as soon as the wheels leave the ground. And everywhere we land, guys line up to fuck The Rose. You know that, you've heard the stories about her. She's a hot lay, and little boys from Philadelphia to San Diego want to brag they've fucked The Rose. Do you think she can resist that? You know better than that. You know how much attention she craves. She *feeds* on it, Sarah. She sees some nineteen-year-old with a big hard-on and she forgets time and place. She always did, and she always will. Tell me something. When she told you the long, sad story of her life, and I'm sure she did, did she tell you about the time she took on the whole high-school football team in her hometown?"

Sarah gasped, and two spots of color appeared in her cheeks. "Nnn . . . no."

Rudge laughed harshly. "I'll just bet she didn't. Why don't you ask her? Go ahead, ask her about it."

He leaned forward over the table and put his hand on Sarah's. She winced slightly, and attempted to pull her hand away from his, but Rudge held on very tightly.

196

"You do see what I'm sayin', don't you? I'm tryin' to tell you that Rose is two different people, herself and The Rose. You've only seen the good side of her so far. But if you want to be subjected to a monster, come along. I'll guarantee you that your love affair will be over in less than two weeks. She'll have you running her errands and scoring her dope and bringing her booze, while she spends every spare minute in bed with her latest stud. Is that what you want to be? A go-fer for a Star? She'll lose all respect for you, and you'll wind up hating each other. Now, if you'll take *my* advice, you'll get out of town before the tour leaves, so she can't put any pressure on you. That way, you'll preserve what the two of you have, and Rose will come back to you and be her old self."

"I see," said Sarah slowly. "I suppose you're right."

"Of *course* I'm right," grinned Rudge. "Don't I always have Rose's best interests at heart? For God's sake, girl, we're partners—50-50. It's in my interest to see that everything works out for Rose. Now, why don't you plan a little vacation? Leave as soon as possible, and be certain to be back home in six weeks' time. As soon as the tour is over, we'll be back in New York."

"All right," said Sarah without spirit. "I'll go to Rome this afternoon. I have a friend with a villa outside Ostia. I'll stay with her."

"Good. You won't be sorry. Rose will come back to you hotter than ever." He managed to keep the triumph out of his voice, but he couldn't resist a gleeful grin as he settled the check.

To Rose, he sang another tune.

"You're right, Rose. The road's no place for Sarah. She's used to luxury. She'd croak at a Holiday Inn. Besides, you know all those beautiful chicks who gang up on you. A knockout like Sarah would be God's gift to them. And there's no reason for her to play Little Miss Faithful while you're fuckin' your brains out. If you're gettin' yours, why shouldn't she be gettin' hers?"

197

The Rose had no answer for that one. She couldn't imagine anybody staying loyal to her. In her life, she'd had more than her share of rejection.

So Rose went home to an empty duplex to pack. There was a brief, loving note of good-bye from Sarah, and an address and telephone number in Italy. And a promise that in six weeks they'd be together again.

Rose asked the operator to dial the number.

"Pronto?" said a strange female voice. A beautiful voice. Rose put the receiver down.

"See?" said Rudge the following day, as the limo carried them out to LaGuardia Airport. "I knew she'd let you down. These rich bitches don't have staying power. They don't pay their dues. Besides, in six weeks on the road you'll have more nookie than you'd get in a year in New York. You'll forget her."

Rose said nothing, but kept her face turned to the smoked glass of the car's window, so that Rudge wouldn't see her crying.

Rudge was right. That was over a year ago, and Rose hadn't seen Sarah since. Rose hadn't answered the other girl's letters or telephone calls and, sooner than she'd expected, they'd stopped.

"I missed you," said Sarah, biting her lip.

Rose nodded gently, and sat down on the edge of the bathtub, pulling Sarah down next to her. She held onto the dark girl's hand as she talked.

"I gotta tell you, Sarah. Something wonderful's happened to me. This man's like no one I've ever known. He's solid. And he doesn't give a shit who I am or what I am. He makes me happy." She pressed Sarah's hand in loving friendship.

Sarah looked deeply into Rose's eyes. They were shining, her face glowing. Even in the ratty old terry bathrobe with her hair hanging down in wet strings, Rose looked more beautiful than Sarah had ever seen her. The hurt was almost too painful to bear, but there was something else—something beyond the pain of spurned love. There was affection and friendship for Rose, and those feelings made Sarah almost happy for her.

She smiled a tremulous smile. "I'm glad for you, Rose. I'm also jealous. But I *am* glad."

Rose smiled at her tenderly, believing her. Sarah's eyes filled and the tears spilled over. Moving closer to her, Rose put her arms around her in a gentle embrace. Sobbing, Sarah clung to Rose, Sarah's need fierce and all-consuming. She pulled Rose's face around for a kiss. Rose attempted to resist her, but her warm and generous nature could not deny the desperate need of a friend. She let her lips meet Sarah's in a long kiss.

The door to the hotel suite opened and Houston Dyer walked in happily, carrying a bucket of champagne on ice. Rose wasn't in the bedroom, but the bathroom door was open, and he went to it.

Rose and Sarah were sitting on the edge of the bathtub, locked in a kiss. Their arms were wound tightly around each other, and their breasts were pressed closely together.

Dyer stared, silent. A host of feelings rose up to confuse and conflict him. Rose with a woman! Part of him felt unmanned, part of him aroused. He'd never seen Rose kiss anybody else, not as long as he'd been with her, yet he knew how promiscuous she'd been. And he accepted it. But a woman! That was different.

"What are you staring at?" yelled Rose as she pulled away from Sarah at last. Rose felt guilty, torn, but the way Houston was gaping at her made her feel dirty, too. *"I said, 'What are you staring at?'"* she screamed.

Nervously, Sarah picked up her handbag and brushed past Dyer, looking for the way out. That left the two of them alone, Rose glaring at Dyer with defiant eyes.

Without warning, Houston's right hand whipped out and . . . thwack! . . . slapped Rose hard on the cheek.

Her head snapped back from the force of the blow, and she went tumbling backward onto the wet floor and the sodden mass of towels. Dyer stared at her, horrified at what he'd done. His action had caught him as much by surprise as it had Rose.

Scrambling to her feet, Rose grabbed the bottle of champagne and hurled it at Dyer's head. It missed him by a hair, and shattered, foaming and bubbling, on the door behind him. Furious, wild with rage, Rose threw herself on him, kicking, punching, biting, scratching, and cursing. Houston made no move to retaliate; all his energies were concentrated simply on defending himself. He wrestled her down to the floor, hoping to pin her there until she had calmed down somewhat. But, as her shoulders touched the wet bathroom floor, Rose brought her knee up hard and connected with Dyer's groin. That ended the fight.

Doubling over in pain, Houston let her go and rolled onto his back, his knees drawn up. Tears stung his eyes; he was really hurting.

"Oh, my God, are you all right?" cried Rose. She was on her hands and knees, moving over to Dyer.

"No! No! Stay away!" moaned Houston, holding his balls protectively.

"I'm sorry, I'm sorry," babbled Rose in hysterical distress. "Let me get a doctor. Hey, I didn't mean to hurt you, baby. Look, the thing with Sarah—it's all over. Can you believe me?"

But nothing was on Houston's mind except the sharp pains radiating from his groin into his thighs and belly. He managed to pull himself to his feet and stagger to the door.

"Hey, where are you going? Don't go, baby. Please don't go." Rose, panicked, tried to stop him, but he shook her off like a terrier shakes a mouse, and slammed the door behind him, hard.

Sobbing, Rose fell to her knees. "Don't go, don't

go," she wailed, heartbroken. Then anger took over, pushing her to her feet. "You cocksucker!" she yelled at the silent room door. "Wait till I get my hands on you!"

Rudge was, inevitably, on the telephone, screaming into the receiver.

"You bloody fuckin' idiots, when I pay for protection, I expect protection! They mobbed the stage, man, and they *touched my star!* They laid their grubby little hands on Rose, and we had to carry her off! Now, where the hell were those fat bastards of cops when I needed them? I shelled out plenty for that, and I expect every fuckin' red cent of it back, you hear me! Or we'll never play your shithole auditorium again!"

A knock sounded on the door.

"Come in!" yelled Rudge, slamming the receiver down.

Sarah walked in, her exquisite nose wrinkling in distaste at the mess in Rudge's motel suite. The bed itself had vanished under stacks of legal papers, contracts, tally sheets, and piles and piles of banded money. Thousands. A calculator sat in the middle of the mess, its digital readout glowing. On the edge of the bed, in a few cleared inches of space near the telephone, sat Rudge, in Jockey shorts and a cowboy hat.

"How'd it go?"

"You want the details?" asked Sarah coldly.

"Please," grinned Rudge.

"I was upset. She was comforting me and he walked in. You got what you wanted."

"I do what's best for Rose," said Rudge, the muscle in his jaw jumping.

Sarah had a vivid memory of Rudge's "best." "You told me she needed me," she accused. "That's the only reason I came. But you lied to me. Again." Then her bitter tone changed to one of pleading. "Give her some time off, Rudge."

Rudge's eyes glittered with dislike. "She can't afford it. And neither can I."

"She's tired . . . she needs it. There's an edge I've never seen before."

Rudge pushed the cowboy hat down over his eyes. "Sarah, why don't you go back to fucking Park Avenue where you belong? I'll take care of Rose. I know what she needs. She needs *me*. She's a child and it takes a grown-up to hold her together."

"Like you?" asked Sarah contemptuously.

"Like me." He watched her slender form turn to go. "Did you tell her I sent for you?" he asked her suddenly. There was concern in his voice.

Sarah turned at the door, her hand on the knob. "No, I didn't. But I wish now that I had." And she walked out.

"Why can't you *find* him?" screamed Rose, anger and panic working her to a pitch of hysteria. Dyer hadn't come back to the hotel suite all night, and Rose stormed into Rudge's motel room the next morning to confront him. *"Why the fuck can't you find him?"*

"I didn't lose him!" shouted Rudge back, just as angry on the surface, but pleased as hell underneath.

The Rose narrowed her eyes. *"I ain't so sure!"* she shrieked. She'd had all night to put the pieces together, and they just about fit. Sarah appearing from nowhere. So conveniently. Just as Rudge really wanted Dyer out, bad. No, everything was too pat, too much like a one-act play.

But this couldn't be the ending, *couldn't* be. She had to find Houston, to make it up with him, to prove to him that she loved him and needed him. Hell, she'd find him if she had to personally take a fine-tooth comb to the whole fuckin' city of Memphis!

She whirled and strode out of the suite, followed by faithful Mal. Rudge and Dennis stared after her.

"Where are you going?" yelled Rudge.

"If you can't find him, I will!" hollered Rose over her shoulder without looking back.

"We're leaving for Florida tonight. Remember? Hometown? You're going to 'show them all.'" He mimicked her words and her voice.

But the elevator doors had closed behind Rose and Mal, leaving Rudge shouting at nobody.

"If I had my gun, I'd kill her," he muttered.

XII

Three o'clock in the morning, between Saturday night and Sunday, can be the loneliest place in the world. Because it *is* a place, rather than a time, a place the soul wants to occupy with another soul that lives in a warm body to wake up close to late on Sunday. Whew! And when you're in a strange town, looking for a lover who's just walked out the door, and you've had a bottle or two to help you make it through the night . . . well . . . three o'clock in the morning between Saturday night and Sunday ain't on any map you'll ever see. It's uncharted, empty, lost.

He could be anyplace in this whole fuckin' world, thought Rose sadly, as the limo nudged its slow way down Beale Street. But wherever he is, I gotta find him. Gotta find him and tell him . . . tell him . . . what? The cherry brandy had fuzzed up her brain. Oh, yeah. Gotta tell him I'm sorry I kicked him in the balls. Gonna kiss 'em both, make 'em all better. Tell him I need him. Tell him not to go away, The Rose needs you, Houston. Can't do without my sweet honey man and his sweet honey.

"Do you see him anywhere?" she asked Mal, peering down the rain-slicked empty street.

Mal, behind the wheel of the Caddy, shook his head and hiccuped a little. He was damn near as stoned as she was, which is why he was driving at fifteen miles an hour straight down the middle of Beale Street. Safety first.

"Pull up here," ordered Rose.

Mal pulled over to the curb in front of one more bar just like all the others they'd visited that long, weary night. The street was lit by an endless procession of neon signs, in the shape of tumbling dice, spinning wagon wheels, spouting oil wells. Massage parlors crowded next to topless bars. Dyer hadn't been in any of the others, and Mal strongly doubted that he'd be in this one. But something about it musta caught The Rose's eye, making it different from all the rest.

You could hear the music coming through the flimsy wooden walls as Rose stumbled up to the screen door. Memphis—birth of the blues. Yet, every fuckin' bar on this strip was playing country & western on its jukebox, mostly Billy Ray or Dolly Parton.

Outside the bar, low-riders and pickups jammed the little parking lot. Inside, topless waitresses in bouffant wigs and G-strings served beer while their tits jiggled and their asses jounced. This was the hot place to be on a Saturday night.

"Hey!" yelled Rose in through the door. "Is there a dude by the name of Houston Dyer in there?"

The guys nearest the door turned to look. They saw a flakey female hippie beating on the screen. A chorus of jeers and catcalls greeted her.

"Aaanhhhh, yer sister chews gorilla balls!" hollered the defiant Rose.

Mal ran to pluck her off the screen door before the massacre began. "Take it easy. Take it easy." He followed Rose to the curbside, where she plopped down, ignoring the rain and the dirty sidewalk. She laid her small head down on her arms and sighed deeply.

"I was such a good lay. How could he *go* like that? Jeee-zus, I really should have gone to college." Rose always had an idea that college would have made her into a lady.

"I don't know, Rose, but don't worry. He'll come back." Mal's heart was breaking for her. How could anybody walk out on Rose, the most wonderful, smartest, best . . . if he ever got his hands on Dyer, he'd . . . he'd . . . pop him one.

"No, he won't come back," wept Rose. "Do you really think he'll come back?" The makeup around her eyes was smudged into a mask, and her nose was running, but Mal thought she was the most beautiful thing he'd ever seen.

"Sure he will, Rose. He loves you."

"Nah, how could he love me? Do you think he does?" asked Rose childishly. "Nah, how could he?" she answered her own question in maudlin tones.

"I know what, Mal. I know what. Let's get something to eat. I'm starvin'. Let's get us another bottle and eat us some delicious Aquavit. That's nourishin', ain't it, Mal? Aquavit's full of vitamins."

The thought of vitamins brought her to Houston again, and she burst out crying. Mal patted her back awkwardly, shyly. He wished he were Houston Dyer and could really take care of her. Seems like Dyer was the only man who knew the secret of Rose's needs.

"The hell with him," said Rose suddenly, wiping her eyes. "I don't give a damn about him."

Mal looked at her sharply. "You positive?"

"No." Tears welled up again, but Rose fought them back. She wasn't gonna look for him anymore. Let *him* come lookin' for *her*. Besides, she had no idea where to find him, and he knew exactly where to find her.

"There's only one thing left to do," she told Mal, standing up and brushing at her wet jeans ineffectually.

"What's that?"

"Go home," said Rose.

206

The bus passed through the gate and stopped at the shed inside. The door opened and a handful of uniformed enlisted men, weary from drinking and fucking on overnight passes, stepped down sleepily and filed through to report to barracks. Houston Dyer was the last man off the bus.

He walked slowly down the corridor toward the noncoms' quarters at the end. A sign on one door read: "Sgt. 1st Class J. Hargraves; Sgt. 1st Class H. Dyer." A ribbon of light showed under the door. With one bone-tired hand, Dyer pushed the door open and stepped inside.

Julius Hargraves' impassive face showed no emotion when he saw Houston. But his eyes registered instantly the fact that Dyer's hair had grown, longer than the regulation cut, and that he'd lost weight. Late as it was, Hargraves was still wide awake, sitting at the desk under a bare lightbulb, drinking slowly and steadily from a bottle of whiskey.

Houston stood in silence, looking down at his closest friend. They had trained together, served together, in the States and in Vietnam. Julius Hargraves was a tall, massive black man with large, work-worn hands and a pair of eyes that had seen too many battles. He wore his uniform, hashmarks halfway up the sleeve, immaculately pressed, a professional soldier. Houston felt dirty and scruffy as Julius' eyes flicked over him without expression.

"You look like you turned into some jive junkie or something," said Julius calmly. He reached into the desk drawer and came out with a dusty tumbler. Filling it nearly full of Wild Turkey, he handed it to Houston.

"I know," said Dyer wearily, accepting the drink. He collapsed on his cot and took a long swallow. He'd spent most of the night riding on a cold bus with bad springs.

"You got travel orders for Saigon," remarked Julius.

207

"Yeah," said Dyer impassively. He was too tired to deal with it.

"You got back just in time. According to my knowledge of Army rules and regulations, in two more days you'da moved from the AWOL list to the deserters' roster. Coverin' the bases for you this long is like to push even an old fox like myself past his considerable limits. They've been blowin' a whole lotta smoke up my black ass around here, good friend."

Houston nodded. "Thanks, Julius," he said quietly.

The black man smiled for the first time. "Would you believe I just reupped for another four?"

"That doesn't surprise me."

"I put in again for 'Nam," said Hargraves without expression.

"That surprises me." Reinlistment was one thing, combat another. Combat meant death, somebody's death, ar.d Houston was sick to his soul of death and killing.

Julius laughed, a harsh bark. "I don't want to be no janitor, man. I can't stand the smell of white people's piss." He took another swig from the bottle, and laughed once more; this time his laughter was self-mockery. "Julius Hargraves is no good for anything but killing."

Silence fell between the two men, a very heavy silence. The room echoed with it. Then Dyer said, very softly, "I lost the taste for it."

Hargraves shook his head. "You never had it anyway," he replied, just as softly. "You got civilian eyes, man." He looked at the boy with an intuition born of long years of hard work and harder experiences.

"Thanks, Julius," said Houston. He held out his glass. Hargraves refilled it and the two men drank together in silence. Each one knew what the other was thinking.

Daylight is a different state of mind. The Rose woke up from her drunken sleep with a surprisingly clear head.

208

It was the smell of the Gulf that had entered her nostrils and awakened her to the sunshine of the morning.

"Stop!" she called to Mal, and tumbled out of the back seat of the car. She was wrinkled and messy, but her eyes were clear, and the wind off the water brought fresh color to her cheeks. She pulled off her spike-heeled shoes and dug her toes into the yellow sand of the beach. It was deserted at this hour of the morning; she and Mal had it all to themselves. They sat on the fender of the car, looking out at the waves rolling in. There was an offshore rock formation that created breakers here, too strong for swimming or surfing, and to Rose the high crests of white-capped water appeared to be marching toward her like a big brass band, welcoming her home.

She felt strong and confident suddenly. She was only a few miles from home; Houston would be there waiting for her; the whole town would greet her like a hero; she'd sing her ass off for them, just to show them that she had *always* been The Rose, even back then, no matter what they thought. Oh, yeah, life could be very tasty indeed.

Her hair blew back away from her face, ruffling like golden feathers in the strong morning breeze, and her large blue eyes caught the color of the water and sent it back dancing.

"Jesus H. Calhoun, I love the ocean," she said joyfully. "Don't you, Mal?"

"I'm not sure, Rose," said Mal doubtfully. "Not much ocean to love in Indiana, where I come from." He took the bottle from Rose's hand and carefully poured two drinks into paper cups. They clicked the cups together in a silent toast, and drank the sweet liquor down.

Rose's mood, always a fragile thing, changed almost instantly, like the sea. "Who's gonna buy me a drink when I'm forty?" she asked Mal mournfully.

"I will, Rose," declared Mal loyally.

"Sure ya will, baby," sighed The Rose. She opened the door to the limousine and crawled into the back seat. "Wouldn't ya think he'd at least phone?" She looked longingly at the telephone in the front seat, a working symbol of her status as a star. "I mean, he knows the goddamn number."

"Don't worry, Rose," said Mal for the thousandth time. "He'll be there. He'll be waiting for you."

Neither of them noticed the bottle cap wedged by accident into the bell of the telephone, killing the sound so that, when it rang, they couldn't hear it.

"Did you find her?" asked Rudge with his mouth full. He was wolfing down a huge breakfast—pancakes, eggs, ham—without tasting it. It would probably be his only meal of the day, and he was treating it like fuel, not food.

Dennis shook his head as he sat down at the counter next to Rudge and ordered coffee. "No. She and that kid tore up downtown Memphis last night looking for Dyer. They never came back."

Rudge bit into a piece of ham savagely, tearing it with his strong white teeth. "She better show tonight, or I'll break her fuckin' feathers for her. Did you try the phone in the limo?"

Dennis nodded, taking a scalding sip of coffee. He'd been at it for hours, tracking down The Rose. "I dialed it a hundred times. No answer. Don't worry; she'll show. This hometown concert is the most important thing in her life."

"It fuckin' well better be more important to her than that Texas shitkicker stud. Try the limo again."

Dennis sighed wearily and got down off the stool. When this tour was over, he was going to buy an island somewhere, without telephones, without automobiles, and, most of all, without rock 'n' roll managers.

It was another little Gulf town just like half a dozen others they'd passed through. Mal had stopped looking out the window, except to keep his bloodshot eyes on the road. Rose, sitting by him in the front seat, stared out at the dusty village, pulverized by the morning sunshine. There was the local high school . . . a gas station . . . the post office. She knew them all . . . all. She was home.

"Hey, Mal," she said softly. "This is it."

"What?" And then it dawned. "Lawrence?" He looked around curiously. A dead burg. Only the oil rigs were alive.

"Uh-huh. The old hometown. Tonight I'm gonna show them all, ain't I, Mal? Tonight's the night. Right, good buddy?"

"Right, Rose. This is it, huh? Born here?"

"Born *an'* raised. Boy, what a shithole. But it sure brings back memories. Turn down Main Street, would ya?"

"Anything you say, Cap'n." The limo, battered and dusty, hubcaps creased and mud on the license plates, sailed down Main Street like a big old ocean liner, once grand, still proud. Rose was becoming more and more excited with every sight she remembered.

"An' there's where I took piano from Mrs. Spohn. . . ." She pointed out a pale-blue stucco house with ecru lace curtains. Mal craned his neck like it was some historical monument.

"She was always rappin' my knuckles with a ruler. Said I didn't understand music. Well, maybe I didn't. She gave 'Peter and the Wolf' to Mary Jane White t' play at the Christmas concert, 'steada to me like she promised. I did scales. Nobody clapped." Her eyes darkened at the memory.

"See over there?" Rose pointed one long finger at a small stucco bungalow. Outside, a middle-aged man was mowing a small scrap of lawn, while a stout woman in an apron hung socks up on a clothesline.

211

"Yeah," said Mal, following Rose's finger.

"That's my mother and father," said Rose quietly.

"Hey! Ain't that something!" Grinning, Mal took his foot off the gas pedal, slowing down the car. Instantly, Rose leaned over and pressed her foot over his, hitting the gas and speeding up.

"Let's keep going," she said, slumping in her seat and turning her face away from the street so she wouldn't be seen.

Mal was puzzled; they looked like nice enough, ordinary people. But, whatever Rose wanted . . .

"Hey!" called Rose suddenly, putting her hand on Mal's arm. "That's Leonard's grocery, where we used to sneak smokes an' drink Dr Pepper." A quick grin, mischief shining in her blue eyes. "Whaddya say, kid? You want a Dr Pepper, buddy?"

Mal pulled up in front of a one-room country store, surrounded by dusty, raggedy palmetto hedges, and shimmering in the ninety-five-degree heat. The paint was peeling off the old structure in long strips, and the two concrete steps leading up to the screen door were cracking. Even the sign over the door was showing its age.

Rose climbed out of the Caddy and dusted herself off. Not that it made a helluva difference. Barefoot and dirty-faced, she was rumpled beyond the help of any mere dusting. The binge of the night before, sleeping for hours in her clothes on the seat of a car, had matted her hair. Sweat stains showed at the armpits of her thin blouse. In the strong sunlight, she looked ratty—ragged and ratty.

Mal was half asleep, half stoned, and the other half a wipeout, but he hung in there with her gamely, out of loyalty. Together they climbed the cracking concrete steps, and he pushed the squeaky screen door open for her, a gentleman to the bitter end.

Leonard's grocery store was like a hundred thousand others, all over the map of the Union. It stocked a little of this and a little of that—flashlight batteries, sodas, playing cards, baked beans, ballpoint pens, Campbell's soups, cheap transistor radios made in Taiwan. It even boasted a record rack, and two teeny-boppers in pedal pushers were pawing through the records with grubby fingers. In the back of the store, a couple of black men were trying to decide whether they could afford Tabasco sauce for the catfish, and Mr. Leonard, five years older, stood patiently behind his counter.

Rose paraded slowly down the aisle to let Leonard get a good look at her. He was to be the first person in her hometown to lay eyes upon The Rose since she had become a star, and she really wanted to savor his reaction.

"Somethin' I can do for you, ma'am?" he asked her as politely as he could, seein' as how she looked like a fifty-cent hooker.

The air seemed to go out of The Rose, and she deflated, her mouth working. She felt tears stinging her eyelids, but she refused to let them out.

"Don't you know who I am?" she asked in a disappointed, very small voice.

Mr. Leonard shook his aging head from side to side. "Nope, can't say I do."

Rose took a deep breath. " 'Gimme a Dr Pepper, Mr. Leonard,' " she said, mimicking the voice of a child, her old voice.

He reached into the cooler for the soda, then stopped, coming up smiling at her. "Why, it's Mary Rose Foster," he said, recognizing the little girl buried in this strange, dirty, exotic creature. "How you been, Mary Rose? What brings you back to these parts?"

What brings you back to these parts? It was her worst nightmare, coming true. The nightmare in which she knew everybody, but nobody knew her. The bad dream that had haunted her for years.

He didn't know her at all, or even who she was! "Jesus Christ!" she breathed. "Jesus CHRIST!"

Mal put his arm around her but she shook it off impatiently. She was mad, now, fit to be roped and tied. Furiously, she stalked down the counter to the record rack, pulling out her latest album. She reached over the counter and grabbed one of the ballpoint pens Mr. Leonard carried in a plastic pocket protector in his shirt pocket. Angrily, she scribbled her autograph on the record.

"Next time you'll know who I am! I'm The Rose!"

Slamming the album down, she turned to go, then turned back. She dug deep down into her poke and threw a bill onto the counter.

" 'Scuse me. I forgot to pay for the album." And, followed by Mal, she rushed out of the store.

Mr. Leonard stared after her, completely bewildered, smoothing out the hundred-dollar bill with absentminded fingers. The two young girls, galvanized into action, grabbed the album and hugged it, staring at the autograph.

"It was *her!* It really was HER! Oh, heaven, that was *The Rose!*" they squealed, totally overcome.

But by that time Rose was too far away to see or hear them.

It took her fully fifteen minutes to bounce back even a little. She sat slumped in the front seat beside Mal, wrapped in coils of black depression that left her unable to talk. At last, the gloom began to lift a little. For God's sake, she told herself shakily. Why *should* he recognize me? I changed a lot, didn't I? And why the fuck should he know who I am? How many fans do I have over sixty? At last, her natural resilience won out, and Rose began to take some interest in life.

She brightened as they approached a new imported-car showroom on the edge of town. There were carefully tended flower boxes outside, and the brass doorknobs wore a high polish. In the window were two low-slung beauties, real sporty, and over the door a sign that proclaimed

EDDIE POMPADOUR FERRARI

"Eddie Pompadour! He gave me my first kiss! Stop the car, Mal."

She led the way into the showroom, yelling at the top of her lungs. "Hey!!! Where's Eddie Pompadour?" Boy, would he be surprised to see her. Bet he told everybody in the world that he gave the one, the only Rose her very first kiss.

A salesman with polished, manicured fingernails came toward her, an expression of distaste written clearly on his features. "He's not here," he said with the meagerest amount of politeness possible.

The other salesmen in the opulent showroom stared at her openly but without recognition. Rose felt the nightmare coming back, but she fought it off like a tiger.

"Hey, is everyone asleep? Don't you sell cars in this shithole?" At once, every back was turned to her, cutting her off. The salesman who had spoken to her vanished in a cloud of polyester doubleknit.

Frustration was choking Rose to death in this goddamn sterile place. She wouldn't give in to these assholes! She'd make them acknowledge her. "Fuck you very much, ladies and gentlemen," she shouted. "Fuck you very much!"

The youngest of the salesmen had obviously been delegated, as the junior man, to get rid of this whore and the hulking bear she had with her. Uneasily, he made his way toward them, his eyes fixed on Mal as though he expected him to attack. No telling what these two were on; they were evidently drug-crazed and dangerous. Making certain to keep the Ferrari on the showroom floor as a barrier between himself and the hippies, he cleared his throat.

"Excuse me, miss. May I help you?" he asked through dry lips.

"How much is this turkey you got here?" demanded Rose, pointing to the car. It was a lipstick-red Ferrari, stick shift, air conditioning, white sidewalls, leather-covered racing wheel, tape deck—the works.

"Nineteen thousand dollars," replied the young salesman automatically, his eyes still fixed on Mal.

Rose dug around in her shabby poke, coming up with a huge wad of bills, double-wrapped in thick red rubber bands. It took her a few seconds of struggling to get the rubber band off the roll, but when it was free, she began to peel thousand-dollar bills off the top until nineteen of them were sitting on the low hood of the car. "I'll take it," she said casually. "Wrap it up."

Everybody was staring at them now, open-mouthed, and the young salesman was so dumfounded he couldn't speak.

"What's the matter with you?" demanded Rose. "Don't ya hear good? I said, 'I'll take it.'" She paid no attention to the stares or the whispers that were running through the showroom.

"Uh . . . excuse me for a moment," said the salesman. He turned away, but Rose called after him.

"Hey, ace!"

The young man froze in his tracks and turned back with a gulp. "Yes, miss?"

"You forgot to take your money, son." Rose nodded graciously at the thousand-dollar bills still sitting on the Ferrari's hood. She wrapped the rubber bands around the rest of the roll and tucked it back deep into her poke; there was plenty left. Plenty. The Rose believed that, if money talked, hers would shout so loud everybody could hear it.

216

The salesman made a dive for the money, handling it as though it were contaminated, and vanished into the inner office. Through the glass Rose and Mal could see a knot of people gathering around the desk to examine the money; one of them actually held a bill up to the light. Rose allowed herself the ghost of a smile. It was legal tender, earned the hard way, by shakin' her ass and singin' her head off. Now several people had come down to the glass partition and were staring frankly at The Rose, at her ragged clothes and her bare, dirty feet. After a minute, their own salesman returned.

His entire manner had changed from one of suspicion to one of extreme deference. The lady had just bought a car, therefore she must be a lady. At the thought of the commission he'd just earned—and all of it in cash —he was practically chirping as he approached them.

"If you'll kindly just follow me," he burbled obsequiously, "I'll be more than happy to fill out all the necessary papers." He grinned at them, delirious with joy. "It's going to be a beautiful day out, isn't it?"

"This thing got a jack?" demanded Rose.

"Certainly," purred the salesman. He opened the brand-new trunk of the car with a flourish and produced the jack and the jack handle, as though pulling a rabbit out of a hat.

Rose took the jack handle from him, and hefted it, testing its weight. Then, raising it over her head as high as she could, she brought it down with all her strength on the shiny red body of the car.

Wham! A terrible dent appeared in the Ferrari's perfect rear fender. The young salesman uttered a loud gasp; his face went white, and his eyes widened to dinner plates.

Bash! Crash! BLAM!! The sound of crunching metal split the sacrosanct air of the showroom, this temple built to wheels. Rose, keeping the jack handle for herself,

217

thrust the jack at Mal, who took it and followed her around the car, demolishing it right and left. First the fenders, then the roof and windshield. The windows went next in a crunch of broken glass, and Rose got to the dashboard and killed it.

It was over almost as soon as it had begun. The car lay totaled in the middle of the showroom, murdered, its twisted wreckage bleeding parts. Shocked into catatonia, the salesmen stood rooted to the spot, unable to lift a hand against this wanton destruction. What could they have done? It was, after all, bought and paid for.

Rose threw the jack handle down on top of the destruction, and Mal tossed in his jack.

"Give my regards to Eddie Pompadour," she called across the showroom, as she and Mal walked out calmly and climbed into the limousine.

Once in the car, Rose sank back against the cushions, her entire body trembling. She knew that what she had done had been foolish, wasteful, and even cruel. At the same time, she'd managed to discharge a lot of negative energy. Every time she'd hit the defenseless Ferrari, she was beating on somebody's head. She was getting something back for all the shit she'd had to eat lately.

WHAM! That was for you, Rudge. For not letting me rest. For driving me without mercy, without love.

And BAM! that was for you, Dyer, for slamming me in the face and walking out on me, you creep!

And CRASH! That was for all you nerds in my good old hometown, with your warm welcome to The Rose. What do you know about anything, you dumb cracker assholes? Don't even recognize a Star when you see one.

The poor Ferrari had paid with its life, but Rose was feeling a little better, a little stronger. This act of retribution had been boiling up in her for a long, long time. The angry steam just had to escape or she'd have exploded—gone up like a rocket and disappeared.

218

Still, and she started to giggle, she'd give a pretty penny to see Eddie Pompadour's face when he saw the mess o' broken shit in the middle of his nice, clean showroom. That would be worth nineteen thousand smackers.

XIII

Rudge sat in front of a mountain of papers, checking the comp list against the manifests to see how many tickets had been given away, to whom, and why. Outside the office, the lighting technicians were working the stadium lights, section by section, for The Rose's concert tonight. Everything had to be perfect—lights, sound, weather guaranteed. This climactic concert was to be the biggest one yet, with the largest audience, coming all the way from Tallahassee to the north and Key West to the south. Hitchhikers were on the road even now, hoping to make it to Lawrence Stadium in time, hoping against hope to score for a ticket.

Dennis, haggard and totally wiped, came into the office and threw himself into an overstuffed chair.

"I checked out every hospital and sheriff's department in four states, Rudge."

A heavy scowl drew Campbell's brows together, and his eyes glinted like cold iron. "Don't worry, she'll be here," he rasped. "She'll crawl back on her knees begging to do every date I can get her. It will be magnificent and touching to the heart." He smiled sourly, showing all his teeth.

Annoyed and frazzled, Dennis snapped, "You're a real prince, you know that, Rudge?"

"Kiddo, in the next life I'll be everybody's pal. Right now I'm too busy trying to keep alive." He turned back to his papers.

Outside, the battered Caddy limousine rolled up to the stadium gate. Beyond the gate were long ranks of gray wooden barricades, waiting to be put into place to hold the crowds who'd be showing up in only a few hours. A white-haired old guard flagged the limo down.

"You can't go in this way, folks. Sorry."

Jesus Christ! Don't I have a face anymore? Isn't there any human being in this whole fuckin' town who has ever seen or heard of The Rose? She looked blankly at the old man for a moment, then she stamped down hard on the gas pedal, elbowing Mal aside, and the car took off with a leap. Tires screeching, the limo plowed straight into the rows of barricades guarding a ramp to the field. She sent them flying, knocking them over like bowling balls, zooming across the artificial turf and whitewashed stripes and dyed end zones. She was leaning on the horn, which echoed and re-echoed across the empty stadium like a howl of pain.

"I'll be damned!" yelled Dennis, leaping out of his chair and running to the window. "It's her."

"What did I tell you?" asked Rudge in triumph. But underneath the triumph was relief, and underneath that, deep, dark anger. And under the anger, a plan to make Rose pay for all this bullshit worrying, a plan to keep her very much in line for the future.

The horn stopped abruptly, and Rose climbed out of the limo. She was wobbly in the knees from the crazy ride, and totally exhausted by the events of the past two days and nights. She could barely lift her head as she walked tiredly into the office of the stadium owners' suite.

"I'm here," she said, her voice almost inaudible.

"I see," said Rudge calmly.

221

Rose walked over to the window and pressed her aching head against the pane, so that the air-conditioned glass would cool it. "I've been thinkin', been doin' some serious thinkin'," she told Rudge.

"Yeah?"

"And it's definite. I'm takin' a year off."

"Uh-huh," said Rudge pleasantly. This made Rose very nervous. When he yelled and screamed at her, she knew exactly where she was. But when he was pleasant, she was swimming in foreign, shark-infested waters. Over her head, unable to touch bottom.

"And . . . uh . . . and . . ." she began to stammer.

"Yes, go ahead," Rudge smiled.

Rose shut her eyes and pulled it together. "But I'm not going to hurt the band. I want to keep everybody on full salary after tonight. Until I decide what to do"— she was gaining some confidence from her words—"you know, when to come back and all, stuff like that. . . ."

"You finished?" asked Rudge after a second or two of silence.

"Yes," said Rose.

Without a word, Rudge walked over to his desk, spun the combination lock on his case, and pulled out a long document of several dozen pages. "You know what this is?" he asked her in a matter-of-fact tone.

The Rose glanced at it and shook her head. "No."

"You ought to," remarked Rudge calmly. "You signed it two years ago."

"My contract?"

Rudge smiled, as at a clever child. "Good. I've been reading it, and thinking about it. For the past two nights I've been thinking about us." He moved closer to Rose. "I've been thinking about all the toilets we played. All the nickel-and-dime hustlers I had to bargain with every time you opened your mouth. And not all for you. For me, too. Because I loved it! I loved finding a raw and wild

222

and hopeless brat and turning her into a performer they're willing to mortgage Australia for. Do you want to play Brisbane? Do you want to play Tokyo? Do you want to play Paris?"

Rose stood frozen at the window, her eyes shut, Rudge's words beating against her brain. Beating, beating.

"Then, suddenly, last night," Rudge went on in that same unemotional voice, "I woke up. And I said to myself, fuck this. Did we go down the road together or didn't we? And I came to a decision. You fulfill *all* the commitments you asked me to make for you. Or you fulfill none of them. Got it?"

It took Rose a minute to figure out exactly what he was telling her. Then she turned, angry.

"Bullshit!"

"You're not singing tonight." It was uttered in a tone of such finality, so totally devoid of emotion, that Rose flinched.

"You're crazy!" she shouted. "I *gotta* sing tonight!"

"The concert's off," said Rudge calmly, folding up the contract.

"What the hell are you talkin' about? They'll nail you to a barn door and set it on fire!"

But Rudge shook his head. "It's my show. I'm the promoter of this concert, I'd remind you. If I want to blow it, I'll damn well blow it. I'll pay everybody off. Nobody will lose a cent. And, by the way"—he held the folded contract out to her—"go find yourself another manager. I don't want you in my life anymore."

Rose stood speechless, unable to move, or to hold out her hand in protest, or to take the contract. With perfect calmness, Rudge dropped the document at her feet.

"You can start your fucking vacation right now," he told her. "You're fired." He turned and walked out the door, leaving it open, not even deigning to slam it.

Stunned, Rose stood in the center of the room. She couldn't believe her ears. It hadn't happened. It *couldn't* happen. Fired? What the fuck was he talking about? She rushed to the window and looked out. Rudge was walking across the field slowly. "Fired?!" she screamed. "Fuck you!"

Fired? What . . . how . . . she saw the contract on the floor at her feet, and a sudden feeling of panic gripped her, sending her reeling as though struck in the face. Fired? *NO!*

Terrified, she ran out of the office and down through the corridor, screaming "Rudge! Rudge!"

RRRUUUUUDDDGGE! Shrieking, Rose ran down a ramp and found herself on the stadium seats. Rudge continued walking across the field, not turning his head, evidently not even hearing her screaming after him. He ignored her totally.

"I'll kill you! I'll kill you, you son-of-a-bitch!" sobbed Rose, clambering over the seats. "Don't you walk out on me. I walk out on *you!* You need me! I don't need you! I can get any fucking manager I want! Don't you walk away from me! Turn around, you motherfucker! RUDGE!"

But Rudge had reached a TV remote truck, standing on the field for tonight's special, and had climbed into it. This time he slammed the door behind him, never giving Rose so much as a backward glance.

Crying bitterly, Rose dropped helpless to her knees.

"Don't you walk away from me," she wept. "Nobody walks away from me. I'm talkin' to you . . . come back . . . I'm talkin' to you. . . ." She broke down completely, folded over, her small body tucked between benches on the concrete bleachers of the stadium.

A sound reached her. Footsteps. Rudge? She looked up through smeared eye makeup, through a mist of heavy tears. Dyer was standing on a ramp about thirty feet away.

"Houston!" she yelled, and pulled herself to her feet. She ran toward him, threw herself on him. He lifted her easily into the air and hugged her little body close. She looked like shit, but, man, was he glad to see her!

"Oh, Houston," she sobbed, kissing his neck, his hair, his shoulders and face . . . anywhere she could reach. "Where've you been?" she wailed.

"Taking care of business," said Dyer shortly. "I came back as soon as I could. What the hell is goin' on?" He pushed back her matted hair to look at Rose's tear-stained face.

"Rudge just fired me," she sniffled.

"Fired you!!" Houston couldn't believe what she was telling him, but she was nodding her head rapidly.

"I came all the way to see him and talk and stuff and he fuckin' fires me!" She broke free from Dyer and ran to the chicken-wire fencing that enclosed the ramp, shaking it with ferocious anger.

"He *can't* fire you! He *works* for you!" shouted Dyer, to get the absurdity of it into her head.

Rose turned on him fiercely. "What do you know?" she shrieked. "I mean, who the hell are you, anyway?"

Houston recognized all the signs of hysteria, and moved to fold Rose into his strong arms. "I'm Dyer. Houston Dyer," he told her in her ear. "Your own private brown-eyed motherfucker, remember?" His hands worked to soothe her, gentle her.

Rose nodded miserably and allowed herself to collapse on his chest. "What's gonna happen now?" she wailed. "What am I gonna do? I feel so bad, honey . . ."

Houston held her at arm's length so that he could look into her face. "Let's get out of here so we can breathe," he urged her. "Before it's too late."

But Rose was shaking her head vehemently from side to side. "All I can do is sing, man! I can't walk out on that for some fantasy! You just wanna save a rock 'n' roll queen, don't you *see* that? My life is fallin' apart, and you wanna buy me a sleepin' bag. Jesus fuckin' Christ!" She slumped forward onto Dyer's shoulder, completely done in. "I gotta sing tonight," she whispered.

Houston folded his arms around Rose and rocked her gently against his body. She was his baby. He had to save her, protect her. He could feel her weariness penetrating his body like a chill.

"We'll just go until we don't want to anymore," he told her.

"Where are we going?" She looked up into his steady brown eyes, trusting him.

"Mexico." Dyer was convinced they couldn't extradite him once he got over the border.

Rose grinned up at him through her tears. "Jesus, I eat this adventure shit up. I wanna tell y' something. Come here." She reached up and tugged his head down to hers. "C'mere." Into his ear, where nobody but just they two could hear her words, she told him. "I love you," she whispered. "I really love you. I wanna sleep with you in Mexico or any other damn place on this planet you want to go."

He pulled his head back, looked long and deeply into her eyes, and nodded seriously. The look on his face was so loving that Rose found herself blushing, warm with embarrassment.

"Do you think you really love me?" she asked in her smallest voice, and shut her eyes with joy when he smiled down at her.

Although there were still a couple of hours to go before the concert, a battalion of Florida state troopers had already arrived at the stadium. The special picked cadre were off to one side, getting briefed. These men, whom Rudge had amply compensated, would be Rose's

226

personal bodyguard, ringing the stage. TV crews were getting cameras 1, 2, and 3 in place, laying down miles of color cable, setting up monitors to check the action and the cameras. Roadies were connecting the amps, and the boys in the band were checking out their instruments.

It was time for the sound check; the engineers were ready. Apart from the concert itself, the sound check was probably the most important part of the activity. Every musician had to be in balance with all the others and with the singer. Each amplifier was connected to giant speakers, as was the keyboard and the control panel. Everything had to sound perfect—these people hadn't come all this way and paid all this money to hear shitty sound. In an outdoor concert like this one, the sound check was doubly important. There would be no great acoustics, like some indoor auditoriums had, to help them along. They'd be in competition with every jet plane on the flyby to Miami Beach or Fort Lauderdale.

The television people were particularly antsy. They had no great love for rock 'n' roll; filming this concert as a special was just a business to them, a highly technical, highly profitable, highly competitive business. They weren't messing around; they wanted The Rose and they wanted her right away. There was such a schedule as color check, makeup, lighting—they had to meet it.

"I think you better get her here pretty soon," said the director to Rudge in no pleasant tone.

"She'll be here soon," Rudge assured him.

Dennis and Danny knocked on the door of the TV control-room tape truck and came in quietly. Dennis pulled Rudge aside, whispering urgently into his ear.

"Danny just told me we're an hour late with the sound check. You're outta your fuckin' mind. Find her and get her to come sing. Forget those other commitments! I think you're insane—"

227

"Goddamnit!" exploded Campbell. "I don't pay you to think!"

Dennis's temper had been sorely tried these past few days, and now it snapped. "Jesus Christ, Rudge, why the hell don't you tell somebody that you don't even know where she is?!"

Rudge's fuse was short, too. "Because I've been in the trenches for two years with a certifiable Section 8 and two years is enough! I want *all* the marbles! I played my ace-in-the-hole with her!"

Dennis shook his head doubtfully. "It may end up working, but it sure smells pussy to me," he said.

"We got to hang in a little longer—"

"And pray we don't get our asses kicked," Dennis finished for him.

As Dennis headed for the door, Rudge motioned him back. "Try the phone in the limo," he conceded.

"She never picks it up," complained Dennis. "I musta tried it a couple hundred times."

"Try it again," ordered Rudge. "And again."

"So that's why you didn't answer your phone," said Dyer, pulling the bottle cap out of its wedge. "This fucked up the connection."

"You mean you were calling me?" asked Rose. Her face lit with delight.

"Every hour on the hour."

Rose snuggled closer to him on the front seat. "I really worried. Thought I'd never see you again."

Houston looked at her in surprise. She really meant it. She had no real confidence, in herself or in anybody else.

The Caddy was all gassed up and making good time on the road south. The windows were rolled down, and Rose sniffed the air, enjoying the dusk. There was a strong scent in the evening air, compounded of equal parts of night-blooming hedges, offshore oil, and diesel fuel from the monster rigs on the highway. Rose took a deep breath.

"Ah, ain't nature wonderful," she cracked. They both cackled with laughter, Rose feeling as free as the wind that blew her hair back from her face.

"Haulin' ass down t' Mexico!" she said joyously. "Gotta make myself beautiful." She began scrambling around the seat and the floor of the car, looking for her personal belongings, which were strewn everywhere.

"You already are beautiful," smiled Dyer.

"You supposed to wear glasses?"

Up ahead, at the side of the road, was a neon rainbow blur advertising Monte's Bar.

"Pull over there, okay?" Rose's face was as excited as a child's.

"What for?" frowned Dyer.

"I haven't been to Monte's since I can't remember when. I used to sing there. Remember? I told you that. Saturday nights and waited on tables."

"I thought we were going to Mexico," protested Dyer. He pressed his lips together angrily.

Rose grinned at him lovingly. "Gimme a break," she wheedled. "Aw, please, it means a lot to me. I just wanna see if they still know who I am."

"They know who you are," said Houston shortly. He didn't like this, not at all. For her sake as well as for his, he wanted to be over that border soon. And they had a lot of miles between them and Mexico.

"Please, Houston," begged The Rose, a little girl pleading for candy.

Taking the cutoff more sharply than he had to, Dyer swung the wheel over and they left the highway, bumping over the divider into Monte's parking lot.

Impatiently, he followed Rose out of the Caddy, although all his instincts were telling him to stay in the

229

car. If he stayed behind, chances are she'd finish up her business in a hurry and start missing him. Yet, he followed her into Monte's Pink Flamingo, his senses tingling with an impending sense of disaster.

As soon as he came in the door, Dyer's inner voice told him he'd been here before. A thousand times. Not in this very bar, maybe, but in a hundred just like it. Exactly like it. A workingman's bar that catered to the younger folks, good ole boys who hadn't yet developed the overhanging beer bellies they'd have in later life. A redneck crowd, but fast on its feet. Hated hippies and freaks, but agreed with them on two things—grass and gun-control laws. In favor of the first, against the second. Supported Nixon and the war in Vietnam. And came here on a Saturday night to get tanked up, score with some chick, and wake up in a strange place on Sunday morning. This could be a friendly crowd, or it could be tar-and-feathers city. No way of telling in advance.

There was a tiny stage at the back of the room, where a three-piece band was laying down some heavy bluegrass—guitar, violin, banjo. The crowd at the bar was paying it mixed attention when the front door burst open and a blond tornado whirled in.

"Hey, everybody, The Rose is here and it's time to get down!!"

They paid her mixed attention, too. Some of them recognized her and applauded; a few of these were even her fans. But most of them had been raised on country & western, and rock 'n' roll was some kinda degeneracy having to do with the Commies and the peace movement. They didn't know who she was. They saw some wild-haired chick with big boobs and they grinned. Hell, any excitement was welcome on a Saturday night.

Rose and Dyer approached the bar; Rose hopped joyously onto a stool and waved to Monte. Standing near the bar stool Dyer selected was a tall, beefy man with large shoulders and a powerful body, now running to fat. He was a good ole boy; Dyer could sniff him out a thousand yards away. Although hunting season was over, he wore a red hunter's cap and a nylon windbreaker. Easing on over to Houston, he snickered, "Does your mommy know you're with a hippie freak?"

Houston had no time for this sumbitch. Better get it over with. He clenched his fist and began his move, but Rose cut in and pulled at his arm.

"Same to you, Milledge," she sneered at the big man familiarly. Then, to Dyer in an undertone, "He's really okay."

"We heard you were here," Milledge said to The Rose in an offhand manner.

Rose turned her back on him. "Are we gonna do some serious juicin' or just a lotta talkin'?" she hollered. "The usual, okay, Monte? Only make it a double." She seemed to be determined to draw everybody's attention to herself, and Dyer checked out his watch, wondering how soon he could pry her loose.

Monte had freed himself from his other customers and came down the bar smiling, to give Rose a kiss. He was a tall, thin, balding man with a permanently morose face and sore feet from standing on them all night.

"Sure, honey. It's good to have you back. But what are you doin' way up here tonight? Aren't ya supposed to be singing at the stadium? Posters have been up all month."

"Came to see you," smiled Rose. "Let's have some service here, Monte." She turned to Dyer. "You don't look happy. Monte, give him a Thunderbird 'n' ginger ale. Chase it with Ripple." She was in a wonderful mood, feeling at home in her hometown at last.

"If you'd just sing one song, it's all on the house tonight, Rose."

Rose lit up. This was more like it. Requests from

her adoring fans at last. "You got a deal, Monte." She moved her small rump down off the stool.

Dyer grabbed her by the arm. "Where are you going?" he demanded.

"I'm going to do my thing," she told him, radiant, heading for the little stage. The men and women standing at the bar cleared a path for her, and she waved to them as she blitzed on by.

The little band knew her well, and as she mounted the stage, they broke into an introduction, a few bars of "Fire Down Below," which broke her up. The leader put his hand down and hauled Rose up to the stage before she could climb the steps, and she gave him a big kiss on the nose.

With her back to the audience, and her voice down low, she asked, "Anybody got any reds?" The guitar player put his fingers into the little change pocket in the front of his jeans and passed her a small plastic bag. Rose swallowed one Seconal furtively and dropped the rest into her poke. Then the band began to vamp for her, and she broke into a loud laugh, shaking her hips, fluffing out her hair.

"Now you-all just turn to page 438 in your hymnal and we'll all sing together."

Everybody in the bar gave a whoop of laughter; she was getting them, she was getting them. Even those men who had never seen or heard of her were watching her closely, and she grabbed the dinky little microphone and began to get down. To get down *to* it. ALL RIGHT!

"Are you with her, man? Huh?"

Dyer turned at the voice. A shifty little weasel of a man, prematurely bald and with a bad complexion, was standing at his elbow.

"Wanna score? You with The Rose? I'm holding the best stuff in the world—dope, uppers, downers, Tuinals, acid, junk, snow—" he recited his pharmaceutical litany. "The Rose likes junk." His voice trailed off at the ugly glint in Dyer's eye. This big sucker was one mean mother, decided the dealer, and he'd better fade. Maybe he could speak to The Rose privately, later on. He was a big fan of hers.

The Rose was singing her head off, bright and sassy. Somebody handed her up a drink and she grabbed it and emptied the glass without missing a beat. This was it, man. This was the hometown concert! Fans at last! People who knew who and what she was! The bright little face was a road map of joy, and that round little butt of hers was wigglin' away to beat the band.

Dyer watched her perform with strangely mixed feelings. He always loved watching her go, listening to that amazing voice as it growled, tore, shredded, coaxed, moaned, wailed, and purred its way through a song. But tonight . . . tonight she was larger than life. She was too big for the little stage and the three hillbilly musicians. She overpowered the crowd, dominated it. They were entertained, but they weren't with her. Not the same way the kids who slept outside the ticket booths all night to score a concert ticket were with her. Not the way the kids who danced in the aisles at her command were with her. There was a wall between Rose and these people, a wall of jealousy and hostility that she could never break down. Why couldn't she see it? She was still too colorful, too freaky, too *alive* for this colorless, dull, dead little town.

Standing at his side, the big guy, Milledge, shook his head and marveled grudgingly. "Well, that pig always could sing!"

Dyer suddenly found it hard to breathe. Oh, God, he knew what was coming. And he was powerless to stop it. The hairs on the back of his neck bristled.

Milledge opened that great yap of his—two of his front teeth were missing, rotted away on red pop and

233

yelled out, his huge voice carrying over Rose's and drowning it out.

"LINE FORMS RIGHT BEHIND ME!"

He turned to Houston in a ghastly fellowship. And his next words . . . Houston heard them echoing in his brain before they were even spoken. *Before they were even spoken.*

"Me an' the guys on the football team gang-banged her before the Lake Worth game," he laughed. He'd laughed about it for years. It was the best joke he knew.

And she woke up on the fifty-yard line, thought Dyer, and threw the punch. He let go with a bone-snapping right into Milledge's face. And there went the rest of the teeth. Bits of splintered bone and teeth, and gushing gouts of blood shot out of the man's nose and mouth as, with one groan, he hit the floor, out cold.

Rose, still struttin' and shoutin' onstage, saw and heard nothing, but the people nearest Dyer moved away, giving him a wide berth, just like in the John Wayne Westerns.

Monte looked down over the bar at the unconscious bulk of Milledge bleeding on the floor.

"I think y' ought to get her out of here, son, before there's some real trouble," he told Houston seriously.

Dyer nodded and made his way through the crowd to Rose. She bent to listen as he whispered in her ear.

"Sweetie," she protested, "these are my people down here. They're good to me, babe. Let's stay a while longer."

No, Rose, these are not your people. If anybody is your people, it's me. And only me. But he couldn't speak those words. Instead, he yelled over the music, "We've got to get out of here now!" He was getting a little frantic. Any moment now, the fuzz might be all over the place. As an AWOL—no, a deserter—from the Army, he couldn't afford to mess with no cops.

And he felt disaster impending for Rose, too. His

sense of doom had not been dispelled by the brief bout of violence. He tugged at Rose's arm.

"Listen, for Christ's sake, these are my friends!" yelled Rose, and the music behind her stopped abruptly. "I can't just walk out on my friends, can I?" She shouted this into the microphone, so that everybody in the bar heard it.

"NOOOOOO!" they yelled back.

Rose turned back to the band, and beckoned them to start playing again. But Dyer, using all his strength, literally dragged her down from the stage and in the direction of the door.

"We're leaving," he told her firmly.

"Let go of my arm!" hollered Rose, furious, her face twisted in rage and pain.

"C'mon!" urged Dyer.

Rose planted her feet so that he had to drag her. "No! I wanna sing!" she shouted fiercely.

Ignoring her protests, he moved her firmly to the door, through the jeers and the catcalls of the cheated, hostile crowd. At last he got her outside and over to the limo, where he pitched her into the front seat.

"I hate you, man! I fuckin' hate you!" shrieked Rose, kicking and punching at him.

Undisturbed, he walked around to the driver's seat and climbed in. He understood why she was angry, and he was sorry he had to do this to her. When she calmed down, he'd explain it and she'd understand and it would be all right between them again. As for now, all he wanted to do was to get her out of here and down to Mexico.

"Who the hell do you think you are?" hollered The Rose, but Dyer refused to argue. He wasn't gonna get mad at her. He understood just how much she craved acceptance in her own hometown, and he understood also that she'd had all that she was gonna get from this kind of crowd, and that it wasn't enough, didn't satisfy her. Well, they'd work that out later.

The telephone rang.

It startled both of them, the ringing of the car phone, and it exacerbated Rose's already raw nerves. Picking up the phone, she shouted into it, "Fuck off!!"

Suddenly, her eyes widened, and she clutched the receiver in both hands, listening intently. Covering the mouthpiece with one hand, she turned to Houston Dyer.

"It's Rudge, man, *Rudge!*" she told him breathlessly. "He wants me back. Anything I want . . . He's crawlin', honest to God!" Excitement lit up her features and made her voice tremble.

Dyer leaned over her and took the receiver firmly from her hand, hanging it up without a word. He sat staring at her, trying to piece it together in his head. No way. He couldn't understand her. Parts of her, yes. Her needs, her pains, her sorrows. But how she fulfilled those needs, and what she gave up of herself to fulfill them— that he'd never understand. And God knows he'd tried. He'd been truer to her than he'd been to himself. He sat looking at her silently, hoping that she'd come to her senses.

"Please don't look at me like that," moaned Rose.

Now anger took hold of her. He didn't understand her, would never understand her. He thought she could be some long-haired old lady in a mountain cabin, milking goats and making pottery, while he went out to shoot deer for supper. The hippie dream. She was a Star, man, and he'd never dig on that. And she needed to sing, to stand up and be seen and heard and applauded and loved. Why couldn't he get behind that? That was her *thing,* and he was always trying to take it away from her, or her away from it. Look at him now, staring at her with those big brown eyes of his, passing judgment on who and what she was.

236

"I said, *'Please don't look at me like that'!*" Without thinking about it, her hand came out and slapped him hard in the face, just as he had once slapped her.

She gasped in astonishment and dismay, and melted down small right before his eyes. "You love me?" she pleaded, sobbing. "Oh, I wish you loved me." She was now totally without dignity.

That was it. There was nothing left for him to say or do. He had tried to save her, maybe for reasons of his own having nothing to do with her. Maybe he just had to save a life to make up for all the lives he'd seen so wantonly destroyed. Maybe because, to him, she represented everything that was good and warm and vital. But he had tried to save her life, and he couldn't. She wouldn't let him. She'd never let him. It wasn't what she wanted. Rose would always prefer boogeying on the thin crust of an active volcano to a life of peace and quiet with a man who truly loved her. That was it, then. Time to go.

He took one last, long look at her, the pain showing in his eyes. Then he opened the car door and swung his legs out. Without looking back, he began to walk on down the highway, heading north.

Disbelieving, Rose watched him go. In the glare of the highway's mercury-vapor lights, she watched him, stunned, until his figure disappeared in the distance. Even after he was gone, she sat unmoving, watching the road.

Then her mouth opened, and from it issued a scream so loud and so long the veins in her throat and forehead stood out like cords.

"PLEASE!!!" Then, in a whisper, "Please. I'm sorry."

She climbed out of the car and ran a few feet as though to follow him, but some deeper, wiser instinct penetrated her madness and told her it was impossible; he was gone; some big semi had already stopped for him and was carrying him away.

237

Weeping piteously, Rose sank to the ground, beating the earth with her fists, hitting the highway that was taking her lover away forever. "Everybody goes away!" she sobbed. "Everybody always goes away!"

Tears ran unchecked down her face and onto her blouse, staining it dark. Her nose ran and she wiped it with the back of her hand, but she couldn't stop. All the sorrow, all the exhaustion, all the rejection and the heavy dues of her young life, everything came back to her at once, pressing her to the earth, weighing her down in misery. She wept out of loneliness and fear, and out of the deepest, truest feeling that she had nowhere to go, nobody to be with or trust. "Everybody walks out on me," she sobbed, knowing it was true.

"Hello, sweet lady," said a voice.

Rose brushed the damp hair out of her eyes and looked up. It was the dealer.

"Damn, Sam," she croaked hoarsely. "How in the hell have you been?" Her pretense, that she wasn't sitting there smack in the middle of the highway, crying her damn fool head off, was graciously accepted, and the weasely man helped her to her feet and ushered her over to her limousine.

"I will now take the liberty," he told her, reaching into his jacket pocket, "of putting a gratis balloon in your purse of some. . ."

"Hey, I don't . . ." protested Rose, but he cut her off.

". . . of the finest shit this side of Marseilles. It's the best, Rose, the real pure stuff. And for you, my own personal works,"—he threw in the syringe along with the glassine bag of heroin,—"because I love you and I love your music. Enjoy, Rose."

Like the serpent in the garden of Eden, he made his pitch and slithered away.

Rose rested her head on the wheel of the Cadillac. Oh, Christ, what a scream! Here she was, in her own hometown where she was born and raised, and the only fuckin' person in the whole damn town who loves her and honors her and pays her attention and is *good* to her is a slimy little connection. What a howl! She began to giggle, and then to laugh, and then she passed the point where she was able to stop.

XIV

She tried desperately to hang onto the wheel, but it had been a long time since she'd had to drive herself anywhere and the big Caddy had been through hell with her in the past few days. Rose's idea of driving was to floor the gas pedal and to hell with anybody in the oncoming lanes! The red she'd swallowed, mixing with the booze in her belly, didn't make it easier for her to concentrate on the road. There was a strange buzzing noise going on in her head, and she tried to escape it by going faster.

The limo fishtailed as it hit the shoulder, and an explosion of gravel and dirt flew up from the wheels. Swiveling and rocking, the car turned completely around, so that it was facing oncoming traffic.

"Shit!" swore Rose.

She *had* to get there. She'd been calling Rudge for half an hour, but the goddamn problem with these car phones was that they used airwaves, not telephone wires, and often the airways were choked with busy signals as the channels were all used at once. Frantically, she punched the buttons again, but all she got was bits and pieces of other people's conversations, and no Rudge.

As panic set in, Rose wrestled the car around and stopped for breath. Think, she told herself, think! I need something to help me think. She dug into her poke and found a long-forgotten half pint of vodka, almost full.

She used it to wash down another couple of Seconals. They would reduce the anxiety that made it impossible for her to get her shit together. They'd have a calming effect. Okay, she felt better now, drowsy but more tranquil.

First. Rudge wanted her to sing; he'd called her, begged her to come and sing her hometown concert. But wait, second. Dyer had hung up on him before Rose could say "Yes," and she hadn't been able to reach him since. Third. You didn't just call a big concert off like that, not with every ticket sold and the TV cameras standing by to film a special. So, fourth. Rudge was waiting for her right now, and she was late and she had to get there and she wasn't even sure where the hell she was because it was dark but she knew she was miles from the stadium.

And here came the panic again, threatening to engulf her.

A phone booth. Why the fuck hadn't she thought of that before? To hell with this goddamn fancy status-symbol automobile telephone that wasn't worth shit when you needed it. A good old Ma Bell phone booth, where you put in your dime and dialed. No buttons to punch. Yeah, find a phone booth.

She peered around her hopelessly; the Caddy sitting on a stretch of highway, but after a few seconds it dawned on her that she *did* know where she was, because she knew the number of the exit right up ahead. Familiar territory. Old home. All she had to do was to get this big gas-guzzling motherfucker off this highway in one piece.

Swinging the Caddy through the exit, Rose drove down a two-lane blacktop, zipping through a side street, past Leonard's grocery, and the house where she took those long, unsuccessful piano lessons, past all the bits and pieces of her former life. There it was, Lawrence High.

There was a telephone booth there; all the kids used it. They used to put slugs in it, Rose remembered. Phone calls were a nickel then. Even so, a nickel was big money in those days.

The car screeched to a halt on a cinder track surrounded by wooden bleachers. The old football field, deserted now. The old high-school football field. There was a telephone booth about fifteen yards away.

Rose tried to get out of the car, but her legs felt suddenly heavy, too heavy to be moved. She was nearly overcome by the urge to put her head down on the seat and go to sleep. Sleep. She couldn't remember the last time she'd slept. Or eaten, for that matter. Today? Yesterday? It didn't matter. Only the telephone booth mattered. Y' gotta make it, girl. One foot after the other. Sleep later. After the concert.

She moved dreamily to the booth and pulled the door shut behind her. The light went on. Hallelujah! Now all she needed was a dime. A dime. Finding a dime in that oversize poke of hers was like finding a grain of sand in the Sahara. Feverishly, she pulled out the contents of her bag, scattering some of them to the floor of the booth, piling the more precious of them—her big wad of cash money, her pot of eye makeup—on the little metal counter. Oh, hey, there were her vitamin pills. She'd need a couple of those. And, as long as she was swallowing pills, maybe another red.

A dime. She fumbled with it, nearly dropped it, but managed to hang onto it. A precious dime. It was a good sign, good luck, good karma. Cherry had talked about good karma. "You owe a debt to the universe," he'd told her, a few weeks before he'd freaked out on bad acid. Well, she was tryin' to pay it, wasn't she? In the only way she knew how. By singin' and dancin' and shakin' her tits and makin' 'em smile.

Rudge. She had to reach Rudge. With dismay, Rose realized that she'd been calling the motel from the car, and certainly Rudge was in the stadium. He couldn't be anywhere else. Somewhere in that giant stadium she had to find one man. And she didn't know the number. Her hands began to shake, and she nearly dropped the dime again, but managed to push it through the slot. She dialed "0."

"Operator, Operator. Give me the stadium. . . . No, I don't *have* the fuckin' number. . . . What do you mean, Information?"

Impatiently, she jiggled the hook, automatically disconnecting the call. She heard the click as her dime was collected, then nothing. Blank. Zero.

"Awww, shit!" She banged on the telephone helplessly, but it stared back at her enigmatically, dead.

Get it together, she told herself. Now! You're almost there, Rose. All you need is another dime. By now, her hands were shaking uncontrollably. She reached into her huge bag and began pulling out more things. The bottle of honey hit the floor and smashed. What the fuck was this? Shit, it had been a long time since she'd carried works in that poke of hers. A long time. She looked at the little package in her hand and shuddered. A long syringe, filled with colorless liquid—cooked heroin—and a red rubber tube for tying off the vein and making it bulge for the needle to enter. A small glassine bag of junk . . . the pure stuff, so he'd said. The perfect high that junkies were always reaching for.

She put the works down on the counter. That was such a long time ago. The scars had healed. Well, the scars on her arms had healed. The scars on her soul were a different matter. Would they ever heal?

No dime. Never mind, here were a handful of quarters. Hell, let Ma Bell have a play party with the extra fifteen cents. She dropped the quarter in the slot and took a very deep breath.

"Operator," she said with all the control she could summon up. "Please help me!" The word "help" as she uttered it released a flood of emotion, and Rose began to weep into the phone. "Thank you. Oh, thank you. Please,

the stadium . . . *No,* I don't *know* the fuckin' number!"
She slammed the phone down on the cradle, sobbing and
biting her knuckles.

Information. All you had to do was call Information.
They were paid to give you the number, right? They'd
help her. They *had* to. It was their job. She fumbled with
the quarters and dropped in another one. 611. No, 811.

No. She remembered now. 411.

Careful. The quarter supply is running low. Don't
fuck this up.

"Information, may I have the number of the stadium? Yes, thank you. No, not the box office, the main
office. Yes, I have it. Thank you. Thank you so much."

Exhaling a long breath, she dialed the number.
The phone rang. It actually rang. Rose slumped against
the wall of the booth, listening to the music of the ringing. The beautiful ringing.

"Hello? Give me Rudge. This is The Rose."

Connection. Somewhere out there, at the sound of
her voice and her name, somebody was actually running
to do her bidding. Somebody out there recognized her,
paid attention. This was more like it.

"Hi," she said in answer to Rudge's anxious voice.
"I'm at school. My high school. No, you'll have to come
get me. How's the house? Really? I'll be waiting. The
phone booth in the parking lot. I'll be fine. Don't worry.
I'll be fine." She hung up the telephone, and a surge of
happiness lifted her on wings. All she had to do was stay
here and be cool. Rudge was coming. Rudge would get
her and bring her to where she had to be. Rudge would
make it all right. It would be just like old times. All she
had to do was hang in there, be cool, and wait.

Rose ran her hands over her damp hair. It was so
hot in here. So goddamn Florida hot and muggy. Crack
the booth door a little, just a little.

What the hell was that? Something was moving on

244

the football field. I thought the goddamn place was deserted. Who's out there? She peered into the gloom of the field. A couple of lights had been turned on at the goal posts, and two squads of the varsity team were practicing drills, exercises, running plays. In the dimness, their white numbers shone with a ghostly light.

Shit, for a minute there I thought I was seeing ghosts. Maybe I am seeing ghosts. God, it's hot. I don't want to think about it, not about that night. But the reds working in her system, combined with the alcohol, lowered her resistance to the memories, and they came flooding back.

She'd been . . . what? Fifteen? Skinny and homely and with the biggest tits in the state of Florida, or so they said. And, oh, Jesus, how badly she'd wanted a boyfriend, somebody who would love her and go out with her proudly and take her to the sock hops and tell everybody she was his girl. She had dates every night she could get out, but they were all with different boys, and they all ended the same way, in the back seat of the borrowed car, with Rose's sweater pushed up and her panties pulled down. And they never called back . . . unless they got horny for her again.

Rose had her crushes, a different one every term, until she was fifteen, when she fixed on Bobo Milledge. He was the captain of the football team, tall, strong, and not very bright, But who cared? Those shoulders and that brush cut of his, so masculine, turned Rose on. If only he'd look at her! But he didn't; he was going out with Suzi Anna Chandler, one of the cheerleaders, and they whispered that Suzi Anna was giving Bobo b.t. That meant "bare tit," and was about as far as girls went in those days. Nice girls, that is, not Mary Rose Foster. They didn't bother to whisper about Mary Rose, they laughed out loud, both to her face and behind her back.

245

Everybody knew about *her*. She was crazy, too, pretending she could sing, yelling and carrying on and making faces. Everybody knew that lady singers kept their voices down low, and wore long gloves and net strapless formals.

"Hey, Mary Rose, why don't ya come out tonight and watch us practice?"

"Ya mean it, Bobo?" He knew her name! She couldn't get over it. And she knew exactly what it was he wanted from her, but she was willing to give it. Willing! Hell, eager!

It was a hot, muggy night, not unlike this one, and she'd sat in the stands with a big bottle of wine, holding it for Milledge. Between plays, he'd sneak over to her, and they'd take long sips from the half gallon, and he'd run his hands inside her sweater, feeling her boobs.

"You got nice big juicy tits, Mary Rose. I love big tits."

"They're all yours, Bobo." God, she was hot for him.

"I'll be back."

By eleven o'clock, he had pulled her down from the stands and under the bleacher section at the fifty-yard line. They were both smashed on the thick, red wine, and Bobo was so drunk he could hardy get it up.

"Suck it for me, Mary Rose. That'll make it hard." There wasn't a girl in Lawrence, Florida, who would take it in her mouth, except for Mary Rose Foster. As she bent her head to his lap, he pulled at her nipples, twisting them, hurting them. Suddenly, with a long, passionate shudder, he came in her mouth, pulling her head tightly to his belly, forcing her to swallow.

"Take your clothes off," he said thickly. "I'll be right back."

Flushed with excitement, Mary Rose pulled off her sweater and her skirt, and slid down her underpants. She left her shoes and socks on. She was hot, and ready.

246

And there he was suddenly, still in his uniform; only his fly was open. He was on her, pressing her back against the damp grass, penetrating her instantly. The heavy shoulder pads and knee protectors bruised her skin.

She flung her arms around him and attempted to kiss his mouth, but he twisted his face away from hers, grunting and panting.

"Wait a minute," she whispered. "Not so fast . . . take it slow and easy."

But it was too late. With one last grunt, he had spurted inside her, and pulled himself out of her and was standing up, zipping up his fly.

Disappointed, Mary Rose uttered a small cry of protest, but Bobo Milledge's loud voice drowned her out.

"LINE FORMS RIGHT BEHIND ME!"

Instantly, another player threw himself on Mary Rose, his dick hard. She tried to struggle upward, to sit up and throw him off, but he was too strong for her. She felt a mouth groping for her tit, and somebody splashed wine between her lips, getting it all over her face and into her hair. Ohhhhh. It was starting to feel good, and she began to move with it.

Again and again and again. Fourteen of them from the two squads were with her that night, many of them more than once. Somebody went for more wine, and Mary Rose drank more than her share. They wanted her to, they wanted her good and shitfaced, so that they could try out on her body all of the things they'd read about in Bobo Milledge's dirty books.

All night long they kept her there, and then, before the sun rose in the morning sky, they pulled up their pants and made for home, leaving her there, an unconscious wreck.

"I woke up on the fifty-yard line," she'd told Dyer, making a joke of it. But the fifteen-year-old girl who came awake that day wasn't laughing. She was hurting, inside

247

and out. There wasn't a part of her that hadn't been used and abused, and the taste in her mouth made her gag. Her body was covered with black-and-blue marks, patches of red wine, and sticky gobs of . . .

They'd gone home, all of them. But how was she to go home. How could she ever go home?

Funny, laughed Rose, propping herself up on the wall of the booth and watching the ghostly players move around the field chasing an invisible football. Funny, here I am more than ten years later, and I still got the same problem. How can I ever go home? And where the hell *is* home?

Aw, Jesus. I feel so low, so flat-out tired. I'm totaled, man. No rest for the weary. Gotta pep things up a little before Rudge gets here. Told him I was fine, and here I am a stoned-out wreck. Those fuckin' pills. Never shoulda taken two pills. Two? Four was closer to it, maybe five, to tell the God's own truth. Five reds. Whew! No wonder I'm asleep on my feet. Gonna snore my way right through my hometown concert. Eyes are closin' now. Gotta do somethin' about that . . . need to be high, not low.

Rose's woozy hand closed around the syringe. Been a long, long time, but a junkie never forgets. Never forgets the high, the excitement, the feeling of euphoria as the junk speeds through the veins. I need that, thought Rose groggily. Need that high. Can't sing without it. Don't worry, she said to nobody in particular, I'm clean. Never gonna do it again. I'm clean. Kicked it long ago. No tracks on my arms anymore. Just this once.

Just this once. She wrapped the rubber tubing tightly around her bare upper arm, holding one end of it in her teeth. She felt for the vein, found it, stuck the needle in.

The rush struck her at once and sent her staggering.

Wow! Good shit! Gooooood shit. A warm glow ran through her veins; she'd sing her goddamn ass off tonight. She'd show them, show them all . . . they'd find out who The Rose was. Goddamn peckerwoods in this crappy little town, not even knowing who she was. And this was supposed to be her home.

Home. Was she ever gonna get home?

There was one quarter left in her hand, slimy with cold sweat from her palms. She dropped it in the slot, hearing the distant bong, then dialed a number. Her golden head bent over the receiver, which she held clutched tightly in both hands. She listened with her eyes closed to the ringing . . . once . . . twice . . . five times. At last, the phone on the other end was picked up.

"Hello, Mom? Yeah, it's me. What're you watching? Yeah, he's good, I like him. You sound close, too. What? No, no, no, you don't have to come. It'll be all crowded and everything. So much traffic. You don't want to drive all the way out there. Hi, Dad, that you? On the other phone? How are ya, Dad? I miss you, too. I miss both of you. No, no, it's okay. I told Mom I didn't want you to come. It's too much trouble. Yeah, I'm doing great! Everything's wonderful. No, we're taking right off for New Orleans, but I'm gonna try to get back for Easter. Yeah, I promise. I'm gonna see to it. Well, I'll just tell them, that's all. I'm tired of the road . . . so tired . . . I wanna stop so bad . . ." The phone trembled in her hands, and she clutched it more tightly.

"There's only one way. You just have to make your mind up to stop. Yep, that's what I'm gonna do. It's a promise . . . a promise. Say 'Hi' to Marge and Karleen. I love you. 'Bye." Nothing had changed; nothing would ever change.

Rose hung up the telephone. Her last quarter was gone. Now all she had to do was wait for Rudge . . . stay cool and wait for Rudge. It was getting very late.

The stadium was packed to the roof, just as Rudge had predicted, with screaming, stomping, shouting fans, hollering happily for their star, wanting only The Rose. They had been waiting a long time, but they were used to that. The bigger the star, the longer-delayed the appearance. But The Rose was worth the wait. They were here to see The Rose.

The band was jamming on the stage, keeping the audience cool and together, but an undercurrent of tension was sparking the entire stadium, with its tens of thousands of happy fans. The Rose! They were gonna see her, their hometown hero, the girl from Lawrence, Florida, who made it out of this dingy little shithole to become a Star . . . the Star of stars. She was gonna come and sing to them and show them how she did it. Show them how maybe *they* could get out of here, too. The Rose was free . . . everybody knew that. She was what freedom was all about.

A sudden spotlight hit . . . the sky, not the stage. A helicopter was coming in, and thousands of eyes turned up to heaven. A scream rose up from thousands of throats as they realized what was happening. As one, they broke into a chant, stomping their feet on the benches.

THE ROSE! THE ROSE!! THE ROSE!!!

A space had been cleared near the stage for the helicopter to land, but hundreds of kids were rushing it, hoping to get a close view of their idol, hoping even to touch her, touch all that magic with their own fingers. No chance. The troopers came down on them like cattlemen, rounding them up and herding them away.

The helicopter landed and Rudge climbed out, then turned to help The Rose through the door. She hung onto him for dear life, the downdraft catching her hair and whipping it around her face. But it wasn't only the downdraft that was knocking her off her feet. Her eyes squinted shut in pain, and she stumbled and nearly fell.

She was completely disoriented. Rudge grabbed her before she could hit the ground.

"I'm all right," she babbled. Her teeth were chattering. "Hey, listen, I'm all right."

Dennis came running over to help Rudge get her up the steps to the stage. "She looks like hell," he muttered to Rudge. "She looks sick as a dog. You can't let her go out there."

But Rudge shook his head. "She says she's all right. If she can walk, she can sing."

But could she walk? Rudge shook his head at the light man, vetoing the spotlight. He didn't want her seen until he was certain The Rose would be standing up. She staggered over to the microphone, Dennis at her side, and held onto it for dear life.

Then, as the band went into the first notes of her first solo, the pinspot hit her full in the face.

Instantly, there was bedlam in the audience. A frenzy of enthusiasm came thundering across the stadium and over the stage. Rose stood motionless, hit by a wall of love so high she couldn't look over it, so wide she couldn't move around it. She had to just stand there and feel it pouring over her, washing her in love.

She couldn't believe it. She couldn't believe her ears. Or her eyes. It was getting hard to see. Why was it so hard to see? Maybe it was the lights. But she could see enough to tell that every man, woman, and child in the audience was on his feet, cheering her and calling her name.

Her name. Up there, on the scoreboard, was her name, spelled out in big lights. THE ROSE. In big lights. They knew who she was. *These* were her people. They had been here all the time. Waiting for her. Waiting for The Rose. She'd been looking in the wrong places.

She shivered a little. Why was she cold? Florida

nights were hot as hell, and the lights on the stage usually made her sweat. But now she was cold, so cold. The palms of her hands were icy, and she was breaking out in gooseflesh. Well, there was only one way to get warm. Right? She grabbed the microphone off the stand, summoning every bit of strength her wiry little body and tough spirit possessed.

"It's so good to be home," she told them. "You're my people."

With one voice, the audience roared back its adoration. The Rose fed on that, it made her stronger. Maybe it could even warm her.

"I didn't mean to be late. Will you forgive me?" she asked them, loving them all. All.

"YESSSSSSSSSSSSSSSS!!!!!!"

The Rose smiled. "I forgive you, too." Only she knew what she meant, how much forgiving she had to do. Now she turned to the band, which was vamping behind her.

"Well, what are you waiting for?" she hollered.

And she sang. Where the energy came from nobody would ever know. She pulled it out of the muggy air, manufactured it from the love that shone in the stadium, dragged it up from the deepest part of her soul. But she held that energy up for all of them to see, a bright, crackling thing that moved with her slender body. And she brought that energy out for all of them to hear, a voice so full of pain and meaning, of woman blues and woman love, so high it touched the dark sky in which the stars were eclipsed by the popping flashbulbs, so low it brought tears to the eyes of those who watched her in silence. To Dennis's eyes, and Mal's, and, incredibly, even to Rudge's.

"She's a genius, a bloody fuckin' genius," he muttered, lost in awe. "She's the other half of me. I'm nothin' without her."

252

The song wound and twisted from crescendo to crescendo, and came to an end at last, leaving Rose white and shaking, barely on her feet.

They're not applauding, she thought. Why aren't they applauding? Did I fuck up? She peered past the lights out into the audience.

They were standing, all of them, clapping and cheering more wildly than any audience she'd ever had in her life. But why couldn't she hear them? They were so far away. Everybody was so far away. She couldn't see them anymore.

She wanted to take a step forward, to walk out there and move among them, getting a hug from one and a kiss from another. Ah, she wanted hugs and kisses so bad. And her hands. They were so cold, so cold. Won't somebody come and take my hands and warm them up? Somebody, please?

But there wasn't anybody. They were all receding . . . fading . . . the stage . . . she looked around it. . . . Where were the guys? . . . Where was Rudge?

"Hey," she said feebly, "where is everybody going?"

Then she fell, with agonizing slowness as Rudge rushed toward her, into the blackness and into eternal cold.

The Rose had gone home.

Houston Dyer, his hair cut very short, was packing his duffel bag for Vietnam, when the news came over the radio, followed by fifteen minutes of her music, uninterrupted by commercials, a final tribute to The Rose. Oh, Christ! I shoulda been there. Maybe, just maybe, I coulda saved her if I'd stayed and tried again. But he knew that he couldn't have. It wouldn't have made any difference. The Rose had simply been too tired to go on. This was her way out. God, I'm sick to death of death, thought Dyer. And he knew what happens to a man who goes into combat not wanting to kill.

Rudge Campbell moved very fast indeed. Three weeks after her death, a memorial album, titled "The Rose," had been put together from previously discarded takes and cuts and was already shipping platinum.

THE BEST OF THE BESTSELLERS
FROM WARNER BOOKS

REELING
by Pauline Kael (83-420, $2.95)
Rich, varied, 720 pages containing 74 brilliant pieces covering the period between 1972-75, this is the fifth collection of movie criticism by the film critic *Newsday* calls "the most accomplished practitioner of film criticism in America today, and possibly the most important film critic this country has ever produced."

P.S. YOUR CAT IS DEAD
by James Kirkwood (82-934, $2.25)
It's New Year's Eve. Your best friend died in September. You've been robbed twice. Your girlfriend is leaving you. You've just lost your job. And the only one left to talk to is a gay burglar you've got tied up in the kitchen.

ELVIS
by Jerry Hopkins (81-665, $2.50)
More than 2 million copies sold! It's Elvis as he really was, from his humble beginnings to fame and fortune. It's Elvis the man and Elvis the performer, with a complete listing of his records, his films, a thorough astrological profile, and 32 pages of rare, early photographs!

A STRANGER IN THE MIRROR
by Sidney Sheldon (81-940, $2.50)
Toby Temple is a lonely, desperate superstar. Jill Castle is a disillusioned girl, still dreaming of stardom and carrying a terrible secret. This is their love story. A brilliant, compulsive tale of emotions, ambitions, and machinations in that vast underworld called Hollywood.

STAINED GLASS
by William F. Buckley, Jr. (82-323, $2.25)
The United States must stop a war with one man and one man alone. His name: Blackford Oakes, super agent. His mission: Kill his friend for the good of the world. This is Buckley at his spy thriller best, with the most daring, seductive, and charming hero since 007.

BEST-SELLING BOOKS OF MOVIE HITS FROM WARNER...

CLASS OF '44
by Madeline Shaner (89-585, $1.95)

They graduated into an era of ration stamps, college hazing, love songs — and a war everybody wanted. Hermie and Julie belonged to the Forties Generation. Driven from childhood by the storms of the world's last war, and the passions of their first mature love. They grew up fast — but they lost something important along the way. . . .

THE OTHER SIDE OF THE MOUNTAIN
by E.G. Valens (82-935, $2.25)

In 1955, Jill Kinmont, in the last qualifying race before the Olympic tryouts, skied down a mountain crashing to earth at forty miles an hour. She never stood up again. Now Jill had another kind of mountain to climb, back up from total helplessness to a useful, meaningful way of life. This is the story of that superhuman struggle and her incredible, inspiring victory.

THE OTHER SIDE OF THE MOUNTAIN Part 2
by E.G. Valens (82-463, $2.25)

Making a life again when your body feels dead from your neck down. Pursuing a career when you cannot move without a wheelchair. Now, E.G. Valens, who wrote the original biography that became a bestseller and a record-breaking film, tells PART 2 of her story. Now you can read of Jill Kinmont's ultimate achievement — accepting the challenge of love.